The Grounded

Rider Edition

Taloa Douglas Ross

TALOA HOUSE
PUBLISHING

—◎—

The Grounded (Rider Edition)

© 2025 Taloa Douglas Ross

Published by Vestige & Veil – Taloa House Publishing

Long Beach, California, USA

VestigeandVeil.com

Print ISBN: 979-8-9995312-2-3

First Edition

Edition Note

This is the Rider Edition

—⊚—

This is the Rider Edition.

This edition carries the full architecture of *The Grounded*, as it was witnessed, recorded, and arranged by the observer within the story—called simply, the Rider.

The Rider is not a savior.

Not a hero.

Not a voice above.

The Rider is the one who walked between the Grounded and the Untethered—never lifting a weapon, but never safe from consequence.

This is the edition they left behind.

It is not neutral.

It remembers.

Dedication

—⊙—

For the ones who carried nothing and still bore the weight.

For the ones who carried everything and set it down too late.

For the builders who spread instead of rose.

For the recorders who remember without absolving.

For the children who drew a circle—then stepped back into it.

For the harmed.

For the healing.

For the world that refuses to be violent to stay upright.

—◎—

"The earth did not strike back.

It refused to rise."

—◎—

The Grounded (Rider Edition) — Table of Contents

Book I – The Drop

Book II – The Shape Between

Book III – The Breath That Remains

—◎—

Prologue – The Pulse

"Law arrived without verdict."

THEY NEVER FIRED A SHOT.

No cities turned to glass. No ships darkened capitals. No countdown echoed across nations. Only a pressure—felt in the teeth and the hinge of the jaw—moving around the earth faster than thunder.

When it passed, some of us tried to stand and could not.

Kian, a grandfather, dropped with his blade still sheathed. His granddaughter sat cross-legged beside him in the dust so he would not be alone. Knees held. Ankles held. But the will to rise met a softness that would not yield, the way deep water refuses a match.

We were not paralyzed. We were not sick. We were simply stopped at thirty-six inches, as if height itself had become a closed door.

THOSE WHO HAD EVER TAKEN a weapon in hand with intent to harm—not idly, not in play, not as a passing thought, but with true readiness—found the air above three feet unwilling. We could sit, crawl, roll, reach, build, drag, climb by arms and elbows. We could love and learn and work. We could keep our weapons—many did. But our lives were now measured at the height of a child's desk.

The rest of the world kept moving. The Untethered—those who had never taken up a weapon with willingness to use it —rose, walked, ran. Not better, not chosen. Only unbound.

They built ramps we could not use. We built corridors they did not need. Between us, a new country appeared at knee-level: markets, schools, lullabies. We named it Belowline.

Above, streets kept their names. Between lay a strip of shared ground we called Threshold.

No council was called. No treaty signed. The law that needed no letter had already arrived.

Some said judgment. Some said mercy. Most said nothing and learned to hold their breath between the two.

IN THE FIRST HOURS, arguments outpaced water.

Is imagination a weapon? Does a promised blow weigh the same as a struck one? What of the girl who never acted but planned the angle and time? What of the boy who lifted a knife and changed his mind?

Answers came like rain on different roofs—uneven, local, sometimes late.

We learned this much: It was not contagion. You could not ground another by touch or wish. The Pulse had not deputized us as instruments—it had measured us as we were, and as we meant to be.

Those who tried to rise by machine could, briefly. The world did not shatter their bones or burn their skin. But something else failed—an echo went dark, a breathmark vanished, a belonging loosened. A breathmark is the imprint of belonging itself, carried in breath. To lose it is not to lose life, but to be cut away from the weave that once held you. The cost was not pain. The cost was severance.

We learned, too, that disarming was not release. You could set the rifle down, bury the blade, melt the brass. The height did not return. The tether was not to metal—it was to the moment you were willing.

CHILDREN ASKED FASTEST and most clearly: *If I think bad, am I broken?* We told them the truth we had: the law did not punish fear or feeling. It held only choice and readiness.

Many children chose, without being asked, to live low beside us. They called it kindness. Some called it courage. We called it a mercy we did not deserve and would spend years learning how to hold.

By dusk, hospitals re-drew their beds. Barracks evaporated into empty squares. Courts became rooms for telling, not deciding. A dancer learned to shelve books with her chin. A carpenter invented a chair that let mother and daughter sit face to face without one stooping or the other rising. A trader chalked a circle on Threshold and named it *listen*.

. . .

NIGHT CAME. The earth hummed once, the way a sleeping animal acknowledges a hand. We listened for a second strike.

None came.

We began.

Not with peace, not with war. With consequence.

We are not paralyzed.

We are grounded.

Interlude I — The First Broadcast

The world broke on camera before anyone knew its name.

THE WORLD BROKE on camera before anyone knew its name.

The anchor in Washington steadied his papers, adjusting his jacket slightly over the concealed weight at his hip. "We're receiving simultaneous feeds from four major capitals—Paris, Beijing, Delhi, Johannesburg." His voice carried the practiced calm of decades behind the desk, but something flickered in his eyes as the screen split into quadrants.

Four cities. Four simultaneous collapses.

In Delhi, generals in polished boots toppled sideways across parade grounds, their ceremonial rifles dragging behind them like the limbs of the dying. Police officers sprawled motionless at busy intersections, their service weapons scattered in the dust around them. The camera lingered on a constable's outstretched hand, still reaching for his radio.

Paris brought no relief. Riot squads that had stood moments before now crawled on their knees through the streets, shields still strapped to arms they could no longer lift. Their batons lay abandoned on cobblestones slick with the first autumn rain.

"We're told this is some kind of coordinated—" The anchor's words died mid-sentence. His hand froze above his papers. The chair tipped slowly, inevitably. His pistol clattered to the studio floor—a small, sharp sound that the silence swallowed whole.

He writhed against the polished tile, muscles straining against an invisible weight. The camera held steady, merciless in its witness. An empty anchor desk. Scattered papers drifting in the studio's recycled air. And below the frame, just visible, his body pressed flat like every soldier, every officer, every armed citizen across the globe.

The feeds from the other capitals painted the same impossible picture:

• Beijing's tanks sat motionless at the edge of Tiananmen Square, their hatches sealed tight.

• In Lagos, a naval commander dragged herself across the dock with her fingernails, saber useless at her hip.

• Moscow's security forces clawed at the granite steps of the Kremlin, knives strapped tight against thighs that would no longer rise.

Across six continents, microphones caught only the sound of breathing. Armies that had never known defeat collapsed without a shot fired, without an enemy in sight.

The world would not call it *The Grounding* for several days yet. But in that moment, as cameras in a dozen capitals held their unblinking vigil, nations watched their own power learn to crawl.

Codex I – First Laws

Filed nowhere. Witnessed by none. These are the laws that needed no writing.

The Law of Intent

The moment you mean to harm, you fall. No blade, no gun, no hand raised is required. Will alone is enough.

The Law of Height

Those bound by intent cannot rise higher than three feet. The earth refuses them, gently but forever.

The Law of Continuance

The Pulse was not a single day. It lives on. Each new intent anchors fresh.

The Law of Equivalence

It makes no difference why. Vengeance, justice, defense, fear—harm is harm. The ground does not weigh motives.

The Law of Command

A word can kill. A signature can kill. To order harm is to bear it yourself. Power offers no escape.

The Law of Silence

No warning is given. No voice explains. You know only when you are down, and cannot stand again.

The Law of Permanence

There is no undoing. Regret does not lift you. The tether does not forget.

The Law of Age

Children are not spared. The ground measures only will, not years.

The Law of Possession

You may keep your weapons. The ground cares nothing for objects. It answers only intent.

The Law of Refusal

No one floats above. The Untethered walk. The Grounded crawl or ride low. That is the divide. That is the sentence.

Threshold

The Divide Made Visible

THRESHOLD IS NOT ANOTHER WORLD. It is the same streets, the same stone, the same air—but cut open where two classes must be seen together.

Threshold is universal. It appears in every city, town, village, and commune after the Pulse. It runs through markets in India, temple gates in Japan, courtyards in Brazil, plazas in Europe, township squares in Africa, and avenues in the United States. Wherever Grounded and Untethered live together, Threshold forms the seam.

It takes shape as plazas, stairs, and corridors at the civic midline. Not designed, not perfected—altered under necessity. Benches cut down, counters trimmed unevenly, stalls rebuilt quickly. None of it equal, all of it visible.

For the Grounded, Threshold is a ceiling pressed at eye level. For the Untethered, it is freedom of motion: to stand, to bend, to kneel, or to lie close beside those they still love. That difference defines every exchange.

. . .

FUNCTIONS OF THRESHOLD

• **Commerce** — trade at the line. Goods and coins are set or lowered where the Grounded can take them.

• **Justice** — benches and platforms cut just above the ceiling. Authority sits slightly higher, visible to both classes at once.

• **Procession** — every march, every gathering, every ritual must cross here. Banners carried near the ground, others lifted into the air.

• **Memory** — families and friends meet across the divide. Children move freely until the law takes hold.

MARKS OF THRESHOLD

• **The Line** — rubbed smooth where thousands of hands have reached and been stopped.

• **The Steps** — the ceiling rises with each tread. The Grounded stop when the next pull would raise their torso past it. The Untethered may descend fully.

• **The Ash Pits** — refuse, cloth, and bodies are burned here. What fire reduces is no longer bound. Ash drifts across both classes, the only substance that crosses the line. Cremation is the final release.

THRESHOLD IS NOT FAIRNESS. It is not balance. It is the scar of the law made visible, the place where a city cannot look away from what it has become.

Breathnote — The First Step

Not verdict. Not decree.

Only stone waiting.

The city held its silence, layered and low, until a hand touched plaster, a cheek pressed close, and a body learned to move within it.

Stone had spoken long before people did.

Now it waited for one voice, one breath, to begin.

UR-I: The Standard of Height

(Upper Registers — Depositions of the Untethered)

THE CHAMBER WAS no marble hall, no senate, no tribunal. Only a long bench cut to the old measure—thirty-nine inches from the floor, polished smooth by centuries of leaning arms. It had never been questioned.

Until a child laughed.

She stretched from Belowline, fingers brushing the wood, and shouted, "Almost." The word rippled through the stair like chalk struck in stone. *Almost.* Not enough. Not fair.

That night the stair filled. Untethered and Grounded alike crowded shoulder to shoulder. **No authority ruled them; no council remained. The old order had collapsed. What happened next was not law but improvisation.** They argued, pressed close, and at last called the carpenters. Three inches fell away beneath their blades, chips scattering like bone. At dawn the bench gleamed at thirty-six, level with the new law none had written but all now felt.

Merchants cursed; their ledgers slumped awkward. A judge turned his back, insisting height itself was his robe. Mothers wept as their children, half-grounded in play, at last rested arms without dangling.

Violence was present. She pressed her fingers to the fresh edge and whispered, "I am not gone. I have only moved lower."

The city learned that day: to change a bench was to change a law. To change a law was to invite fracture.

Part One

Book I – The Drop

Where height was broken, and silence first claimed law.

Not war. Not peace.

Only the last unmeasured moment—

before consequence had a name.

Chapter 1

Delta Stair

"Every river begins the city; every stair divides it."

THE RIVER SPREADS WIDE before the city, its surface broken by reeds and the ribs of barges left half-sunk. Silt fans gray along the banks where houses leaned toward the water before the Pulse. Salt creeps into the soil, staining walls white. The plain is a mirror of flood and retreat, breathing in seasons the way lungs take air.

From this yielding delta floor, the stair cut the city in two, rising toward the high plazas in defiant ascent. Its steps were chipped by countless feet, patched where floods gnawed, darkened where hands have clung. The middle risers hollow inward, worn by knees as much as feet—each depression a testament to those who crawled when walking failed them.

At the top, Tribunal banners flap unreadable from below— cloth hoarded, colors fading, each strip a sign of privilege in a city where even rags are contested. At the base, where the stone meets salt-stained earth, chalk spirals mark where children linger at the boundary between water's mercy and the city's judgment. The spirals fade fast; chalk is rationed, salvaged from schools and quarries, crushed from shells when no other source remains. Each line is precious, yet children still press it to stone, proof that play survives scarcity.

The stair is no simple passage. It is argument made vertical, lifting the city's people from the delta's soft forgiveness toward the harsh geometry of power above.

Chapter 2

Belowline

The ground is closer than the sky, and everything presses down.

CORRIDORS TWIST LIKE VEINS, ceilings low, air damp with mildew. Pipes run naked along the walls, sweating rust. Drain grates clatter under hands that drag across them. Mats lie flat on stone where stalls stood before the Pulse.

Drains hum even when dry, echoing floods through channels cut beneath Crawlways. What trickles down carries only rain turned black with soot, threading through warped covers worn smooth by palms that grip them as handholds.

Above this buried network, cables sag between buildings—frayed arteries patched with desperate knots. Some still hum faintly, sparks stolen from batteries wired desperate to keep one light alive. Most hang dead, dangling like severed nerves.

At night, lamps sit at ankle height, jars of fireflies set where they will not be crushed, each one rationed: a glow for two hours, never wasted in daylight. Smells pool here: damp flour, sweat, wet wood. A child counts steps in silence to keep fear away.

Here, silence is not absence. It is weight. It is memory. It is the ground's refusal to forget.

Chapter 3

Breath & Night

"A city exhales in water and in wires."

DRAINS HUM EVEN WHEN DRY, echoing old floods through channels cut beneath Crawlways. What trickles down carries only rain turned black with soot, threading through warped covers worn smooth by palms that grip them as handholds.

Above this buried network, cables sag between buildings—frayed arteries patched with desperate knots. Some still hum faintly, flickering against wet stone. Most hang dead, dangling like severed nerves.

Night in Belowline is not empty darkness but layered sound: whispers, trades, the thud of hands against walls. Light survives only by invention—drop by drop, spark by spark—against the weight of loss.

Chapter 4

Ash Market

"Barter speaks lower than coin."

THE MARKET SPREADS along Crawlway bends, stalls marked not by mats or ribbon scraps but by whatever cloth could be spared, each strip cut from shirts or unravelled hems. Grain rests in baskets at palm height, cloth folded on stone, tools scattered like bones—every piece a relic, not a surplus.

Here cloth carries more weight than grain. Every scrap is contested: torn from bedding, cut from shrouds, unraveled thread by thread until only a rag remains. To lay it on stone is to declare life in fabric that was never meant to last this long.

No shouting now, only quiet exchanges. The air smells of damp flour, charred wood, fish salted too long. Ash clings to corners where fires roared before the Pulse, but more than soot lingers here. Ash is trade itself—mixed into poultices, pressed into cloth for marking, scattered from urns when the Grounded chose fire as their only escape. And some pressed ash into their own flesh, black marks that did not fade, as if to say: consequence belongs to the living as well as the dead.

The market is not trade alone—it is survival arranged flat against the earth, and ash is its measure.

Chapter 5

Clinics & Care Rooms

"Care is reach, not pity."

COTS LINE NARROW HALLS, frames lowered until even a crawler can lift a cup from the floor. Shelves sag with jars of gathered herbs, bottles of lamp oil pressed into service, and shawls unraveled thread by thread until nothing remained. Beside them sit bowls of sifted ash, mixed into poultices to seal wounds or dry fevers, black dust pressed into service when nothing else remained.

The air is sharp with vinegar and coughs that echo against tile relics that outlasted the walls around them. Consent boards lean against doorframes, words burned plain into wood: Ask at the same height as the service.

Care here is not mercy. It is adjustment carved into every beam.

Chapter 6

Schools & Study Courts

"Learning bends to the height of its pupils."

CLASSROOMS SIT IN HALF-LIGHT, chalkboards lowered to waist height, slates scattered on mats—salvage from before the Pulse, their surfaces worn thin from too many hands. Chalk comes in fragments now, crumbled from broken sticks or ground from limestone, each mark rationed, each line fading fast.

Teachers kneel beside students, voices carried no higher than a child's shoulder.

Children read in circles, passing the few books left flat across the floor, spines frayed, pages already loosening. Cloth strips mark their place, and when pages warp with damp, ash is rubbed gently along the edges to keep them dry.

Knowledge does not climb here. It crouches, waiting to be lifted.

Chapter 7

Shelters & Halls

"Even bowed walls remember their voices."

TENEMENTS lean into each other like drunks, balconies collapsed, stairs blocked by debris. Rooms are divided not by walls but by fabric hung low, patchwork and threadbare, stitched from shirts and bedding and shrouds, whatever scraps could be spared.

Civic halls stand hollow since the Pulse, pulpits lowered, benches cut down. Churches, mosques, temples—each bent toward the ground. Bells hang silent since the Pulse. Domes dark. Yet chants and prayers remain, pressed into railings as strips of cloth, though every strip torn away for devotion is cloth no longer shelter, no longer warmth. Still the songs hum at the level of knees.

Chapter 8

Cemeteries & Memory Grounds

"The earth remembers longer than marble."

GRAVES TILT where floods softened soil. Stones carved low, some no taller than a hand. Ribbons and jars mark the fresh earth—flowers wilt too fast, and every strip of cloth tied here is cloth no longer worn, no longer warm.

Mausoleums stand cracked, stairs unreachable by Grounded knees.

The living visit low, pressing palms into dirt, whispering names into soil. Memory seeps sideways, through earth and breath. Yet for many, the only escape from height is fire: bodies returned as smoke that rises, and ash that drifts low enough to be carried—pressed into jars, folded into cloth, or borne upon the skin of those who refuse to forget.

Chapter 9

Rooftops & Skyways

"Height without care becomes its own exile."

ABOVE THE CRAWLWAYS, bridges lace rooftops together. Untethered children chase across planks while Grounded listen to the thump of feet they will never match.

Gardens sprout in gutters—small things only, herbs clinging to silt, weeds coaxed from scraps of soil, washed away with each hard rain. Laundry snaps, threadbare and patched, cloth stretched past its years.

Up here the air is cleaner, but the cracks show too—boards warped, ropes frayed, corners leaning toward fall. The city's roof is no safer than its floor—only higher.

Chapter 10

Soundscape & Atmosphere

"Silence is never empty; it is layered."

AT DAWN, gutters drip into cisterns like muted drums, their stone seams streaked with hairline leaks. Pipes groan with old air. A severed cable flickers high and sharp, not from any grid but from scavenged cells wired desperate to hold one last spark.

Voices move sideways through Crawlways: barters whispered close, laughter bent low, arguments colliding in echo. Prayer does not rise in chorus—it settles.

At night, jars of fireflies pulse, boards shift, a child counts steps to keep fear away. The jars last only hours, their wings stilled by dawn, glass dulled by condensation, cloth seals blackened with use.

Here, silence is not absence. It is weight. It is memory. It is the ground's refusal to forget.

Codex II – Of Jars and Light

"Earthbound stars, trembling against the dark."

THEY WERE NOT BORN for us. They were born to hold food, pills, pickles, oil. Found in cupboards, kitchens, broken markets, their glass chipped and uneven. We called them back into service.

At first we carried them empty, rattling reminders of a world that once stored abundance. Then children pressed fireflies into them, sealing the mouths with cloth and resin. Wings beat against the glass, and the dark was broken.

A single jar glowed two hours before dimming. Three jars together could hold a night, but always at cost—spent wings scattered at dawn, glass fogged with condensation. In other jars we burned oil, cloth strips blackened where wick met flame. Both kinds failed by morning: some hung dull, their captives stilled, others reeked of smoke and ash.

We did not waste them in the sun. Daylight was ration enough. But in Crawlways, where no window reached, or at night markets beneath the stair, they were our constellations. Earthbound stars set low, steady as breath.

Some called us jar-bearers. Others, knot-binders, spiral-chalkers—names that tethered us to tasks as if to say: you belong, you endure.

We knew the truth: jars were not symbols. They were necessity. Yet in their fragile light we glimpsed something more—a reminder that even in capture, even in exhaustion, wings had once moved against the dark.

Breathmark — The Descent

"The Breaking of Silence"

THE CITY HAD SPOKEN in stone, in water, in ash, in cloth, in jars of failing light.

It could go no further on its own.

Now the silence waits to be broken by breath.

Now the ground waits to be measured in bodies.

Now the years begin in people, not in place.

Chapter 11

The Weight

"Stone remembers longer than flesh."

RAEL KEPT his cheek to the wall because it was the only thing that did not lie. Cold, damp, unmoving—it anchored him when air and voices slipped. He breathed into plaster that smelled of mildew and lime and counted the way he always had.

Seventeen. Pause. Four. Pause. Two. Stop.

If he lost the count, he feared he might lose breath, balance —himself.

He learned it the night the world's loudest sound collapsed into silence.

IT HAD BEEN A CONCERT—WALLS of speakers stacked like towers, bass so deep it rattled ribs, strobes cutting the dark like blades. Thousands packed shoulder to shoulder, a storm of youth sweating and shouting in one vast pulse. Rael had been there as a cable hand, part of the crew that made the noise possible. Invisible, but inside the hum.

Then panic. A bottle shattered. A mic stand lifted like a spear. Somebody swung a wrench. Fists tore through the crowd, rage spreading like fire in dry grass. One shove became ten, became hundreds.

And Rael, pressed in the crush, shoved back. His hand rose —empty, but meant to strike. That was enough.

THE PULSE HIT. Not thunder, not lightning—weight. Every will bent to harm folded at once. Knees slammed stone. Screams cut short. The bass died mid-beat, lights froze, and silence fell heavier than any gravity Rael had ever known.

Seventeen beneath the west truss still breathing when the smoke cleared. Four lifts to drag the collapsed rig off them. Two breaths between heaves. The foreman's cadence became law, and Rael carried it into his marrow.

Seventeen. Four. Two.

NOW THE CRAWLWAYS gave him what music once had: a rhythm he could feel against stone. A drip into the gutter run. The iron tang of rusted pipes. A whistle sliding down from Threshold Square. Each sound set a distance, each echo marked a turn. The walls spoke truer than people.

His scar—a shallow hook along his cheek—rubbed the plaster like a second palm. He had cut it himself after the Pulse, proof to other grounded boys that he belonged where they were. He regretted the blade, not the mark. The scar told him who he was when words failed.

Memory still pressed at him—flashes of smoke and glass, of his own hand raised in panic—but the count kept it down.

Seventeen. Four. Two.

Above, reed mats unfurled on stone. The square woke: a trader's cough, a tin jar lid skittering, a guard's staff cracking against a post just to be heard. The sound slid down the stair like a warning.

Rael tapped his scar twice, sealing the cadence back inside. The wall held. So did he. With palms and knees set firm, he pushed toward the light.

Codex III – The Inverted Covenant

"What bends in love makes upright what would have fallen."

AMONG THE CHILDREN OF THRESHOLD, it is written that two sisters were bound by a single, sacred reversal.

Mira bent low, though bending was not her birthright. She chose to shield another, and in that instant her will hardened to harm—the Pulse claimed her, tethering her spirit to earth and shadow. She bore the weight of silence, kept the ledger of sorrows, and carried scars as the price of her protection.

Nessa rose high, though she might have been the one to bend. Her sister's sacrifice spared her from that fate, and so she walked untethered beneath open sky. Yet she did not waste her freedom on flight or hollow triumph—instead, her very standing became a shield of its own kind.

Thus did the covenant turn upon itself: the Grounded became protector through silence and sacrifice. The Untethered became guardian through presence and defiance.

The Witnesses call this the Inverted Covenant—the truth that love, once freely chosen, does not end with a single act of sacrifice. Love reverses, continues, doubles back upon itself. One sister bends low so the other may stand tall. One stands tall so the other may still draw breath.

And so long as breath flows between them, their bond—like a braid of light and shadow—holds fast against all breaking.

Chapter 12

Mira, Thumb Black

"Ink stains deeper than silence."

By NOON the clean half-moon at the base of Mira's thumb was black again. She sat cross-legged on the registrar's floor, shutters breathing mildew and light, the clock stuck forever a minute past noon. Two ledgers, one cracked-nib pen, a pencil stub, a jar of soot-steeped ink, and her grandmother's eraser wrapped like medicine—this was her kit against forgetting.

On the top line she dated the day the way they did now—by flood height and bread allotment, not by any calendar that had betrayed them. Names she wrote gently, because names had weight.

Outside, a messenger boy rasped at the shutter. "Recorder? The school books."

"Bring them," she said, and took the swollen notebooks, their pages smelling faintly of chalk and old perfume. She preferred to write in margins that had already held a life.

"Is it true the stones remember you?" the boy asked, not going.

"It's true the city remembers," she said. "Sometimes it borrows a hand."

"Which are you?"

"A person with a pen," she said, and, after a breath, "and a decent eraser."

He grinned and fled with three clean spines for the clinic. When he'd gone, the hum found her—low, like a whetstone drawn once across iron. It rose through tile into her teeth. The ledger warmed.

"You may use my hand," she told the pressure, quiet, practiced, "but not my name. You may say what is true, but not what punishes."

Her wrist steadied. The words that came were plain enough to live: *Stone keeps what law forgets.*

She let them stand, pressed the eraser lightly—just to feel the ink seat—and closed the book. Her thumb left a black oval on the cover on purpose. People would ask. Some would demand. The stain said she knew the weight of what was inside and would not spend it lightly.

Chapter 13

Nessa, Charms Bright

"The gift that became legacy."

MIRA OPENED HER PALM. Two small studs lay there, silver bright. Beside them, their father's ledger, the leather dark where his thumb had worn it smooth.

"These were hers," Mira said. "You'll keep them better than I will."

Nessa wasted no words. She fastened one stud in her left ear, one in her right, then set her father's hammered coin-fireflies beside them—quarters filed to light, no value left in trade, all of it in witness. The metal caught light without a sound.

Stud and fireflies. Plain and bright. Both now hers.

Mira took the ledger, tracing the thumb-dark margin. They divided inheritance without quarrel: Nessa carried light; Mira carried record.

They would love each other fiercely and fight like alley cats. But when Nessa's fireflies flashed and Mira's thumb stained black, both would remember who had made them and why.

Chapter 14

Salliwith, Strips of Cloth

"Fray is honest."

SALLIWITH'S SHAWL had once been whole, dyed indigo in her mother's basin. Now it hung in long torn tongues, each strip already promised to some corner of pain.

She sat at the bend of Threshold where shadows swallowed the stairs and tore another length slow, the fabric whining in her grip. Her shoulders were bare where the cloth had thinned. She tied the new strip low at rail height—witness where hands could reach.

"Why cloth?" a boy asked.

"Because it frays," she said. "And fray tells the truth about use."

Her husband, a joiner, had died with his mallet still at his side. Her Untethered daughters had gone up into Upper-ways and did not come down. Cloth was what she had left that still answered her hands.

Mira passed later, touched the knot with two fingers, and moved on. One recorded. One remembered. It was enough.

Above, banners snapped. Below, barter murmured. Salliwith pressed her palm to the knot and exhaled. Witness always cost. She paid in strips.

Chapter 15

Kess, Straps and Weight

"Fiber does not lie."

KESS DREW her gloves on before anything else—boiled leather, seams turned outward so they wouldn't bite. She rubbed a thumb of tallow across each palm until the grain went matte and true. Flex once. Twice. No squeak. Ready.

HER CANVAS ROLL lay open on the stone. Inventory by touch, not sight: crooked awl, smooth file, waxed linen line, two pine slats shaved even, three apron straps trimmed and burnished, cord coiled by thickness, a sliver of soap, a tin of tallow. She tapped each with a knuckle. The kit answered back.

"COUNT IT," she said.

THE KNOT-BINDER CHILD at her side repeated the list without faltering. Kess gave a single nod. "Method holds when memory fails."

. . .

SHE CHALKED a rectangle low across the floor. "This is our lane. Nothing crosses it unless we set it there. If it isn't tied, it isn't true."

FAR OFF, Guards scraped their staves. Kess didn't turn. Noise is weather—note it, allow for it, never argue with it.

SHE SET her awl and spoke the words that had become her litany: "Level. Cross. Lock. Test."

FIRST STRAP DOWN, cheek near the floor. "Level." A shim of linen scrap until both sides lied to her hand the same way.

SECOND STRAP BENEATH THE FIRST. "CROSS." Tension drawn until the fibers sang a single low note.

KNOTS SHORT AND DOUBLED. "LOCK." She slid her glove across each tie, trusting grain over sight. "Your glove knows."

THEN SHE LEANED IN SHOULDER-FIRST. "TEST." The strap hummed steady. Not loud, not slack. True.

. . .

"Where do you want the light?" a jar-bearer asked.

"In the crooks," Kess said, "where strap meets post."

A hoop was lashed and set. The jar settled. No rattle. No swing.

They brought her a child on a blanket—fever bright, breath shallow. Kess laid a slat beneath, looped a strap so the pull would spread. "We don't lift what we can slide. We don't slide what we can roll."

She set two bottle-necks wrapped in cloth as rollers. "No hero pulls. If your shoulders climb, you're wrong." The boy shifted smooth across stone, breath easing as weight traveled true.

"Check," Kess said.

The child apprentice repeated, hands at the ready: "Level. Cross. Lock. Test."

. . .

KESS LISTENED to the line's low hum. True.

A STAVE JABBED down from the stair, jerking sideways. The span flexed. Kess dropped her weight into the crossing and let the pull finish into the post. "Don't fight the drag," she told the kids. "Finish it where you choose." The stave came away chalk-marked and empty.

MIRA CROUCHED NEARBY, ledger closed against her chest. "Name this."

"UNDERLINE," Kess said, adding a diagonal strap beneath the pair. "Put it low if you write it. Low is what lasts."

KARINE MARKED anchor points in chalk. "Your lens is different."

"GLOVES ARE A LENS," Kess answered. "So are straps. They tell me what the stone wants."

AT THE CLINIC THRESHOLD, she lifted her chin. "Check."

. . .

Voices rose in chorus without her prompting: "Level. Cross. Lock. Test."

Kess flexed her hands inside her gloves. Tools kept, method steady. Work didn't finish when one line held. Work finished only when the next line held, and the next.

"Next load," she said, already chalking the route back. "Work's not finished. Work's working."

Chapter 16

Night Workshop, Grip Cart #1

"Pride breaks before leather."

THEY WORKED BY JAR-LIGHT, a ring of soft gold breathing against the square's stone. Kess spread her canvas on the ground: two scavenged wheels with crooked hubs, a broom handle filed down to an axle, four short slats, a coil of cordage, three straps cut from aprons long ago retired from cooking to carry the city instead.

"Low first," she said. "Everything after."

A knot-binder child steadied the nearest wheel with both knees. Another held the jar close without shaking—fireflies pulsed, patient and bright. Kess chalked a rectangle on the stone, the size of a pallet and no higher than a palm stacked on a fist. She marked a cross through its center.

"Keep the load low," the children murmured, following her chalk.

"Cross the strain," Kess answered, and drew two more lines —a second set of diagonals to keep the platform from racking when the ground turned mean. She drilled with the crooked awl, twisted the broom handle through the hubs, shimmed the wobble with shaved slivers of slat. The axle squealed. She mixed soap scrap and ash with a thumb and worked the paste into the wood until the squeal narrowed to a whisper.

"Two knots tell the truth of one," she said, lashing the front struts, then lashing them again where leather met wood. She passed the strap to the smallest pair of hands. "You start. I'll finish."

They tightened together, a call-and-response of tension until the leather sang its quiet note of held. Kess set a pad of folded cloth on the platform—old wool, clean, thicker at the hip rests. She fitted a looped harness to the front, the pull point low enough that knees would not catch and shoulders would not lift beyond the law's hard ceiling.

"That's too low," one boy said, doubtful but brave.

Kess nodded. "Test the doubt." She shortened the loop by two finger-widths. "Now drag."

He leaned. The cart inched. The wheels found their path along the shallow runnels years of crawl had carved. No lift. No catch. A soft roll and a steady strain.

Mira arrived with her ledger hugged closed against her ribs, breath white in the cool. "Name?" she asked.

"Grip Cart," Kess said. "First."

"Grip Cart, One," Mira wrote in the margin and left the rest of the page blank, the space a promise.

At the clinic threshold a woman raised a hand: "We've got a man who can't be carried in arms. Spine."

Kess looked at the cart, then at the children. "Lesson time."

THEY PUSHED the platform to the threshold. Kess knelt, eyes level with the boards as if the cart were an animal to be gentled. "Corner ties here and here. Pad thick at the sacrum, thin at the shoulders. Don't let pride choose speed. Pride breaks before leather."

"Pride breaks before leather," the children echoed, and their hands moved. Pads set. Straps crossed. Knots doubled. The man was eased onto the wool with breath-held care, his grimace knotted to the same rhythm as the lashings.

"Lift nothing you can roll," Kess said. "Pull nothing you can share."

Two kids took the harness. A third walked at the rear, palms light as air on the frame to keep sway from becoming swing. They set off, slow and level, down the line chalk had drawn through the square earlier that day. Firefly jars preceded them like small patient stars.

RAEL'S CHEEK rested against his wall as they passed. He tapped twice—the old test for true—and the sound came back clean. Kess didn't look up. She could hear truth when the wheels spoke it.

At the step lip the cart shuddered—one wheel caught a chip where stone had risen like a tooth. The boy at the harness stiffened.

"Breathe," Kess said. "Weight is a language." She slid a spare strap under the lifted edge and cinched it to the rail, making a temporary ramp out of leather and will. "Now the load has a sentence it can finish."

They went over without jolt. The man's jaw loosened. The boy's shoulders dropped. The cart rolled on.

At the clinic door, hands took the frame and the man both, and Kess let them. The harness fell slack against the stone. The children stood panting, bright-eyed and proud in the way pride is allowed: not about being right, but about getting someone through.

Mira lifted her ledger and, instead of lines, pressed her blackened thumb once beside the new name.

Karine, who had watched from the stair with her cracked lens, drew a small square on the lowest step and labeled it in white: *Carry*.

Kess crouched and ran her knuckles along the strap where it had borne most strain. The leather was warm. The knot was honest. The boards had not lied.

"Nothing holds alone," she said, mostly to herself, and then aloud so the children would hear it and keep it: "Nothing holds alone."

The jar-light dwindled as lids were closed. The cart rested at the rail, waiting for the next call. Kess rolled her tools back into the canvas, the edges stained with soap and ash. Her palms stung again—the good ache—and she welcomed it. It told her what the city had asked and what it had agreed to carry in return.

By dawn, Grip Cart One would earn its first scuffs and a second name. By dusk, there would be a list.

Chapter 17

Karine, Cracked Lens

"A fracture becomes map the moment it is named."

KARINE CROUCHED at the base of the Tribunal stair like a scholar studying ancient texts, her cracked magnifier catching the slanted light of afternoon. The lens her father had pressed into her hands on his last conscious day—rim bent, surface veined with fractures that split light into rainbow shards—still magnified enough truth to make the invisible undeniable.

Through the web of cracks in her lens, she read the deeper cracks that mattered: hollows worn smooth by ten thousand desperate knees, edges sharp enough to draw blood, seams where marble had finally given up pretending to be eternal. The stone bore witness to every body pressed against it, every palm scraped, every tear fallen into its pores.

Her chalk moved with surgical precision, tracing each scar as if drawing a map of the city's secret heart. Where her father's lens revealed damage, her hand made it permanent —visible to any who cared to look. She placed small pebbles at exact points where knees would catch, where elbows would scrape, where flesh always met stone.

. . .

"WHAT DO YOU SEE DOWN THERE?" a child asked, dropping to his knees with the fearless curiosity of youth.

Karine held the chalk still, then lifted the cracked lens so the world fractured into honesty. "The places where the city remembers us," she said. "Each mark is someone who knelt here. Someone who bled here. Someone who refused to disappear."

He helped her place the pebbles, his small fingers learning the geography of scars. His wonder at each groove and scratch reminded her why the work mattered. Someone had to teach the young to read the language of stone.

MIRA PASSED with her ledger wound tight against her wrist, ink-black thumb already seeking the next truth. Their eyes met—one mapping the body's testimony, the other preserving the voice's witness. Word and line, same labor.

Karine bent back to her work. For a heartbeat the fractured lens caught the sun just so, its cracks aligned with the stair's, broken things reflecting broken things until the scar blazed like lightning. Then the light shifted, and it was chalk on stone again.

THE CHILD TRACED one of her marks, already learning to read the city's hidden language. Already understanding that some truths can only be seen through cracked glass, only mapped by those who keep working after breaking.

The stone remembered. The chalk held. And somewhere between fracture and function, between damage and documentation, the real work of resistance continued—one mark, one pebble, one scar at a time.

Codex IV —On the Act of Naming

"What is named cannot be erased."

To the Untethered, names were decrees written from balconies, banners painted in gold, signatures pressed into wax that flaked and faded. But the Grounded knew better.

A name spoken from height can be ignored. A name traced in chalk at the base of a stair cannot. It is seen by every hand that drags across it, every knee that grinds against it, every child who follows the lines with a fingertip and learns to read the language of scars.

Karine's cracked lens did not reveal beauty. It revealed truth: stone fractured by weight, corners sharpened by grief, seams widened by the mathematics of suffering. Her chalk wrote those truths where none could deny them.

This was not ornament. It was indictment.

Not decoration. Documentation.

When a fracture receives a name—*Hunger*, *Ash*, *Oath*, *Burden*—it ceases to be silence. It becomes map, ledger, testimony. The Tribunal's laws crumbled, but chalk held. The names clung. And each name bound the city tighter than any chain.

To erase a word was to admit the word had power. To leave it was to confess the world remembered.

So the Grounded named their own history, line by line, crack by crack, until the marble itself became a book that would outlast all golden letters above.

Chapter 18

The Children

"Too light to be tethered, too cruel to be ignored."

THEY WERE NEVER ONE THING.

Most walked tall—Untethered—darting between markets and crawlways, running where no adult could follow. Their feet barely kissed the stone before they were airborne again, voices carried on winds that couldn't catch them. A few, fewer than one in five, lived low already: knees raw from scraping stone, palms calloused from catching falls, bodies pressed into a world they were too young to deserve. Those were the Grounded children—bound by dares that went too far, by rages that burned too bright, by moments they could not take back.

The Untethered mocked them without mercy.

"Half-grown forever," one boy sneered at a girl dragging a knife-scored knee across the market stones. "You'll never stand taller than my belt," another laughed, towering just enough to sting, his shadow falling across her bent form like a taunt made solid.

. . .

CRUELTY CAME QUICK WITH CHILDREN. But so did honesty, sharp and clean as winter air. They pointed out truths adults swallowed like stones: "Your banner hangs lower than her jar." "Your staff sounds hollow when you think no one's listening." "The ledger may rip, but it still remembers every mark you tried to erase."

And sometimes—*sometimes*—they laughed when no one else could.

They turned the city's solemn chalk lines into spirals of play, leaping in and out as if ancient decree were nothing more than a skipping rope drawn in dust. They released captured fireflies only to chase them again through twilight streets, calling the sacred code "hide-and-seek for the dark." They tied the ceremonial cloth not with reverence, but in knots shaped like cats and crooked hearts, until the judgment rails looked less like instruments of law and more like carnival banners swaying in the evening breeze.

NOT ALL THEIR cruelty stayed harmless.

Some Untethered walked a line so thin it scraped their own shadows raw. They shoved Grounded peers toward stair edges, dangled water jars just beyond desperate, reaching fingers, mocked the constant scrape of knees and elbows against unforgiving stone. They laughed, yes—but always with fear flickering behind their eyes like candle flames in wind. For they knew the law was always listening, always watching, always measuring. One shove too deliberate, one vow spoken with true malice in the chest, one laugh sharpened from play into genuine intent—and they would drop instantly, shackled to the very height they had scorned.

No adult needed to warn them. They could feel it in their bones: the ground itself waited, patient and silent, taking measurements of every heartbeat, every breath, every moment of choice.

Animals moved freely among them—dogs bolting fearless across judgment rails, cats perched smugly on ledges just out of human reach, birds wheeling overhead in mockery of earthbound rules. The children laughed when animals did what the Grounded could not: leap, climb, escape the weight of consequence. They also wept when those same dogs returned to owners who could no longer stand, licking faces now pressed forever against cold stone, whimpering at the scent of tears they couldn't understand.

The children had no council. No titles. No charter written in official hands.

Yet their games outlasted the banners that proclaimed civic order, and their taunts outlived the decrees that shaped their world. In scraps of cloth and lines of chalk, in broken jars and wild laughter that echoed off stone walls, they made the city's harsh law their own—not through rebellion, but through the strange, terrible alchemy that transforms play into fate.

Not verdict. Not decree.

Only games that turned into permanence when no one expected it—least of all the children themselves, caught forever in the moment between laughter and consequence, between the lightness of youth and the weight of forever.

Chapter 19

The Circle

"A shape begins the moment breath finds rhythm."

THEY GATHERED at dusk in the hollow where crawlways crossed like broken bones. No decree summoned them, no Tribunal order carved in stone. The ground itself pulled them together—six bodies drawn by gravity older than law.

Rael came first, always first, pressing his scarred cheek to the wall's cold truth. He counted under his breath—seventeen, four, two—the numbers a lifeline thrown to lungs that had nearly drowned. His chest caught, stuttered, but the rhythm steadied him like a hand at his back.

Mira followed, ledger cord looped at her wrist, thumb already black with ink. She hated opening it, but she feared forgetting more than she feared remembering.

Nessa dropped into the hollow with a grin sharp as broken glass, earrings flashing in the jar-light. "Don't look so grim," she said. "We're still breathing. That counts for something."

Salliwith lowered herself slowly, joints grinding, shoulders bare where her shawl had dwindled to threads. She tied one strip to the rail and exhaled as though breath itself was tribute.

Kess unrolled her canvas wrap. Gloves already on, she set slats and straps before her like an offering. The leather was worn, but her method was not. "Level. Cross. Lock. Test," she murmured, fingers tracing each knot as if the circle itself depended on their holding. She lashed a short span between two rails—not for weight tonight, but to prove truth. The straps hummed their steady note. The children nearest her grinned and whispered the words back: *Level. Cross. Lock. Test.*

Karine crouched last, cracked lens fogging with each breath. She mapped lines across stone, chalk tracing cracks like a surgeon's hand marking bone: *Fray. Bend. Hold.*

AND THEN THE children drifted in, as if summoned by pulse more than voice.

Jar-bearers set glass vessels low, amber glow pulsing like heartbeats in the growing dark. Knot-binders tied fresh cloth where Guards had torn the old, their small fingers repeating Kess's patterns until the rail looked stitched by dozens of careful hands. Spiral-chalkers widened rings around them all, turning the hollow into something more than stone.

A breath-counter picked up Rael's numbers, dared others to follow. The cadence spread—seventeen, four, two—threading itself into the straps Kess had braced, into the chalk rings Karine had traced, into the ledger Mira held closed against her chest.

. . .

THE CIRCLE BECAME MORE than six. More than stone. More than shadow.

Mira's thumb tapped once against leather. Nessa's earrings caught the last light. Salliwith's shoulder leaned heavy into the rail. Karine's chalk whispered across each fracture. Rael breathed "Hold" like a vow. And Kess, palms gloved, checked each strap twice, then taught the children to check a third time.

The shape breathed.

Above them, Guards barked orders from marble stairs, voices sharp as their staves. But down here, in the hollow where crawlways crossed, none looked up.

The circle breathed. The circle held.

And for now, that was enough.

Chapter 20

Provenance of the Tribunal

"No crown made them. No Archive named them."

THE CHAMBER WAS shallow as a wound cut into stone, its ceiling no higher than a child could stretch. No dais rose above three feet; no bench towered over the crowd. The Tribunal sat level with the law itself—measured low, restrained by the same tether that bound them to earth.

They were Grounded. Not Untethered, not spared, not clean. Each bore the scar of intent, the weight of having once chosen to strike. Yet it was they who presided, three voices set to balance the city when hunger and riot first tore Threshold in two.

CHIEF ARBITER TENRIC Halvorsen

He leaned upon a ledger thick as brick, knees aching from years pressed against stone, though his conviction never bent. A mason's son who once raised a hammer in fury, he had dropped with the rest on the day of the Pulse. Since then, he treated precedent like mortar—each case laid atop the last, every ruling a wall against collapse.

He did not call it mercy or cruelty, only weight measured fairly, stone upon stone. His flaw was the same as his strength: he trusted walls more than breath.

Defender Magistrate Elara Mora

She wore her shawl in tatters, wrist wrapped in a strip torn from the day of her own trial. Once, she had shouted at guards with such fire that she was dragged into judgment herself. She had not struck, but she had *willed it*, and the Pulse had claimed her body low.

Since then, she burned to protect others from the machinery of law she knew too well. Her voice cracked like flame on wet wood—bright, furious, never steady for long. To some she was a savior; to others, reckless tinder waiting to ignite.

Canonister Brannic Raal

He sat apart, silent but for the sound of his fingers on the shard of first Accord stone that hung from his throat. He had been a scholar before the Pulse, teaching the philosophy of restraint, yet in secret he had carried a knife for fear of his own students. That knife had condemned him to the ground.

Now, his silence was scripture. To him the first Accords were not suggestions but commandments carved into breath. He would rather see a child crushed by consequence than see the law bent by pity. People feared him most, though he seldom raised his voice.

.   .   .

THE TRIAD

Together they formed the triad: stone, fire, silence. No crown made them, no Archive named them. The people chose, desperate for an anchor. And though the Archive's breath sometimes whispered through walls, it had never spoken their names.

They ruled from necessity, not purity. Their hands were as stained as those they judged, their knees as bruised, their lungs as tethered. The crowd knew this. The judges knew it too. And it was this paradox—condemned men and women delivering verdicts—that gave their chamber its terrible weight.

Outside, cloth strips fluttered in the ash wind. Inside, the boy with the knife waited his turn.

The Tribunal began.

Chapter 21

The Ledger Torn

"Authority breaks first in the margins."

GUARDS SCRAPED down from the stairs like beetles fleeing light, their staves dragging against stone, knees grinding ceremonial cloth into mud and memory. Their boots deliberately blocked the crawlways with cruel precision, arms swinging stiff across rails where children's knots still hung like defiant prayers. From the dais above, the formation appeared orderly. Up close, its gaps betrayed weakness: jars glowed steady in unreachable corners, chalk spirals widened beyond the reach of scuffing staves, and cloth fluttered free just outside armored grasp.

The Herald of the Tribunal raised his hand, voice thin as winter air. Behind him, the Triad leaned close in their failing postures of power.

The Chief Arbiter coughed through a decree, parchment shaking in hands that had forgotten strength.

The Defender Magistrate pleaded for obedience—fear dressed in authority, her words trembling more than commanding.

The Canonister spat mockery loud enough to mask his own terror, venom that fell short of its mark.

The Herald's finger cut through the crowd like a blade.

"Recorder. Surrender the book."

Mira clutched the ledger tight against her chest, heart hammering against its spine. Her thumb smeared fresh ink into the cover—a black oval pressed so deep it resembled a bruise.

"This is witness," she said, her voice steady despite the tremor in her hands. "Not yours to command."

A Guard lurched forward on raw knees, stave scraping stone as he reached for her.

One sheet tore free, caught by evening air, spiraling down the stairs like a wounded bird. Mira's careful script bled where the tear had savaged it, words scattered like broken teeth across the page.

The square held its breath.

Then the children moved.

Knot-binders scrambled on raw knees, chasing the falling page.

A jar-bearer dropped low, lifting glass like a shield against the encroaching dark.

Spiral-chalkers circled the ground where it would fall, claiming the space as sacred before paper even touched earth.

The page settled into ash and dust. A breath-counter whispered Rael's rhythm: "Seventeen. Four. Two." The numbers rose from young lips like an incantation, as if mathematics itself could mend what had been torn.

Small hands lifted the page high—edges smudged with ash, Mira's ink bleeding where her grip had pressed too hard. They bound it to the rail with a strip torn from Salliwith's own shawl, red cloth tying paper to iron. Torn, stained, imperfect—but visible. A banner born of ruin, proclaimed by voices too young to know surrender.

The Canonister shrieked: "Memory belongs to the Tribunal!"

Nessa's laughter answered, bright as breaking crystal. "Then why do you crawl on your bellies to steal it?" Her studs and firefly charms blazed in the jar-light, her inheritance glinting untouchable.

The Guards froze. They had torn one page—and multiplied it into a thousand witnesses. Every child had seen. Every adult had watched. Every strip of cloth tied now carried the ledger's wound as its own.

Rael pressed his scarred cheek to the wall and whispered: "Hold." The word rippled outward until the whole square inhaled and exhaled as one—a single lung, a single vow, a single refusal to be erased.

The ledger was no longer whole.

But it was louder than it had ever been, its torn voice echoing off stone that would remember long after the guards had scuttled back to marble safety, long after the Tribunal had retreated to chambers where they dared not admit the ground itself was listening, measuring, waiting for their own fracture.

Chapter 22

Children Answer Back

"The smallest answer louder by lowering."

THE GUARDS SCRAPED into the square on knees and elbows, staves dragging like crutches across stone. Authority made ugly by posture—crawling men pretending to stand. They tore cloth from the rails, ground it beneath their palms, smeared witness into mud. They dragged wood across chalk spirals until dust rose choking.

But the knot binders knelt again. Small fingers threaded fresh strips into iron faster than boots could grind them away. Spiral-chalkers crouched low, tracing circles under the Guards' own elbows, chalk rings widening even as staves scuffed them thin. Jar-bearers slid glass between rails, fireflies pulsing gold where no stave could reach without shattering dignity. A breath-counter whispered Rael's rhythm into the stone: *seventeen, four, two.* Others picked it up until the numbers beat steady through the dust.

The Guards pressed harder, knees barking against stone, arms swinging stiff with rage.

Nessa leaned from the circle, earrings catching jar-light. "See? They'd have to crawl lower than us to win." Her smile cut like glass.

One Guard swung his stave toward a jar. A girl darted beneath him, chalking a spiral so close he would have to flatten his body to erase it. White dust streaked his knees.

Another ripped cloth from the rail. A boy tied two strips back faster, laughing: "You'll need three arms to keep up!" The crowd laughed with him, relief bubbling sharp as survival.

The Triad sagged on their dais. The Chief Arbiter coughed through his decree, parchment wilting in his grip. The Defender Magistrate whispered "Please" like a prayer to silence that had stopped listening. The Canonister shrieked, "Children cannot decree!" His voice cracked, thin as a snapped strap.

Salliwith pressed another ribbon low to the rail, bare shoulder trembling but steady. "Witness begins in strips," she said.

Karine bent over her cracked lens, marking the scuffs where stave met stone, naming each one: "Break. Bend. Again."

Mira pressed her blackened thumb to the spine of her ledger, whispering, "Answer written in cloth and chalk."

Kess knelt with her gloves still on, guiding a knot-binder's hands. "Level. Cross. Lock. Test." The girl repeated each word, pulling the strap tight until it hummed. The sound carried, low and steady, cutting beneath the Guards' noise.

Rael exhaled against his wall, and the breath-counter echoed him. "Hold."

The Guards' jeers wavered. Their staves sagged. Crawling men met crawling children—and lost.

For the first time, the Tribunal saw it plain: law rising from hands too small to silence, written lower than decree, stronger than shame.

Chapter 23

The Firefly Game

"Play becomes law the moment it survives a night."

AT DUSK the jar-bearers returned like pilgrims, lids loose, fingers gentle on glass that held captured starlight. They lowered jars into the crawlways with reverence, fireflies pulsing gold against stone. Too swift, too low for any decree to cage.

The Guards crawled in at the edges, staves clattering like angry crutches. "Child's play," one spat, his knees grinding chalk spirals into dust. "Bugs and babies."

But play has gravity. And this game was already pulling minds into orbit.

A girl whispered to her brother: "One jar means safe passage." A boy called from across the square: "Two jars side by side means danger coming." Another voice added: "If we break one, everyone scatters—fast as water."

By full nightfall, the rules had spread like fever through the ward. Jar-light flickered from corner to corner, a wordless code of survival. Spiral-chalkers circled each vessel with bright rings, claiming the glow as sacred ground. Knot-binders tied cloth to jar handles, their knots steady under Kess's watchful eye. The jars no longer wobbled—they held.

Kess crouched low, gloves tight, teaching children to brace jars with leather hoops and test the lashings. "Light wobbles if the strap lies. Hear it hum." She plucked one taut cord; the jar answered with a faint note. "That's truth. No hum, no law." The children echoed her chant—*Level. Cross. Lock. Test.*—until the whole square whispered the method like prayer.

A breath-counter matched Rael's rhythm to the beating wings: "Seventeen. Four. Two." The numbers stitched themselves into the flicker, math woven to light, survival bound to pattern.

Laughter rose, sharp as defiance. Children darted between glowing markers, daring Guards to strike at shadows. A boy dropped a jar at a Guard's knees, insects scattering gold across his crawling hands. "Careful!" he cried, grinning. "They outrank you now."

The crowd laughed with him—relief sharpened to joy.

On the marble dais, the Tribunal stiffened: The Chief Arbiter coughed through parchment that sagged like wet cloth. The Defender Magistrate whispered, "It is only children," as if prayer could undo truth. The Canonister bellowed, "You kneel to toys!" But his voice cracked high and thin, desperate as a broken stave.

Nessa tilted her chin, earrings blazing like their own constellation. "Better toys than thrones," she said, and the laughter doubled, carrying farther than banners ever could.

Mira held her ledger closed, thumb pressed black against its spine. "If I write it, I'll kill it," she murmured. "Let play be its own record."

The fireflies pulsed on, law written in wings and knots, straps and chalk. Play had survived its first night, and in surviving, it had hardened into truth.

By dawn, when the Guards retreated to barracks and the Tribunal to chambers, the jars would dim, the chalk would blur. But the rules would remain—unwritten, unspoken, yet real as gravity.

Law born not from decree, but from game. Law held by hands too small to silence. Law that would outlast the night.

Codex V – Spark

"A law whispered is already written."

MORNING LIGHT FOUND the jars still glowing like patient stars. Some wings had stilled overnight, but the chalk rings around each vessel shone bright, and cloth on their handles fluttered like prayer flags. What began as children's play had not vanished with sleep. It had hardened.

A spiral-chalker crouched low, retracing the night's rings, whispering meanings soft as secrets: one jar safe, two jars danger, one broken scatter. The crowd leaned close, repeating each phrase until memory held.

Karine bent over her cracked lens, sketching each formation into her fracture-map. The flawed glass split the morning sun into shards across stone. She named each pattern as she drew: Safe. Flee. Warning.

A breath-counter lifted Rael's rhythm into the square. "Seventeen. Four. Two." The numbers pulsed steady as heartbeats, syncing breath to flicker, survival to mathematics.

Mira opened her ledger without fear and wrote in clean hand: *Codex Spark: one jar = safe passage. two jars = danger approaches. broken jar = scatter like water.* She closed the book on those words—truth distilled, nothing added.

Salliwith touched the fresh page with ash-stained fingers. "Witness," she said. "Even if paper frays, this moment holds."

But it was Kess who gave the code its spine. She moved along the rails, gloves on, tightening every knot, checking every strap, refusing drift. "Level. Cross. Lock. Test." Her mantra carried as a low hum beneath the children's play. She lashed jars tight against iron so no Guard's stave could spill them. She underlined chalk with fiber, laughter with leather, play with permanence.

"Without straps, it scatters," she said, plucking one cord until it sang its note. "Law needs tension. Test it. Then trust it."

The children echoed her—*Level. Cross. Lock. Test.*—tying fresh strips until the rails hummed like instruments.

The Triad stirred above, uneasy: The Arbiter coughed into his parchment, decree unread. The Magistrate whispered "It is only play," but her hands shook. The Canonister roared, "Scribbles and insects! Nothing more than noise!" Yet his voice cracked thin with panic, and everyone heard the fear beneath his fury.

But the law had already been tied down. Kess's straps held the jars. Karine's map traced them. Mira's ink named them. Children repeated them.

The first spark of Codex was struck—not in marble halls, but in crawlways where fireflies danced and leather hummed under steady hands.

It would not be extinguished. It would spread, jar by jar, strap by strap, until even silence could not untie it.

Chapter 24

Tribunal Mockery

"Power mocks loudest when it trembles."

AT DAWN, banners dropped from the stair like wounded birds—no gold seals, no vellum, just rough scraps painted in haste, letters broad and cruel:

PLAY IS NOT ORDER. BUGS ARE NOT LAW. YOUR CLOTH IS RAGS.

The Guards dragged them low on staves, crawling forward, knees scraping chalk rings, arms trembling under the weight of their own humiliation.

The Canonister's laugh rang brittle across Threshold, sharp as glass underfoot. "Fireflics and scribbles!" he shrieked. "Insects cannot govern! Rags cannot decree!" His voice climbed higher with every word, shrill as fear wearing another man's mask.

The Arbiter tried to cough authority into parchment, but his script sagged with his breath. The Magistrate pressed her hands together at the rail, whispering, "This cannot be safe," as if mercy still answered marble.

But the crowd did not roar back in anger.

It laughed.

Laughter rolled low at first, then wider, until it shook stone that had heard too many decrees and too few jokes. The sound of people who had finally seen their oppressors crawl.

A jar-bearer lifted her vessel, fireflies pulsing steady gold. A knot-binder tied crimson cloth to a sagging banner, turning insult into ornament. A spiral-chalker circled the Tribunal's painted words, then added her own in steady script: **REMEMBER.**

A breath-counter whispered Rael's rhythm—seventeen, four, two—and the laughter bent into cadence, the square breathing like one lung.

Salliwith pressed her bare shoulder to the shrine's stone. "Witness outlasts paint," she said, her voice carrying clear. "Outlasts panic. Outlasts fear."

Karine marked the sagging banners into her fracture-map, cracked lens catching the light. "Look how low they hang," she murmured. "Lower than our law."

Mira tapped her ledger shut with a sound like a gavel. "Mockery is admission," she said. "They fear it enough to name it."

And Kess—gloves firm, straps taut—tugged at the jars tied to the rail until each sang true. "Level. Cross. Lock. Test." The mantra carried, whispered by children at her side, louder than the Canonister's shrieks. She bound their law again, securing jars against rails so no decree could spill them.

Nessa threw her head back and laughed. "Better toys than thrones!" she called, her earrings flashing firefly-light until she gleamed like her own constellation.

The Guards tried to bang staves for order, but the sound rang hollow, staves slipping in chalk dust. Their formation broke like water through fingers.

The Tribunal's insults had exposed what no decree ever could: they were not rulers above, but grounded like everyone else, pressed lower than the children they mocked.

And in the growing light, one truth stood brighter than banners, stronger than mockery:

The Codex held. The straps held. The laughter held.

Chapter 25

Branding Attempt

"Marks meant to shame burn longest as scars."

By DUSK, the Tribunal's laughter had soured to something thin and desperate. Mockery had failed them. Cloth still knotted the rails like banners. Jars still pulsed with captured starlight. Chalk spirals widened with every hour. What they had meant to erase had only multiplied.

The Chief Arbiter fumbled with his velvet pouch, fingers trembling. From it he drew a branding iron, the word **IRREPARABLE** carved deep into its tip. He tried to lift it to the brazier, but his hands shook; the iron clanged against marble, the sound ringing like dignity's funeral bell. His cough drowned whatever decree he meant to speak.

The Defender Magistrate leaned close, voice low, face ashen. "This is not protection," she whispered, words carrying farther than she intended. "This will not save us." Yet she kept her hands folded, complicit in silence.

The Canonister shrieked to the square, spittle flying: "If law cannot be written in books, let it be burned into flesh!" His voice cracked thin as glass, shrill as cornered fear.

The Guards dragged a boy forward—wrists bound, knees bloodied from crawling. The iron glowed white-hot in the coals, heat shimmering like the ghost of justice long dead. The child whimpered once. The silence that followed cut sharper than any blade.

Salliwith lunged forward, shawl gone, shoulders bare, clutching her last strip of cloth. A stave barred her chest but she leaned hard, wood creaking under the pressure of witness.

Kess pressed both gloved hands against the rail, leather straps cutting deep into iron. "Look at his grip," she said aloud, voice steady, carrying. "He can't even hold level." Her words split the square: not poetry, not plea, but a craftsman's verdict. The Arbiter's hand trembled harder.

Karine's cracked lens fogged as she mapped the fracture lines spreading from brazier to stair. Mira smeared her ink-black thumb across her ledger's cover—not to record, but to refuse witness to cruelty. Rael pressed his scarred cheek to stone, whispering his vow: "Hold. Hold."

And then Nessa stepped between the boy and the fire.

She did not crawl. She did not kneel. She stood—Untethered still—her earrings catching brazier-light until they burned like constellation stars. Every eye saw it: Tribunal bent low, Guards crawling, and Nessa upright, a line drawn in living flesh.

"Then brand me," she said, voice clean as water over stone. "But you'll have to crawl lower than I stand. Low enough for all to see you grovel."

The Arbiter's hands shook. To mark her, he would have to bow beneath the child he meant to brand—or rise above her and betray the very law that bound him. Either choice meant collapse.

The Magistrate hid her face in her palms. The Canonister shrieked, but no sound came. His voice was gone, eaten by its own emptiness.

The iron slipped from the Arbiter's hand. It struck marble with a hiss, branding **IRREPARABLE** into dust and ash where it belonged.

Steam rose like ghost-script, an epitaph for cruelty. The boy remained unmarked. The Tribunal sagged on their dais like scarecrows after harvest. They had reached for ultimate cruelty and discovered they lacked even the strength to be truly evil.

The square did not riot. It remembered. And it waited.

For ash does not vanish. It lingers—until someone claims it.

From the Ledger of Mira:

"Defiance stands taller than decree."

- **No mark is law if taken by force.**

- **Refusal is inheritance.**

- **Scars chosen are stronger than scars imposed.**

- **Untethered rises where authority grovels.**

Chapter 26

The Weight of Inheritance

"Ink and laughter make inheritance bearable."

NIGHT FELL heavy after the branding iron hissed its failure into ash, settling over the square like a blanket woven from exhaustion and wonder. The crowd had grown hushed—not from fear, but from the profound weight of having witnessed law itself attempt cruelty and collapse under its own hollowness. The silence that followed was not empty but full, pregnant with the understanding that something fundamental had shifted in the world's balance.

Mira sat with her ledger balanced in her lap like a sleeping child, her thumb already stained black from pressing the cover shut, over and over, as if the pressure alone could keep the words inside safe from those who would twist them. She had become the guardian of witness, and the responsibility sat heavier on her shoulders than any cloak.

Nessa dropped down beside her sister with the fluid grace of water finding its level, stretching her legs long against stone that still held the day's warmth. The small silver studs their mother had left glinted faintly in the jar-light, while beside them the hammered charms their father had shaped

with his own calloused hands hung warm against her skin—
not loud, not showy, but present as heartbeats, substantial as
memory made manifest.

"You're writing again," Nessa teased, nudging Mira's knee
with her own. "If paper could speak, it would beg you for
mercy. All those words pressed so deep they're practically
carved."

Mira shook her head, dark hair catching glints of distant jar-
light. Her grip tightened on the ledger until her knuckles
showed white through skin. "If I don't write it true, someone
else will twist it false. Or worse—they'll let it fade until it
never happened at all."

"Maybe." Nessa tilted her chin toward the scattered lights
below, earrings catching jar-light like ripples in a breeze. "Or
maybe they'll laugh it into legend instead. Not every truth
needs to be caged in books, sister. Some stories live better in
voices than on pages."

Mira looked up from her ledger, ink-stained thumb tapping
restless against the margin where her careful words waited.
"You really think laughter alone can hold us together? Keep
us whole when everything else is breaking?"

"It worked tonight." Nessa's grin bloomed slow as sunrise,
and the charms at her ears caught the light, shimmering like
captured stars. "Did you see their faces when we laughed at
their banners? How small they looked up there, shouting at
fireflies?"

For the first time in days—weeks—Mira felt her mouth
curve upward, the expression foreign but not unwelcome.
The ledger sagged in her lap, transforming from shield to
burden, from necessity to choice. Their mother's laugh

returned to her memory in a flash of recognition—quick and bright as flint striking steel, cut off far too soon by the weight that had pressed them all low.

Their father's hands came back too, steady as mountains as he hammered coins into sparks of light, creating beauty from the scraps the world had thrown away. She could almost feel the warmth of the forge, smell the honest sweat of labor that created rather than destroyed.

"Promise me you won't lose those," Mira said, nodding toward the earrings that carried their parents' love made visible.

"Promise me you won't lose this," Nessa answered, tapping the ledger's worn spine with a finger that understood its weight. "The words matter, even when laughter carries further."

For a heartbeat that stretched like eternity, they leaned into each other—shoulder to shoulder, sister to sister—one carrying memory in careful ink, the other in light that danced against her skin. The ground beneath them offered no comfort, no softness, no mercy. But this inheritance they shared—one book heavy with witness, two earrings bright with love—held them upright in a way that mere standing never could.

They laughed then, both at once—a sound that erupted unbidden from throats that had forgotten joy was possible. Startled, unplanned, almost foolish in its honesty, it rang across the quiet square like a bell tolling hope instead of loss.

A child's head turned toward the sound, small face brightening with the recognition that witness was not only pain, that survival was not only endurance, that sometimes—even in the darkest hours—sisters could find reasons to remember what happiness sounded like.

In that moment, fragile as soap bubbles and fierce as forge-fire, the sisters were whole. Not because their world had healed—the ash of attempted cruelty still stained the marble, the boy's wrists still bore rope burns, the Triad still cowered in their robes of faded authority.

But because they had learned the secret their parents had died trying to teach them: that love shared is weight divided, that inheritance carried together grows lighter with each step, that two hearts beating in rhythm can hold steady against any storm the world throws at them.

The ledger held their mother's final words. The earrings held their father's final gift. And between them, in the space where laughter lived, they held each other—proof that some things cannot be branded, cannot be broken, cannot be burned away no matter how hot the iron or how deep the ash.

Chapter 27

Rael's Fracture

"A vow whispered can split stone."

RAEL PRESSED his scarred cheek to the crawlway wall, the stone's grit cutting familiar grooves into old wounds. For three years the rhythm had carried him—*seventeen, four, two*—a lifeline whispered into plaster, his vow carved as deeply as breath could cut.

Tonight the stone pushed back.

He began as always: *seventeen... four...* But the final number caught, lodged in his throat like a shard of broken tile. His chest heaved, breath snagging. The square hummed around him—cloth fluttering, jars glowing, chalk spirals widening—but the witness had grown too heavy for one set of lungs.

Children noticed first. They always did.

A breath-counter crouched near, repeating his cadence louder, throwing him a rope of numbers. Knot-binders tied cloth at his elbow as if fabric could tether him back. A jar-bearer set fireflies near his hand, gold light brushing skin pale with strain. But Rael's lips stayed still.

His body trembled. His vow cracked.

Mira abandoned her ledger, knees scraping stone as she crawled to him. "Rael," she whispered, tapping the wall twice where scar met plaster—the same correction he once gave her when her hand slipped in ink. The echo rang hollow.

Nessa stood taut above them, earrings catching jar-light like tears. "Breathe, damn you," she hissed, too sharp, but her hands shook as she reached down.

Salliwith tore another strip from her dwindling shawl, tying it low on the wall where his cheek pressed. "The stone remembers," she murmured, voice breaking.

Karine sketched the fractures spreading through plaster around his body, lens fogged, chalk frantic. Each crack mirrored the splitting of his vow.

And Kess—still in gloves, kit rolled open at her side—laid her tools flat on the stone beside him. "Level. Cross. Lock. Test," she muttered, hands checking straps that weren't carrying weight. She knew the truth: fiber tells when it's about to fail. She heard the same note falter now in Rael's breath. "The line won't hold alone," she said, voice shaking.

Then silence. His rhythm gone.

But the square did not scatter. It answered.

Dozens of small voices picked up his numbers—*seventeen, four, two*—until the vow spread wider than any one chest could contain. Adults added their breath, syncing with children. His absence multiplied the sound until it filled every crack of stone.

Mira smeared ink across her cheek like war paint. "We'll carry it," she whispered. "Even if you can't. Especially because you can't."

Rael trembled once more against the wall, then stilled. Whether faint, collapse, or the small death of exhaustion, none could say.

But the vow lived.

The wall remembered. The straps hummed under Kess's hands. The fireflies pulsed steady gold.

And the numbers carried on: *seventeen, four, two. Hold.*

Forever and always, hold.

From the Ledger of Mira:

"A vow whispered can split stone."

• **Breath counts truth.** *Seventeen. Four. Two.*

• **Rhythm holds where strength fails.**

• **Silence carried by many is louder than one voice alone.**

• **Hold is covenant. Hold is law.**

Chapter 28

Kess's Failure

"Fiber holds, until it doesn't."

KESS LAID her canvas roll open in the square, every tool where it belonged. Gloves on. Palms tallowed. Knots rehearsed. She had checked each strap until her shoulders ached, tested every board under her own weight, listened for the note that told truth. The system had held all night. It had to hold now.

The boy waiting in the shadows burned with fever, limp as cloth. She slid slats under his blanket, gloved fingers tightening cords with clean economy. "Level. Cross. Lock. Test," she said—not as poetry but as procedure. Her words steadied the men crouched at the corners, their hands braced to lift.

"At your call," one said.

"Lift even. Keep the span low. If one side climbs, the line lies."

Leather strained. Cord hummed. The sling held true, singing its quiet note through her gloves. The boy's chest eased. Three steps carried him forward, weight spread perfect across the frame.

Then the left strap snapped.

The sound was sharp as breaking bone. The boy spilled sideways, striking marble, breath knocked out of him in a ragged cry that silenced the square.

Kess was already there, gloves on his small chest, checking airway, spine, pulse. Her voice cracked as she whispered to him, to herself, to the listening stone: "The line was true. The strap lied. Fiber doesn't lie—until it does."

Salliwith pressed cloth to the torn strap, knotting it with shaking hands. "Fray is honest," she murmured, though her voice trembled.

Karine sketched the break into her map, cracked lens scattering light as she named it: "Failure."

Mira pressed her ink-black thumb to her ledger's cover but did not open it. Not every truth belonged in ink.

Nessa's earrings caught firefly light, sharp as accusation. "Even the best systems break," she said—not mocking, only cold as winter stone.

On the dais, the Canonister's laughter rang shrill. "Toys and rags!" he cried, but fear warped his voice into something thin.

Kess bowed her head over the sling, hands still steady even as her heart staggered. She had done everything right— every test, every check, every knot pulled true. But truth has limits, and tonight it had broken in her hands.

The boy coughed, shallow but alive. Others lifted him toward the clinic. He would bear scars, but he would live.

The sling remained behind—broken leather, splintered boards, cord frayed to threads. A body of work collapsed into witness.

Kess whispered into her gloves, words too soft for the Tribunal but clear to the children at her side: "Method held. Hands failed. Remember that. Nothing holds alone."

The square held its breath, watching her crouched over the ruin of her craft, and knew: what broke here would not be forgotten.

Chapter 29

Audit Line

'The strap that failed did not vanish; it became the first mark in a line that turned burden into vow."

THE BROKEN SLING lay in the square like a fallen body—straps frayed, boards splintered, knots dark with Kess's blood. She sat apart from it, gloves still on, palms pressed against her thighs to stop the tremor. Her whole life had been method—Level, Cross, Lock, Test—and still the strap had snapped.

The crowd would not let it end there.

A knot-binder child crawled forward first, small hands fearless of blood and breakage. She lifted the snapped strap and tied it to the rail with steady fingers. "So we remember what trying looks like," she said.

Others followed. Spiral-chalkers ringed the blood-marked stone in white. Jar-bearers set their vessels close, fireflies pulsing gold against the ruined fiber until the wreck itself seemed to glow.

Salliwith pressed her bare shoulder against the rail, adding her last strip of shawl to the broken strap. "Witness pays," she whispered.

Karine sketched the outline into her fracture map, cracked lens scattering light across the page. "Break. Mend. Hold," she named each fracture aloud.

Mira pressed the word into her ledger—**Audit**—the letters bold as stone.

Nessa stood with her earrings flashing like sparks. "Fiber lies when it stands alone," she said. "But look—bound together, held by many hands, it holds now."

The Guards on their knees jeered from the stair, but their voices fell hollow against the square's quiet work.

Kess lifted her head at last. She watched children tugging straps, pulling them taut with careful concentration. She heard them whisper her own mantra: Level. Cross. Lock. Test. Check. Their knots weren't perfect, but their voices were steady.

Rael pressed his cheek to the wall, whispering Hold. The vow answered from a hundred throats.

The sling, lashed into place, was no longer wreck. It was contract.

And from that contract, something harder took root.

From the Ledger of Mira: The Contract of Kess

What is tied true cannot lie.

Work is witness. Tools that hold bear more law than decrees that fail.

Method is law. Level. Cross. Lock. Test. Check. The cadence itself binds.

Failure named becomes inheritance. A snapped strap is not shame but scripture.

Law must survive inspection. Inspect. Tighten. Replace. Record. Repeat. Endurance is legitimacy.

Hands are tools. Tools are kept. Gloves guard dignity. Fiber is covenant.

This was not decree, not marble, not ink ordained by height. It was contract written in straps and chalk, low enough for every child's hand to trace.

Chapter 30

Karine Names

"A fracture becomes map the moment it is named."

Karine crouched at the base of the stair, her cracked lens pressed to her eye until the world split into truth. The marble beneath her palms bore the story of years: grooves from knees, gouges from staves, depressions where bodies had pressed too long. And now—freshest of all—the splintered sling tied into shrine.

She set chalk to stone with the steadiness of a surgeon. "This one: Hunger," she said, circling a groove worn by traders who had crawled winter after winter, begging for bread. The crowd repeated the name until the stair itself seemed to answer.

"This one: Ash," she marked where fire-jars had spilled, soot still caught deep. "This one: Oath," she traced along the line Rael's cheek had carved, whisper by whisper.

Children gathered closer, watching her transform stone into language. Spiral-chalkers echoed her marks, drawing white rings until every scar carried a name. Knot-binders tied cloth at the ends of her circles, each tether a vow that the fracture would not be erased. Jar-bearers set vessels along the deepest cracks, fireflies pulsing gold so the breaks glowed with witness.

Kess knelt near the shrine of her broken sling, gloves tugging at straps others had tied. "Mark this one," she said quietly to Karine, laying her hand on the snapped leather bound into the rail. "Name it so the lie doesn't hide."

Karine looked through her cracked lens, saw the strap's torn fibers haloed in firefly light. She drew a bold line across the stone. "Burden," she said, and chalk dust lifted into the air like incense.

Salliwith tied one last ribbon to the word Karine had drawn, bare shoulder trembling with the effort. "Fray remembers," she murmured.

Mira stood apart, ledger heavy in her arms. She did not write Karine's words—some truths were too large for ink. Instead she drew one thin black line across a blank page. "Some names don't need letters," she said.

Nessa laughed once, sharp and clean. "At least they'll answer when you call them. More than law ever does."

Rael stirred against his wall, eyes half-open, lips cracked but moving. "Name it," he breathed. Karine bent close, heard him force out a single word: *Hold.* She wrote it on the stone itself, chalk white against marble.

Above, Tribunal banners sagged, letters already fading. Below, the stair glowed with new names—Hunger, Ash, Oath, Burden, Hold. A map written not by decree but by witness.

The crowd whispered each name, a litany stronger than any law.

And through her gloves, Kess felt the hum of straps lashed tighter by many hands, failure made shrine, shrine made map. Her mantra joined the litany: "Level. Cross. Lock. Test." And for the first time, it was not hers alone.

Chapter 31

Salliwith Exhaustion

"Witness costs until there is nothing left to give."

THE SHRINE STOOD like a testament to broken things made sacred—splintered slats bound tight, straps torn but lashed together by dozens of hands, chalk spirals circling it like arms around a wound. Fireflies pulsed their patient vigil. Karine's names clung bright across the stair.

But nearby, Salliwith sagged against the stone, body weighted by the terrible arithmetic of giving without end. Her shawl was gone—sacrificed thread by thread until the memory of its pattern lived only in strips tied across rail and crack. Skin bare to the cold, she shivered, hands still reaching for cloth that no longer existed.

She clawed at phantom fringe, found only air, and closed her fist around absence. The gesture was small. It broke the square's heart.

A knot-binder child appeared at her side, ribbon torn from her own dark hair. She placed it in Salliwith's trembling hands. Silk caught jar-light like spun silver. Salliwith smiled faintly, shame and gratitude tangled together, and tied it low on the rail. "Fray is honest," she whispered. "Even when it isn't mine to give."

Mira stood close, ledger heavy. She wrote one line—*Salliwith's shawl: exhausted*—then shut the book with a sound like a coffin lid.

Karine crouched nearby, cracked lens fogged, chalk scrawling one stark word beside Salliwith's bent form: *Cost.*

Nessa, earrings dimmed in respect, said only: "We see you." Three words sharper than all her laughter.

Rael whispered "Hold," voice thin as paper. A child echoed him louder, steadying the rhythm.

And Kess—Kess did not stay back this time. She slipped off one glove, pressing her bare palm to the rail where Salliwith's shoulder sagged. With her other hand, still gloved, she looped a strap from her kit around the rail and cinched it tight across Salliwith's back. Then another. She spoke her litany low but clear: "Level. Cross. Lock. Test. Check."

The straps took weight where Salliwith's body failed. The rail hummed true.

"Breathe," Kess told her, voice steady. "The brace will hold. You don't have to."

Salliwith exhaled long and heavy, as though laying down the burden itself. For the first time, surrender did not mean collapse.

Above, the Tribunal shifted in silks and chains, unsettled. They could not mock what they saw: exhaustion braced into dignity, failure underwritten by method, witness kept upright by fiber.

The shrine held. The straps held. The people held.

And in that moment, Salliwith and Kess stood as one truth: love given without limit, and craft built to catch it when it breaks.

FROM THE LEDGER OF MIRA:

"Witness costs until there is nothing left to give."

• **Cloth torn is memory made visible.**

• **Fray is honest.**

• **Strips tied are verdicts stronger than parchment.**

• **To be seen is survival; to see is law.**

Chapter 32

The Rest-Brace

"What shoulders cannot hold, fiber can."

SALLIWITH'S BODY SAGGED, shawl long gone, shoulders trembling with the cost of endless giving. The rail at her back was cold, stone unforgiving. She tried to press herself upright but her arms shook, weight dragging her lower with each breath.

Kess knelt beside her, gloves already on, kit open. She drew a strap across Salliwith's back and cinched it low against the rail. "Level," she said, voice even. Another strap angled higher. "Cross." A third locked into the others. "Lock." She leaned her weight into the ties, listening with her gloves. "Test." The straps hummed steady, carrying what Salliwith's bones could no longer bear.

Then Kess added one more step—one she had never spoken aloud before. She tugged each knot again, then nodded. "Check."

Salliwith exhaled heavy, a sound like surrender—but for the first time, surrender did not mean collapse. The brace held her upright.

Children crowded close, wide-eyed. "Teach us," one said.

Kess set her chalk to the stone and drew five short lines, each marked with a word: Level. Cross. Lock. Test. Check. She tapped each with her glove. "Anyone can do this. You don't need strength—only method. One of you ties, another counts. Rotate. Watch."

A knot-binder repeated her words. A breath-counter added Rael's rhythm beneath them: seventeen, four, two. Together they made a cadence—count for straps, count for lungs.

"Rest-Brace," Kess said, naming it. "Not shrine. Not witness. Work. When a body gives out, we catch it here."

The straps hummed. The child who had asked to learn leaned her cheek against the rail, whispering, "Hold."

The square felt it: a new law written not in marble decree, but in leather and method. What love exhausted, craft would brace.

And for the first time since the Pulse, the people saw that rest itself could be held.

Codex VI – The Maintenance

"What is checked endures."

MORNING FOUND the square littered with chalk dust, loose cloth, jars dimmed to grey glass. The Codex of play had survived the night, but Kess knew survival was not enough. Anything left untended rotted, failed, or lied.

She spread her canvas roll across the rail and drew chalk marks on the stone itself: five small squares, each labeled with a word. **Inspect. Tighten. Replace. Record. Repeat.**

Children gathered in a half-circle, jar-bearers first, knot-binders close behind.

"Law is not only written," Kess said, tugging at a strap until it sang. "It is checked. Every day, every night. Fiber frays. Knots slip. Cloth rots in rain. You think witness holds forever? It doesn't—not unless you check."

A knot-binder frowned. "How often?"

"Intervals," Kess answered. "Jars every dawn. Straps at dusk. Chalk before sleep. Ledger when ink allows." She tapped each chalk square on the stone. "Inspect. Tighten. Replace. Record. Repeat."

Mira stood near, ledger cord wound tight on her wrist. For once, she wrote without hesitation, copying the five words exactly as Kess spoke them. "Maintenance Codex," she said, closing the book with a sharp sound.

Karine added it to her map, cracked lens catching the grid of chalk as if it were a constellation. "Intervals hold like stars," she murmured.

Rael pressed his cheek to plaster, whispering his rhythm. A breath-counter wove it beneath Kess's five words, turning inspection into chant: *Seventeen. Four. Two.*

Nessa snorted from the rail, though her eyes softened. "So now law is knots and calendars."

Kess didn't flinch. She pulled another strap tight, glove creaking. "Law is what survives the night. If you don't check, it dies."

Salliwith, shoulders braced in leather, tied one more ribbon to the Codex grid. Her voice was thin but sure. "Check is mercy."

The crowd repeated it—low at first, then rising until it echoed off the crawlway walls. *Check is mercy.*

Kess stood back, kit at her side, gloves still on. She had no smile, only the certainty of craft done right. For the first time, the Codex was not just firefly play or whispered vow. It was schedule. It was habit. It was endurance.

The Maintenance Codex lived—five words that would outlast panic, decree, or failure.

Chapter 33

Threshold Uprising

"An uprising holds only when tied; law remade in knots cannot be torn by decree."

THE STAIR WAS NEVER SILENT—STONE always carried the scrape of knees, the drag of rails, the low hum of vows. But tonight it shuddered with something new. Guards crawled low across it, staves clattering, knees grinding chalk into dust.

Above, the Tribunal sagged on their dais.

• **Canonister Brannic Raal** shrieked for order, but his voice split like a frayed strap.

• **Magistrate Elara Mora** pleaded for silence, her shawl in tatters, words spent on air that would not listen.

• **Arbiter Tenric Halvorsen** coughed into parchment that wilted in his hands, the scroll collapsing like a wall gone soft with water.

And below, the crowd surged.

Children tied fresh cloth faster than Guards could tear it free. Spirals bloomed under crawling boots, rings bright and defiant. Jars glowed steady where Kess's straps lashed them to rails, humming their quiet note of permanence. Fireflies pulsed like heartbeats refusing to quit.

The uprising did not roar. It bound.

Kess stood at the center, gloves tight, kit open.

"Level!" she shouted, cinching a strap across the rail where Guards ripped cloth away. Children echoed her: Level.

"Cross!" Another strap braced the jars. Cross!

"Lock!" Knots tightened. Lock!

"Test!" She pulled until it sang true. Test!

"Check!" A dozen small hands tugged the line, confirming it held. Check!

The chant carried through the square, louder than the Tribunal, steadier than the Guards.

Rael pressed his cheek to the wall, whispering his vow. Breath-counters spread it into rhythm: seventeen, four, two.

Mira opened her ledger and wrote one word—**UPRISING**—ink so heavy it bled through the page.

Karine traced cracks splitting the marble stair, naming each: **Break. Bend. Hold.**

Salliwith tied the last strip of ribbon at her shoulder, murmuring, "Witness doesn't ask—it answers."

Nessa stood upright, earrings flashing like defiant stars. "See them crawl," she shouted toward the dais. "See who kneels now!"

The Guards pressed forward on knees and elbows, staves swinging. But they struck straps, not skin. They struck jars bound too tight to spill. They struck chalk already redrawn by smaller hands.

The square erupted—not in chaos, but in discipline. The uprising breathed in rhythm, held by method. Straps, knots, chalk, breath, laughter—woven tighter than decree could tear.

The Tribunal watched, powerless. Their law hung high above. But the new law lived here, tied low, braced by hands too many to silence.

The stair had been a scar. Tonight it became a spine.

The Threshold Uprising had begun. And it held.

Chapter 34

Guards Fail

"Lines drawn in crawling cannot cover every gap."

THE GUARDS SURGED FORWARD, staves raised high as if height could return to them by swinging wood. They crawled across the stairs in formation, knees grinding against marble, voices barking like dogs desperate to sound tall.

The square did not scatter. It held.

Straps lashed tight by Kess kept jars steady against the rails, their electric hum traveling through her gloves into every child who touched them. The knot-binders took up her litany—*Level, Cross, Lock, Test, Check*—chanting until the words spread like a second vow through the crowd. Spiral-chalkers ringed the Guards' advance with circles, forcing the soldiers to scrape through chalk-dust witness with every desperate lunge.

A boy darted beneath a raised stave and retied a knot before the Guard could recover from his crawl. A girl slid a jar across the stone, its brilliant light blinding a soldier's eyes for the crucial moment it took to disarm him. Every movement was quick, low, deliberate—taught, not wild.

The Guards swung harder. Their staves cracked chalk lines, split cloth, knocked jars loose—but each time the straps caught what fell, the knots held what broke, and small hands replaced what had been shattered.

"Fiber outlasts fury!" Kess shouted, pulling a line taut against the rail. The strap sang true under tension. Children echoed her words until their chant buried the Guards' hoarse curses.

Rael pressed his cheek to the cool wall, whispering "Hold." The breath-counters took up his rhythm until it shook the stairs like a living drum. *Seventeen. Four. Two. Hold.*

Salliwith pressed her palm against stone, whispering, "We see you." Karine marked each break in chalk, her stylus scratching faster than the Guards could destroy her work. Mira scrawled across her ledger: *They failed because we held.*

Nessa's laughter cut sharp and bright through the chaos. "Crawl faster!" she shouted at the struggling men. "The children write quicker than you can break!"

The Guards' formation splintered. Their tight lines tangled into themselves. Staves knocked against one another in the confusion. One soldier slipped on chalk dust and sprawled flat against the marble. Another dropped his stave entirely to drag himself free, only to be blinded by jar-light flaring gold against his visor.

The Tribunal watched from their high perch, but their commands meant nothing now. Their enforcers were not an unbreakable wall—they were splinters scattered uselessly against stone.

The crowd pressed closer, armed not with weapons but with witness. Fresh cloth replaced what was torn. New chalk circled what was cracked. The straps hummed steady and sure where fury faltered and failed.

The Guards had not been defeated by force. They had defeated themselves—undone by their own imbalance, exposed by their crawling posture, broken against the simple law of hands too many to silence.

By nightfall, the square breathed steady. Straps still hummed their electric song. Jars still cast their golden glow. And the Guards—those who had crawled so low to enforce silence—dragged themselves back up the stairs empty-handed, their mission a ruin.

The square laughed once, short and sharp.

The Guards had failed. And everyone had seen it.

UR-II: The Quiet Guard

(Upper Registers — Depositions of the Untethered)

IT HAPPENED ON THE STAIR.

The Police had claimed the upper risers, uniforms pressed, staves polished, issuing decrees in steady voices. They stood as if the Pulse had never struck them, as if law itself still wore a badge.

Below, the Guards crouched, uniforms mismatched, blades on their belts, eyes hard with hunger. They did not speak in statutes. They spoke in presence—a leg across a step, a stave dragging stone. They guarded height, not people.

That morning the crowd swelled at Threshold: traders with jars, children with chalk, Untethered clerks counting coins. Noise thickened until one Guard barked low, voice raw as iron on rust: *"Kneel if you want to pass."*

The Police captain on the upper riser frowned. *"We do not kneel. Order stands."* His stave tapped marble three times— echo sharp, authority rehearsed.

But his partner shifted uneasily. She looked down at the crowd, at mothers pressed against the barrier, at children straining to lift jars above their heads. She bent one knee, lowering her voice so it carried evenly to both sides: *"Walk slow. No pushing. No blades."*

The crowd obeyed her. They did not hear the captain's decree.

Violence leaned close then, whispering in the man's ear: *"Strike, and you fall. Stay standing, and you vanish."*

He froze. His badge gleamed useless in the stair's half-light. The Guard below laughed once, cruel and low. The Untethered above looked away.

And the city learned: law spoken from on high no longer ruled. Only words delivered at eye level mattered now.

Chapter 35

Tribunal Falters

"When theater collapses, banners hang lower than breath; names fall heavier than titles."

THE GUARDS DRAGGED themselves back up the stairs, staves clattering against stone, knees streaked with chalk dust and blood. Their formation had dissolved, their authority leaking across marble like spilled oil.

The Tribunal leaned forward—three shadows cut against the failing light.

Chief Arbiter Tenric Halvorsen coughed into his decree, parchment shaking in his trembling hands, ink blotting beneath his spit. His voice broke between syllables like a rusted hinge.

Defender Magistrate Elara Mora pressed her palms together, knuckles bone-white. "It cannot hold," she whispered, more to herself than to the crowd below. "Without the Guards... without the line..." Her words dissolved before they found an audience.

Canonister Brannic Raal shouted to drown them both: "Blasphemy! Rags and bugs cannot be law!" His cry rang across the stairs, but it cracked on the word *law*—shrill as panic, thin as a frayed strap.

The square did not answer with rage. It answered with order.

Kess tugged a strap once more, gloves firm against the tension, and it hummed true. "Check," she called. Children echoed across the stone: *Check*. They pulled at knots, tightened cloth, reset the glowing jars. A living system in seamless motion.

Karine marked each broken banner on her map, cracked lens scattering fractured light across the parchment. *Falter,* she named the sagging cloth above. *Collapse,* she wrote beside the broken staves left behind.

Mira pressed her stylus deep into the ledger, heavy enough to bleed ink through the page: *Authority broke first in its own hands.*

Salliwith pressed her palm to the covenant rail, her voice steady despite trembling shoulders. "Witness doesn't bend," she declared. "Even when they do."

Rael whispered his vow into the wall—*Hold*—and the breath-counters carried it across the square until even the Tribunal heard the rhythm echoing back at them, louder than their decrees, stronger than their fear.

Nessa stood tall, earrings flashing like defiant stars against the dimming sky. "Look down," she shouted, voice cutting through the air like a blade. "See what your law has become. See what crawls when children rise."

The Tribunal faltered as one. Their voices clashed instead of uniting, their postures bent instead of commanding.

Tenric sagged against the rail, coughing into parchment that tore beneath his grip. Elara turned her face away, unable to meet the crowd's unwavering gaze. Brannic shrieked until his voice failed entirely, silence swallowing his impotent fury.

And below them, straps hummed their electric song. Chalk held its witness-circles. Jars glowed steady and sure.

The uprising was not riot. It was order—low, disciplined, unbreakable.

The Tribunal faltered because the ground itself had turned against them, and that ground was held by hands too many, too steady, too disciplined to ever let go.

Chapter 36

Constellations in Jars

"When scattered lights are bound, they become stars."

Night fell over Threshold, but the square did not dim. The jars glowed steady, lashed to rails and posts by Kess's practiced straps, cloth tied firm, chalk rings gleaming white and bright in the firefly glow.

The children gathered at the center, breathless with shared purpose. One by one, they lifted jars from the rails—not to scatter them, but to arrange. They crawled across the stone with reverent care, setting the lights in deliberate patterns, chalking connecting lines between them until recognizable shapes emerged from the darkness.

A hunter. A flowing river. A hand open in witness. A sling that never failed.

Each constellation flickered gold, the jars pulsing like captured stars pressed down into the square. Chalk lines bound them into meaning, cloth tethered them against the wind, straps braced them where the stone sloped uneven.

The Guards, still grounded at the stair's edge, watched with slack staves in their hands. They could not break what they could no longer even reach.

From above, the Tribunal sagged in defeated silence. They had crafted no decree against play, no law against making stars.

Kess moved through the square like a conductor, gloves steady, checking each jar as it found its place. She tightened cords with practiced fingers, balanced frames, guided small hands with gentle precision. "Level. Cross. Lock. Test. Check." Her familiar mantra spread like sacred song until even the youngest spiral-chalkers whispered it under their breath.

Mira opened her ledger but her stylus remained still. She could only watch in wonder as the jars transformed into constellations, ink forgotten in the face of law made luminous and alive.

Karine sketched frantically in her map, cracked lens scattering rainbow fragments of their light across the parchment. "Not fractures," she murmured, chalk dancing across the page. "Connections."

Salliwith pressed her palm to the strap-braced shrine and whispered with quiet awe, "Witness shines."

Rael, cheek pressed to cool plaster, breathed his eternal vow —"Hold"—and the breath-counters carried the word until it wove through the star-shapes like a thread of living sound.

Nessa tilted her chin high, earrings blazing like her own twin stars against the night. "So that's what law looks like," she declared, her grin bright as the constellations themselves. "Not written high above us, but shining up from below."

The crowd exhaled as one, soft laughter rising—awed, unafraid, transformed. For the first time in memory, Threshold's night was ruled not by decree or dread, but by constellations born of simple jars, chalk dust, worn cloth, and unbreakable straps.

And everyone who witnessed knew with absolute certainty: these patterns of light would outlast any parchment, endure longer than any banner. Because once scattered lights are bound together with purpose, they become eternal stars.

The square had not just held—it had become something new entirely. Something that could never be torn down, only carried forward in memory and light.

Chapter 37

Map Laid Low

"A map endures when many hands can read it."

By DAWN, the constellations still glowed faint gold, fireflies drowsy in their glass prisons. Chalk lines had smudged under morning dew, but enough remained to reveal the shapes—hunter, river, hand, sling. What had begun as defiant play still held, bound together by straps, knots, and collective memory.

Karine crouched at the stair's base, cracked lens pressed close to the stone. She sketched the constellations into her weathered book, tracing their precise alignment against the fractures she had already mapped: Hunger, Ash, Oath, Burden, Hold. Stars above, scars below the city's true geography unfolding under her careful hand.

But it was Kess who transformed momentary beauty into lasting truth. She moved methodically through the square, gloves testing each strap's tension, chalking fresh lines where jars must sit, teaching the children to measure distance with cord and memory. "Level. Cross. Lock. Test. Check," she recited, tapping each chalk mark with practiced precision. "A map means nothing if it scatters in the first wind. Fix it low, so the next hands can follow the path."

A young knot-binder absorbed her words, then tied a jar exactly where her chalk had marked the stone. "Fixed," the child announced, grinning with newfound purpose.

Mira opened her ledger to a fresh page and drew one straight line across it—a low, unbroken horizon. "Above and below," she murmured, stylus steady. "Fractures and stars, scars and light."

Salliwith pressed her palm against the strap-braced shrine, her voice carrying quiet reverence: "Witness doesn't float in the air—it stays low, where ordinary hands can touch and trace."

Rael breathed his eternal vow into the wall's cool surface. A breath-counter caught his rhythm and traced it onto the chalk lines of their living map, numbers tucked like secret coordinates between the constellations: Seventeen. Four. Two.

Nessa leaned back against the rail, earrings catching the morning light like stars caught in her dark hair. "So we've charted an entire sky in three feet of stone," she observed, laughter sharp but warm with pride. "Looks better than the one they tried to write above us."

The crowd gathered closer, voices soft with concentration as they repeated the names Karine had given each constellation, memorized the precise placements Kess had fixed in chalk and cord, whispered Rael's sacred numbers as navigational bearings for future pilgrims.

The map lived not in fragile parchment or royal decree, but in humble straps and chalk dust, in glowing jars and patient witness. Low enough for every hand to trace its patterns. Simple enough for every voice to repeat its names. Strong enough to survive what the Tribunal had already chosen to forget.

For the first time since the Pulse had shattered their world, the city could be read again—not by imperial edict from above, but by endurance written in stone below. A map laid low and true, inscribed where only the Grounded could reach, where fundamental truth would never be erased by those who crawled too high to see it.

The square had not merely held its ground. It had become the ground itself—unshakeable, eternal, and forever within reach of those who needed to find their way home.

Chapter 38

Circle Breath

"What many lungs measure together cannot be broken apart."

AT TWILIGHT THEY GATHERED AGAIN, drawn not by decree but by gravity older than any law. The jars were placed low where Kess had marked the stone in chalk, straps holding them steady, cloth marking each constellation point like careful stitches mending a wound. The constellations shimmered faint gold against the darkening sky. Fracture lines glowed bone-white in the dusk. The living map was ready to be read.

Rael pressed his cheek to the cool wall, whispering his sacred vow. *Seventeen. Four. Two.* His voice trembled with reverence, but the breath-counters caught it immediately, repeating the numbers until they circled the square like a steady, breathing tide.

Kess moved among the gathered children, gloves secure, repair kit open and ready. She tugged each strap with practiced fingers, nodding approval when it hummed true under tension. "Level. Cross. Lock. Test. Check," she intoned with quiet authority. Children echoed her words faithfully, tying fresh knots, cinching cords until the jars sat perfectly balanced within their chalk circles.

Then something powerful happened—the two rhythms met and merged. Rael's grounding numbers and Kess's ancient litany wove together into one unified cadence: *Seventeen, four, two, level, cross, lock, test, check.* Breath and fiber braided into something stronger than law—into lived truth.

They began to move as one organism. Knot-binders crawled purposefully from jar to jar, tightening lines in perfect time with Rael's count. Spiral-chalkers refreshed their protective circles on his measured exhale. Jar-bearers shifted vessels at each rhythmic *check*, watching fireflies pulse steady and sure with the collective breath.

Mira recorded only one phrase in her ledger, but she pressed the stylus deep: *Circle held.*

Karine marked the sacred moment onto her map, cracked lens fogging with her whispered reverence as she named each point. "Hunger. Ash. Oath. Burden. Hold. Constellation. Connection."

Salliwith braced herself against the shrine, shoulders finding perfect alignment in Kess's Rest-Brace. She exhaled slow, long, deliberate. The children followed her breath until silence itself became another rhythm, another form of communion.

Nessa stood at the circle's edge, earrings catching and reflecting firefly light like captured stars. "Look at them," she said, voice softer than anyone had ever heard it. "The Tribunal would dismiss this as play. But play doesn't hold this steady, this true."

The Guards watched from their positions on the stair, staves hanging useless, knees still stained with chalk dust, their once-proud posture bent and broken. They could not destroy what they could not even begin to comprehend.

And the circle breathed as one.

One rhythm uniting them. One method binding them. One map guiding them forward.

The law of the Tribunal sagged impotent above their heads. But the law of breath and strap pulsed strong below—low enough for every hand to reach, strong enough for every lung to sustain, bright enough for every child to carry forward into whatever darkness awaited.

The Circle Breath held steady and true, and everyone in the square understood with absolute certainty: this was how survival would sound. This was how hope would endure. This was how the future would be built—not from above, but from the ground up, one breath at a time.

Chapter 39

Riot Sparks

"Hunger is the weapon no one can set down; sparks fall harmless when rhythm already holds the fire."

THE TRIBUNAL ROSE from their dais in a flurry of silk and fear.

Chief Arbiter Tenric Halvorsen lifted his parchment high, but his cough shredded the words before they could reach the square.

Defender Magistrate Elara Mora shouted for silence, her voice too thin to cut through the hum of a thousand held breaths.

Canonister Brannic Raal shrieked commands like curses hurled into a storm.

The Guards crawled forward again, staves swinging low, knees grinding through chalk circles as they kicked jars from the rails. This time they did not merely scrape—they lunged, desperate to shatter what would not kneel.

The first jar fell. Glass exploded across stone, fireflies scattering like sparks into the night. The crowd gasped as one. The Tribunal heard it and mistook fear for victory.

But Kess was already moving.

"Circle! Reset!" she shouted, gloves pulled tight, kit unrolled. She seized a cord, tied it to a rail, cinched it hard. "Level!" she barked.

Children echoed her: *Level*.

Another strap drawn taut. *Cross*.

A knot pulled tight. *Lock*.

Small hands tugging until the cord sang. *Test*.

A dozen fingers checking again. *Check*.

The cadence rippled outward—a wall stronger than stone. Spiral-chalkers redrew circles beneath the Guards' knees. Knot-binders tied cloth faster than staves could tear it free. Jar-bearers lifted scattered fireflies into new vessels, setting them where straps already waited.

Rael's voice cracked, but the breath-counters carried it forward: *Seventeen. Four. Two. Hold.*

Mira scrawled one line across her ledger: *Riot caught.*

Karine traced fractures splitting wider beneath the Tribunal's weight and named them, her voice steady: "Falter. Panic. Break."

Salliwith pressed her palm to the shrine, whispering, "Witness doesn't scatter."

The Tribunal shrieked, but their noise was drowned. The riot they had sparked found no fuel. Each shove met a strap. Each strike met chalk. Each broken jar was caught, reset, named.

Nessa tilted her chin high, her earrings blazing in jar-light. "See?" she shouted to the crowd. "They can't break us unless we choose to scatter. And we don't scatter."

The crowd roared—not wild, but measured. Not chaos, but rhythm. Not panic, but discipline.

The Tribunal faltered again, their last weapon—the spark of riot—turned against them. For sparks cannot ignite where breath, strap, and witness already hold the fire in their own hands.

Chapter 40

Council of Empty Hands

"What cannot be carried as weapon may still be lifted as voice."

THE TRIBUNAL DESCENDED THE STAIR, silk dragging in chalk dust, their voices raw from shouting. They gathered at the rail like judges at a reckoning, hands lifted as though gesture alone could bind the square.

The Chief Arbiter's parchment was gone, shredded by his own cough. He raised bare fingers, shaking, with nothing left to hold. The Defender Magistrate clasped her palms together, empty even of mercy. The Canonister clenched his fists, but no stave, no strap, no symbol remained in his grasp.

They stood as the Council of Empty Hands.

The crowd did not kneel. It did not riot. It breathed.

Kess stepped forward, gloves on, kit at her side. She laid her hand on the shrine's strap and pulled once. The leather hummed steady, answering louder than any decree. "Level. Cross. Lock. Test. Check," she said, her voice clear and certain. Children echoed her, their voices carrying across the square like a verdict.

Rael pressed his cheek to the wall. *Seventeen. Four. Two. Hold.* The vow rippled outward.

Karine chalked new words onto the stone beneath the Tribunal's feet: *Empty. False. Spent.* Her cracked lens caught the sagging silk above and she named it aloud: "Collapse."

Mira opened her ledger and wrote a single line, neat and permanent: *Law belongs to hands that build.*

Salliwith tied a final ribbon to the shrine, her shoulders trembling but her voice steady. "Witness holds," she said.

Nessa laughed sharp and bright. "Look at them! Judges with no tools. Priests with no altar. Commanders with no line." She gestured toward the Tribunal with fierce joy. "Empty hands can't hold a city."

The Tribunal faltered, their silence louder than all their shouting had been. The Guards at their knees crawled lower, staves dropped to stone. The people leaned forward, cloth and chalk in hand—not to beg, but to work.

What the Council had tried to claim from above now lived below, low enough for every child to reach. Straps hummed. Chalk marked. Jars glowed. Breath counted steadily onward.

The Tribunal had their chamber. The people had their law.

And for the first time in living memory, it was clear which would endure.

Codex VII – Kess's Breaking Point

"Fiber frays most at the point of strain."

THE COVENANT LOOMED ABOVE HER, straps and boards lashed high against the iron rail—no longer relic, but discipline bound into wood and fiber. Scraps of cloth fluttered in the dusk, chalk dust clung to stone, and jars breathed their steady golden light. It was not memorial. It was method made visible.

Kess knelt there, gloves blackened, her kit spread open on trembling knees. The sling lay across them—broken once, mended twice, bound with knots so fierce they had bitten scars even through her leather. She had sworn it would hold. She had sworn it on her blood and on the lives it carried.

A cry split the Crawlway—a man crushed beneath fallen stone, his breath ragged, legs twisted at angles no body should bear. Panic rippled through the crowd, their voices raw with helplessness.

Kess rose, sling pressed to her chest. "Corners, not shoulders," she commanded, her voice hoarse but unshaken.

"Even weight across the frame. Keep it level or we lose him."

Two men obeyed, steadying at her nod. Straps tightened. Boards braced. Together they lifted, carrying the broken man across stone slick with fear and blood. Leather creaked, wood groaned, her arms shook with effort—but the load held. Each step was a prayer answered by craft.

Then strain hit its limit.

A strap began to fray, fibers screaming under weight. The board split along an old seam. For a heartbeat the world teetered between mercy and collapse.

Kess did not step back. She thrust her body into the gap, bracing with raw strength where the fiber had failed. Her knees buckled, ribs groaned, but she held—long enough for children to swarm close. Knot-binders tied fresh cloth around the failing strap. Chalkers marked the break and sealed it with witness. Stronger hands dragged the man to safety.

Kess staggered, breath torn from her in ragged bursts, gloves split where seams had bitten into her palms. She dropped to her knees, head bowed, chest heaving like a bellows on its last pull.

But she lived. The man lived.

The square held silence for a long beat, then exhaled as one.

Mira's thumb smeared ink across her ledger, but she closed it tight and spoke aloud instead: "She holds. The contract holds."

Salliwith pressed both bare hands to Kess's shoulders, steadying her upright. "Witness breathes," she whispered, fierce as an oath.

Karine traced the crack in the failed board and named it **Burden**, her chalk breaking in half but leaving the word clear on the stone.

Rael pressed his cheek to the wall, whispering through fever: "Hold." The vow ran outward through hundreds of lungs.

Nessa stood tall, her earrings blazing like twin stars. Her voice rang across the square: "See how she bears what none of you would dare touch. See how the law of fiber shames the law of marble."

The altar grew with new offerings: straps tied higher, cloth layered thick, jars set in circles until the covenant pulsed with life. It was not a tomb for failure. It was living law.

Fiber had frayed. Body had bent. Breath had nearly broken.

But the contract of Kess endured—strong as community, fragile as flesh, and alive in every hand that now knew how to hold.

Chapter 41

Accord in Lungs

"When words collapse, lungs remain."

THE SHRINE pulsed steady where straps, boards, and jars had been lashed into a frame that no decree could tear down. It no longer looked like stretcher or repair—it looked like law, humming with knots, glowing with witness, breathing with firefly light.

Kess sat against its base, her ribs banded with leather, gloves still tight over bloodied palms. Her breath came shallow but real. Every strap that held above her head had been checked by other hands now—small hands repeating her litany, binding her contract into the shrine itself.

Silence pressed down across Threshold like a held breath.

Then Rael stirred, cheek pressed to stone, fever burning, voice breaking. "Hold," he whispered.

The sound barely carried. But it was enough.

A breath-counter child echoed him, then another, then dozens, until the square exhaled as one. Seventeen. Four. Two. Hold. The rhythm became tide—low, steady, vast.

Witnesses joined the breathing:

Mira closed her ledger without writing. She smeared her ink-black thumb across its cover and pressed it to her chest, her body itself becoming record.

Nessa tilted her head toward the shrine-light, earrings flaring like captured stars. "Then breathe," she whispered, exhaling with sharp laughter that turned pain into defiance.

Salliwith braced Kess upright, her bare shoulders pressed to hers. "Witness breathes," she murmured, matching her rhythm to the crowd's.

Karine crouched low, her cracked lens fogging as she traced lines that blurred and reformed with each exhale. "The map breathes too," she whispered, chalk dusting her fingers white.

The crowd followed like tide after moon—not chanting, not singing, only lungs filling together across the divide of Grounded and Untethered. Air shared. Rhythm shared. Survival shared.

Above them, the Tribunal sagged. The Arbiter coughed blood onto parchment that curled and tore. The Magistrate covered her eyes with trembling hands. The Canonister opened his mouth but no sound came; his authority drowned in the tide below.

Cloth and chalk had stripped their banners. Jars and straps had mocked their decrees. Now breath sealed what rebellion had begun—not with violence, not with law, but with the simplest covenant: to exist together, lungs aligned.

An accord no parchment could hold. No banner could fray.

Only air, drawn and released, binding every body under the same broken sky.

Kess exhaled slow, a rasp but steady. The strap above her hummed true under a child's tugging hand.

"Still holds," the girl said.

And the square breathed the word back.

"Hold."

"Hold."

Threshold exhaled as one living thing.

Chapter 42

Uprising Holds

**"What survives panic becomes law;
endurance written in dawn is stronger
than decree."**

AT DAWN THE ALTAR BREATHED, jars pulsing their patient glow into the gray of morning. Straps retied and tested held true as promises. Chalk sprawled across the courthouse stairs, bright lines cutting fractures into clarity. Mira's ledger lay sealed in her arms, thumbprints black as signatures pressed by grief and resolve. The vow, cracked but alive, still pulsed in children's lungs like an inherited heartbeat.

Threshold had endured riot's rage, mockery's sting, the kiss of branding iron, and the crush of collapsing stone. Yet as the sky bled pink and gold over a city scarred and trembling, the square did not scatter.

The work continued, quiet as prayer:

• Knot-binders wove ribbons freshly washed in river water, colors bright against ash, each strip a defiance of decay.

• Spiral-chalkers bent to their geometry, retracing lines smeared by boots, circling scars until the very stone seemed to inhale and exhale with pattern.

• Jar-bearers set new glass where shards still glittered, fire-flies pulsing steady as the breath of sleepers.

• Breath-counters guarded the rhythm, ensuring no silence fell unwitnessed, no grief vanished unshared.

The Guards lingered on the stairs, staves slack, eyes hollow. Their perfect lines had dissolved, their charge broken not by force but by futility. They did not advance. What was left to advance against?

Above them, the Tribunal sagged like actors after the play had ended. The Arbiter coughed himself mute, parchment limp in his bloodstained grip. The Magistrate whispered words too soft for air to hold. The Canonister clenched a banner in white-knuckled hands but lacked the strength to raise it. Their height had become exile.

Below, the six witnesses remained—a circle wounded but unbroken:

• Rael pressed his scarred cheek to stone, whispering "Hold." Thin as glass, his voice was caught and carried until it filled the square.

• Mira clutched her ledger shut, her body itself the archive, refusal her most honest entry.

• Nessa stood tall, earrings catching first light until they burned like twin suns, her grin sharper than any decree.

• Salliwith knelt at the altar, bare shoulders bowed, palms pressed flat to wood—her body a declaration that witness does not vanish.

• Kess, ribs bound, gloves split, leaned against the covenant she had built and broken and built again. Her breath was ragged, but her voice was steady: "Level. Cross. Lock. Test. Check." Children repeated it until the litany became law.

• Karine crouched by her map of fractures, chalk trembling in her fingers as she inscribed a single word that outlasted all others: **Endure.**

The crowd pressed close, silence thick as cloth, heavy as shared breath. No banners snapped. No thrones toppled. No proclamations rang from marble heights.

But they had held.

Held through mockery and riot. Through hunger and fever. Through iron lowered, straps frayed, walls cracked. They had held when all that remained was breath and witness, when endurance was the only rebellion left.

And in a world remade by collapse, where everything solid had dissolved to fragments, holding itself had become victory—quiet as dawn, persistent as lungs, unbreakable as people who chose not to scatter but to remain bound together under the same broken sky.

Interlude II – Boardrooms of Dust

"Contracts cannot outlast silence."

In towers of glass and steel that scraped the belly of heaven itself, far from Threshold's humble stones, the boardrooms convened for the last time. They gathered in suits pressed thin as autumn leaves, silk ties knotted like nooses around their throats, golden pens gleaming with wealth they could neither eat nor breathe.

The Pulse had come for them too, democratic as death itself.

Weapons locked in titanium safes had dragged their private guards beneath mahogany conference tables like anchors pulling ships to ocean floors. Security chiefs crawled across Italian marble with pistols still holstered at their hips, steel dead weight now, hauling themselves through meetings on bloodied palms and torn knees. Executives averted their eyes from the spectacle, unwilling to witness the humbling of men and women they had once paid handsomely to stand taller, straighter, deadlier than themselves.

Screens that had blazed with the fever dreams of capitalism stared back blind and black. No ascending charts. No climbing indexes. No graphs reaching toward infinite growth. The electronic hum of server farms had stilled to the silence of graveyards.

"Markets will stabilize," one director whispered, his voice thin as winter air, as if repetition could resurrect the dead. "Contracts remain legally binding," another insisted desperately, clutching a leather portfolio against his chest as if law itself could draw breath without the electricity that had given it teeth.

But their ledgers were only paper now—fragile, finite, mortal—and even the finest parchment smudges when touched by trembling, ink-stained thumbs.

The mighty had been made low:

Directors knelt beneath tables polished to mirror brightness, their bodies unable to rise beyond the height of their own bent knees. Thousand-dollar suits split at the seams as spines curved lower than pride had ever allowed. Laptops that had once blazed with the fire of algorithms lay dark as tombstones, their digital souls extinguished.

Outside the boardroom windows, trading floors gathered dust like abandoned temples. Elevators hung motionless in their shafts like bodies in wells. The air itself tasted of leather and the sharp metallic tang of fear.

Across the globe, the same drama played in different tongues:

In Shanghai's gleaming towers, they argued over phantom cargo that would never sail, ghost profits that had evaporated like morning mist. A chairman clutched his golden Mont Blanc like a talisman but could not lift himself from the floor where gravity had made him equal to his janitors. His lieutenants smeared their palms with fountain pen ink, pressing desperate handprints across Carrara marble instead of signatures—cave paintings for the digital age.

In London's financial district, skyscrapers dimmed at dusk like dying stars. Executives lit candles scavenged from wine bottles, shadows stretching across Persian carpets like prison bars, their light revealing faces hollow with the recognition of their own irrelevance.

In New York's concrete canyons, corner offices sat tomb-empty, million-dollar contracts curling at the edges in bone-dry air, their words becoming meaningless as dead languages.

In São Paulo's rising towers, a CFO took chalk from her daughter's small hand and drew a jagged line across the polished boardroom table that had cost more than most people's homes. Gasps echoed off glass walls. "Vandalism," someone muttered through clenched teeth. "Property damage."

"No," she said, her voice carrying the weight of revelation. "Orientation. Learning which way is down."

Dust gathered in corners that cleaning crews could no longer reach. Suits pressed bodies low against floors they had never expected to touch. Power bent its neck to gravity's ancient law.

Not one contract survived the night intact. Not one deal remained binding when the infrastructure of enforcement crumbled to silence.

When dawn broke pink and gold across the humbled cities, every boardroom bore identical evidence of capitalism's funeral: chalk marks scratched into marble floors, desperate fingerprints smeared across floor-to-ceiling windows, and the profound silence where servers had once hummed their electric prayers to endless growth.

Profit had lost all meaning when no one could stand to count it. Height held no command when everyone crawled equal on the ground. The earth had inherited every boardroom, every corner office, every tower that had dared to scratch the sky.

Gravity, it seemed, was the most honest accountant of all.

Interlude III – The Industrial Silence

"When wheels stop, silence becomes the only product."

In Manchester's brick cathedrals of commerce, mills stood hollow as picked bones, their mighty looms sagging like the ribs of beached whales. Threads hung limp as severed arteries, dangling from machines that had once thundered like gods of steam and steel. Workers sat cross-legged on floors dark with a century of oil stains, their bodies finally at rest after generations of servitude to the rhythm of production. No thunder of shuttles weaving empire. No roar of progress devouring itself. Only hush deep enough to hold prayer, silence sacred as any cathedral.

In Detroit's rust-red graveyards, conveyor belts hung slack as the spines of dead leviathans. Men who had built the world's dreams of motion now crawled beneath machines that would never wake again, wrenches still hanging at their hips like rosaries of a forgotten faith. Their bodies bore the weight of steel that had shaped them, tethered to assembly lines that would stay mute until the end of time. Chrome had promised eternity, but silence proved more durable than any alloy forged in human furnaces.

In Dhaka's sprawling textile temples, garment halls over-
flowed with seamsters whose needles stitched only air. Ten
million hands moved from muscle memory alone, fingers
tracing phantom seams across emptiness, decades of repetition carving patterns in bone and sinew that no stillness
could erase. Some tore their own shirts into strips, weaving
them through ceiling rafters in testimony to labor that had
consumed their lives—witness blooming where no overseer's
orders could reach.

In Osaka's shipyard graveyards, half-born hulls rusted like
the skeletons of iron whales, cranes frozen mid-gesture as if
time itself had crystallized. Children with chalk-dusted
fingers scrawled messages along their towering beams—not
production quotas or efficiency metrics, but the simple
names of what remained: *Hunger. Hope. Here.*

In Lagos's oil fields, mechanical hearts gasped their final
beats before falling forever silent. Gas flares that had
burned like captured suns since before memory guttered
and died, leaving only the smell of crude dreams and abandoned ambition. Children appeared like pilgrims, lining the
silent rigs with mason jars filled with fireflies—living light
replacing the dead flame of industry, small souls glowing
steady where engines had surrendered their ghosts.

In São Paulo's concrete forests, smokestacks coughed their
last breath of soot into dawn air that tasted of ending and
beginning both. By the time sun crowned the city's broken
skyline, factory walls bloomed white with chalk declara-
tions: **WE BREATHE NOW.** The words spread like
contagion, like gospel, like the first honest advertisement the
city had ever known.

Across the wounded world, the great machines fell still:

No loom stirred to weave tomorrow's cloth. No wheel turned to carry yesterday's dreams. No engine fired to burn the future as fuel. Industry itself—that titan that had devoured mountains and rivers and human lives for centuries—finally surrendered to the weight of its own ambition, collapsing not in explosion but in whisper, not in fire but in the simple, profound act of stopping.

The new labor was not the manufacture of objects but the cultivation of presence. Not the production of goods but the creation of witness. The world's factories had fallen silent, but in their ruins, humanity was learning to make something more enduring than any commodity:

The courage to simply be, together, breathing the same air under the same broken sky.

Witness had become the world's most essential industry, and its only product was the irreplaceable miracle of staying alive.

Interlude IV – Dangerous As Decree

"Words written high fracture faster than stone."

In Washington's marble halls of borrowed glory, a senator struggled to his feet from the bench that had become his cage, decree rolled tight in his fist like a weapon forged from paper and impotent rage. "Order must be restored!" he thundered at the vaulted ceiling, his voice cracking with the desperation of kings who discover their kingdoms were always imaginary. The gallery sat cross-legged in perfect silence, bodies forming a constellation of quiet defiance on cold stone. His words echoed once against indifferent marble, then died without progeny. Chalk spirals drawn by children's hands across the Capitol floor outlasted his entire speech, outlasted his career, outlasted the very notion that power flows downward from podiums.

In Delhi's monsoon-soaked corridors of bureaucracy, a minister clawed red proclamations across government walls with fingers that bled authority. His paint ran like wounds in the pre-dawn rain, words dissolving into meaningless streams of crimson water. Children appeared at first light, tying strips of cloth to storm drains where the dissolved decrees pooled, their witness fluttering in the morning breeze longer than any official paint had ever endured on stone.

In Madrid's judicial temples, a magistrate struck his gavel until the ivory handle split like bone, the sound sharp as gunshots in his empty courtroom. Citizens gathered below pressed their palms to courthouse steps instead of bowing to his elevated bench. Their breath, shared and witnessed, carried farther through the building's corridors than any verdict he had ever pronounced from his throne of assumed righteousness.

In Johannesburg's shanty sprawls and glass towers alike, massive posters screamed from every surface: **THE GROUND REMEMBERS.** The words blazed red as fresh blood, black as old wounds, promising memory that outlasts flesh. Afternoon rain peeled them from walls like old skin, but passing feet carried the soggy fragments farther than industrial glue ever could—words becoming pilgrimage, message becoming migration.

In Tokyo's corporate citadels, glass towers unfurled silk banners proclaiming eternal loyalty to Untethered supremacy, their characters painted in gold that caught the rising sun. By noon, wind had snapped them into colorful rags that tumbled through narrow streets. Children claimed them from gutters and trash heaps, transforming proclamations of power into capes for games of heroism, authority become costume, law become play.

In Beijing's Forbidden City, officials shouted orders from balconies to courtyards that answered only with echo. In London's Parliament, MPs read bills to empty chambers where pigeons nested in the rafters. In Ottawa's halls of governance, ministers signed legislation with pens that left no mark on paper grown too damp with tears to hold ink.

Everywhere across the wounded globe, decrees thundered from artificial heights. Everywhere, the ground refused to carry them beyond the first footfall. Gravity had become democracy's truest expression.

It was not silence undoing their authority—silence, after all, can be broken. It was not stone rebelling against their words —stone bears whatever weight is placed upon it.

It was law itself, that ancient river, finding its natural course again. Flowing downward as all living things must flow. Settling where it had always belonged: not in marble halls or corporate boardrooms or judicial chambers lifted high above the people they presumed to govern.

But here, in the dust and chalk and breath and witness of those who had always been governed, who were now learning that they had always been the only source from which legitimate authority could ever spring.

The ground had inherited the courthouse, and with it, the right to write its own laws in languages older than parchment: touch, breath, shared presence under the same merciless and merciful sky.

Chapter 43

The Low Bench Oath

"Even games can bind when played enough times; repetition worn into stone becomes law."

AT DAWN, when mist still clung low in the crawlways, children gathered at the benches cut for Grounded height— stone slabs worn smooth by decades of knees and hands. What had begun as play lingered there, stubborn as chalk dust.

They traced spirals where Guards had scuffed them out. They tied cloth where Tribunal decrees had ordered it torn away. They whispered Rael's rhythm and Kess's litany, repeating each as if the very benches demanded rehearsal.

"Seventeen. Four. Two. Hold."

"Level. Cross. Lock. Test. Check."

The words mixed like call and response. One child whispered cadence, another answered, and soon the benches echoed with rhythms older than any parchment still clutched in marble halls.

Mira watched from the rail, ledger closed against her chest.

"It is oath already," she murmured. "They are writing it by use."

Salliwith pressed a ribbon flat against stone, bare shoulders trembling but steady. "Witness begins here," she said, voice soft but certain.

Kess leaned close, gloved hands guiding knot-binders as they checked each strap with careful fingers. "Play becomes craft," she said, voice rough but unwavering. "And craft endures."

Karine bent low with her cracked lens, sketching the benches themselves into her map, naming them with precise chalk strokes: *Oath-seat. Law-stone. Memory-mark.*

Nessa laughed, sharp and bright, earrings flashing in the early light. "Then the Tribunal has lost twice over. First to breath, and now to benches."

Rael pressed his scarred cheek to the wall, whispering the vow that had become sacred, and children repeated it until their breath shook dust loose from ancient stone.

By the time the sun rose high enough to burn off the mist, the benches had become more than seats. They were altars of rehearsal, low courts where the only verdict was endurance, the only law what hands and lungs had learned by heart.

What began as play had bound itself to stone.

The Low Bench Oath was not written, not decreed, not proclaimed from heights. It was repeated—over and over, until it could not be forgotten, could not be torn away.

And in that repetition, in that rhythm worn smooth as the stone itself, the city learned: even games, played enough times, become law.

Chapter 44

Mira's Single Refusal

"Silence can weigh more than ink; refusal itself becomes scripture when witnessed."

THE LOW BENCH Oath had stretched deep into the night. Children's laughter echoed through the crawlways, their vows cast like pebbles into dark water—some kind, some cruel, all heavy in their own way.

Mira sat apart, ledger open across her knees. Her thumb bore the permanent crescent of ink that marked her as Recorder, a stain she no longer tried to wash. She listened as the oaths multiplied—Rael's vow bent into chant, Kess's litany reshaped as rhyme, the square thick with voices layered like evening mist.

She dipped her pen, lowered it toward the waiting page... and stopped.

From the stair, a Grounded Guard sneered, stave dragging across stone. "What's this, Recorder? Won't you write? If it's not in your book, it never happened, eh?"

Mira closed the ledger with a sharp snap, pressing her inked thumb firm against the cover. The smudge bled darker across the spine.

"This one," she said, her voice quiet but carrying clear across the square, "will live without me."

The crowd hushed. A gasp here, a murmur there. Even the children stilled mid-chant.

"Why not?" asked a boy, his knees chalked white from the oath-bench, jar-light trembling in his small hands.

Mira studied him—wide-eyed, breathless, waiting. "Because if I write it, I trap it in my words. If I refuse..." She let silence fall between them, deliberate as a blade. "It remains free to become what it truly is."

Nessa's laugh cut the air, sharp as struck glass. "Careful, sister. You'll make refusal itself into scripture."

Salliwith pressed her bare palm against the cold stone, her voice low and steady: "Witness always costs something."

Karine bent over her map, chalk scrawling a single word beside the night's geometry: **Silence.**

Rael's cracked whisper drifted from the wall: "Hold." It was assent enough.

Kess shifted close, ribs bound, gloves frayed but still on her hands. She laid one strap across the ledger's cover, cinching it tight. "Method holds what words cannot," she murmured. Children echoed her litany, knotting the silence into vow.

The Guards shifted uneasily, their mockery withering in the quiet. On the dais, **Elara Mora** leaned forward, voice cracking like old parchment. "You cannot choose silence. You owe us the record."

Mira met her gaze steadily. "No. I owe the truth. And truth does not belong to you."

She bound the ledger shut with its leather cord, laid it beside her like a sleeping animal, and folded her blackened thumb into her palm.

That night, nothing entered the Archive.

And refusal itself became the loudest record of all.

UR-III: Marriage at the Bench

(Upper Registers — Depositions of the Untethered)

THEY DID NOT MARRY at an altar. They married at a bench.

Thirty-six inches from the stone floor, polished by a thousand hands, cut to the new measure where both could meet. The Grounded bride, leather straps cinched at her wrists, lifted herself until her chin brushed the wood. The Untethered groom bent from his full height, knees pressed hard to stone, shoulders trembling with the strain of stooping.

Witnesses stood in silence. Some wept, others scoffed. One merchant spat, *"This is misaligned. The law will not hold such vows."*

But the scribe recorded every word.

The vow was not long.

"I will not rise higher than you can reach."

"I will not stoop lower than you can bear."

When it was done, they placed a small crib flush against the bench. Its rails sat exactly at thirty-six inches, where both could touch, feed, comfort. A space designed not for law, not for commerce, but for a child who would know both registers as home.

Violence lingered at the edge of the square, disguised as laughter from the crowd, disguised as a muttered threat about children growing crooked. She could not claim the vows, not yet. But she waited, patient as gravity.

Chapter 45

The Day of Two Bridges

"Every city must choose which span will bear its weight; stone cracks, but breath can bind."

WORD SPREAD FASTER than cloth could carry it: the Tribunal would speak from both bridges. One arched over the Crawlways' murky depths, the other spanned the river's mouth where it met the sea. Twin stages for twin decrees—a final show of authority stretched thin across stone and water.

At the eastern bridge, **Chief Arbiter Tenric Halvorsen** stood with his scroll unfurled, a violent cough shattering every third word. "By decree... order shall be... restored..." Each phrase scattered weak across the water, parchment snapping in the river wind like a dying bird struggling for flight.

At the western bridge, **Canonister Brannic Raal** abandoned all pretense of dignity. He howled at the sky: "Children are insects! Cloth is refuse! Fireflies cannot be law!" His voice climbed higher and higher until it cracked, shrill as a kettle left shrieking over flame.

Between them, **Defender Magistrate Elara Mora** made her last desperate attempt at connection. She knelt at the Threshold rail, leaning toward the people below: "For the people—listen, just listen to me." Her plea drifted like smoke—part prayer, part apology, wholly unheard.

The crowd did not move toward either bridge.

Instead, they wove their own answer. Knot-binders stretched ribbons from parapet to parapet, bright strands pulsing like veins across stone. Spiral-chalkers marked the bridgeheads in widening rings of white and blue. Jar-bearers climbed the balustrades to set glass vessels along the rails, fireflies pulsing steady as heartbeats. Beneath it all, breath-counters whispered Rael's rhythm in unison: seventeen, four, two.

The Tribunal's spectacle bent and broke against this quiet rebellion.

Tenric's cough consumed his words, parchment stained with spit and ink. Elara's voice thinned into desperate pleading that earned only pity. Brannic screamed until his throat tore raw, words dissolving into soundless fury. Their robes dragged in dust, their banners hung limp as dead skin, their authority collapsed into bodies hunched and trembling.

Below them, witness bloomed like wildfire taking dry wood.

• Mira sealed her ledger shut, thumb black against its spine. "This is record enough," she murmured.

• Salliwith pressed her bare palm against the stone. "Witness demands its price," she said. "They cannot pay it."

• Karine marked the sagging banners on her map, cracked lens scattering lamplight into fragments. She inscribed one word beside their image: **Ash.**

• Kess braced herself at the square's edge, ribs bound, gloves patched, calling steady through the children's work: "Level. Cross. Lock. Test. Check."

• Rael whispered his vow from the wall: "Hold." The word spread into hundreds of lungs.

• Nessa stood tall, earrings blazing like stars. "See?" she cried to the dais. "You crawl now. You crawl before children."

The Guards scraped their staves in mounting frustration, grinding bright cloth into grey mud, smashing jars within reach. But their lines crumbled faster than they could reform them—too many gaps to fill, too many spirals redrawn, too many hands raised in quiet defiance. Grounded men trying to unmake a law already written in breath and light.

By dusk, the Tribunal sagged together, three shadows bent low on their dais. Not law incarnate. Not theater of power. Only Grounded. Only human. Only small.

The bridges meant to prove their reach had revealed only fracture.

The people did not cross either span.

They remained in Threshold square, bound not by stone or decree, but by their own bridges—woven from cloth and chalk, glass and shared breath. Connections stronger than any arch, more enduring than law carved in stone.

Chapter 46

Nessa Marked

"To stand upright among the Grounded is its own defiance; to choose one's mark is covenant beyond decree."

THE BRAZIER HAD GONE cold hours ago. The branding iron lay abandoned where it had fallen—blackened and useless, its cruel word burned deep into stone and ash instead of living flesh. The boy who had been dragged forward still bore his binding ropes, but his skin remained whole and unmarked. The square breathed as one body, collective memory settling like dust.

On their raised dais, the Tribunal sagged like broken marionettes, robes limp as funeral shrouds. Their voices had failed them completely. Their decrees lay in fragments, shattered by their own trembling hands.

And yet the ash still waited.

Nessa stepped forward—not summoned, not bound, not commanded by any authority. She crossed the square entirely of her own will, moving toward the very place where cruelty had collapsed upon itself, where sacred iron had branded nothing but indifferent marble dust.

She knelt—not in submission, but in deliberate choice—and pressed her bare palm deep into the cold gray residue. The ash clung to her skin like something newly alive, dark streaks rising across her hand and creeping up her wrist like a shadow that would never wash clean, never fade, never be forgotten.

Then she reached to her right ear. One charm swung low beneath her mother's silver stud—hammered bright, sharp enough now to serve. She wrenched it free, clenched it tight, and without pause drew a spiral into her forearm. Blood welled quick and bright, searing pain stiffened her arm—but she pressed the wound into the ash, sealing it black.

When she lifted her arm high, the mark gleamed—a spiral cut and burned into flesh, blood and ash bound into covenant.

"You call me irreparable," she said, her voice cutting sharp as winter air, carrying to every corner and crevice of the square. "But I am Untethered by choice. I choose my own scars. I claim my own marks."

The square erupted around her. Not in riot. Not in panic or rage. In laughter—fierce, dangerous, intoxicating laughter. Laughter that mocked sacred iron into meaningless ash, that bent holy decree into common dust, that stripped institutional cruelty of its teeth and transformed it into bitter parody.

The Tribunal bent even lower on their platform—not in solemn ritual, but in undeniable defeat. Their sanctified mark had vanished utterly in worthless smoke. Hers remained: chosen freely, claimed boldly, witnessed by hundreds of beating hearts.

And then, as if her courage were contagious, others came forward. Children pressed eager palms into the cooling ash and raised their smudged hands like victory banners. Spiral-chalkers drew bold black spirals across their forearms, mixing soot with their white chalk in deliberate defiance. Knot-binders tied strips of cloth streaked with gray to the bridge rails, each ribbon a small rebellion. Jar-bearers touched ash to their vessels, fireflies pulsing through smudges of chosen resistance.

All of it—every act of defiance, every gesture of solidarity—flowed outward from her single, transformative choice.

The mark no decree could force upon unwilling flesh.

The covenant no iron could burn into submitted skin.

The scar she had chosen freely—hers alone, witnessed by all, and somehow, impossibly, shared.

Codex VIII – Fragment, Day of Ash

From the Ledger of Mira

I DID NOT WRITE the Tribunal's decree. Their words failed before air would hold them.

But I wrote her.

Nessa cut a spiral into her own arm with the charm that once swung from her ear. Blood marked the line first. Ash sealed it after. She dropped the blade of herself into the brazier and left it there. What had been ornament became scar. What had been inheritance became covenant.

Her left arm bears it still—spiral dark as stone dust, cut deeper than decree.

One charm remains. It caught jar-light like a star when she lifted it high, laughing.

I set down only this:

• Scar chosen is stronger than scar imposed. • Ash brands truer than iron. • A spiral cut into flesh can outlast marble law.

Witness does not belong to parchment. It belongs to those who bleed and choose their own mark.

Codex IX – The First Communal Covenant

"Ash carries further than iron; choice carries further still."

FROM THE WITNESS Ledger of Kaelen Thorne, Scribe of the Lower Quarter

Third day of Harvest's End, Year of the Broken Iron

ON THE MATTER of Nessa's Ash

Let it be set down: on this day, before three hundred souls gathered in Justice Square, the ancient practice of forced marking ended forever—not by riot or blade, not by petition or revolt, but by one woman's act of chosen defiance.

When the Tribunal's sacred iron failed and their holy decree crumbled to worthless ash, one among the Untethered—Nessa, of no House, no lineage, no station save what she claimed for herself—rose to transform their failure into her triumph.

What had been intended as punishment became covenant. What was designed to brand became blessing. She pressed her bare hand into the dust of their broken authority and lifted it high, marked not by their decree but by her own unbreakable will. And all who bore witness understood in that moment: the iron held no true power. Only the choosing did.

Within a fortnight, the transformation had spread like fire through dry grass. Children bore ash spirals on their arms like badges of witness. Cloth merchants knotted strips blackened with sacred soot into their wares. The scorched stone itself became hallowed ground—pilgrimage destination where even the unmarked came seeking to claim a sign of their own choosing.

The Tribunal still perch in their high places, muttering hollow edicts into empty air. But their iron lies cold and powerless. The only mark that endures is hers—and those countless others who followed her courage into freedom.

Let the record show for all who come after: this was the day the Untethered ceased to be merely unnamed, and chose instead to name themselves.

The ash remained when the iron could not.

Sealed this day in the presence of Mira the Ledger-Keeper, Rael of the Wall-Watch, and Kess the Stone-Binder, who bore witness to the witnessing.

Chapter 47

The Map That Circulates

"Names are the first roads."

Karine spread her cracked lens across the cold stone, its jagged edges carefully bound in strips of worn cloth so no shard would break loose and draw blood. Beneath its fractured surface, a new kind of map took shape—not of nations or kingdoms, not of trade routes or territorial boundaries, but of the fractures themselves. She traced them with steady chalk until the lines bent and forked like pale veins through marble, marking precisely where ancient walls bowed under invisible pressure, where the Crawlways split and yawned into hungry darkness. Each mark she sealed with her thumb, pressing stone dust deep into memory and meaning.

Children pressed close around her, all sharp knees and elbows against the unforgiving stone. They whispered the names she gave to each crack as if repeating sacred spells: *Shardwalk. Silent Turn. Breathcut. Jarline.* Each syllable carried more weight than it appeared to hold—no scholar's dry label, but survival's hard-earned currency, paid for in scraped skin and careful steps through dangerous places.

When the mapping circle finally broke apart, they carried her knowledge away in fragments: sketched hastily onto scraps of torn cloth, scrawled in the dim amber glow of firefly jars, traced across their own arms in ink that would fade by morning's light. Others carried no visible mark at all, only the rhythm she had burned into their careful steps—counting fractures by instinct and heart until their bodies themselves became living, breathing charts of the city's hidden wounds.

By nightfall, her names had spread farther than her hands could ever physically reach. Traders repeated them in hushed, respectful tones at shadowy market stalls. Children scrawled them beside storm drainage grates in defiant chalk. Even on the Tribunal's pristine marble stairs, someone had dared to chalk a spiral with *Breathcut* written plain and bold beneath it. The map no longer belonged to Karine alone. It lived now in dust and cloth, in whispered rumor and sworn vow, breathing and growing without her guidance.

She lifted the cracked lens once more, watching light scatter across its central fault like a promise broken long ago. Tears did not come—she had abandoned that luxury years past, when survival demanded clearer sight. Instead she bent low over the stone, drew one last hidden line that no one else would ever learn to read, and whispered into the gathering darkness:

"It moves. It all moves."

Chapter 48

Breathmark of Hunger

"An empty stomach counts louder than law."

SMOKE from a thousand cook fires thinned into the indifferent night sky, but no sustenance followed its false promise upward—only the bitter ghost of meals that would never come.

MARKETS that once thundered with fierce barter now stood hollow as sun-bleached bones, their wooden stalls worn smooth by countless dragging hands searching shelves that had nothing left to give. The Ash Market had earned its cruel name twice over, offering only the gray dust of abandoned dreams. Grain bins gaped like starving mouths, clay storage jars cracked open like broken marriage vows, and what little meat remained putrefied in open channels where even the hungriest scavengers had finally surrendered hope.

CHILDREN LEARNED to measure the depth of their hunger by the rhythm of their breath: slow and steady at first, then ragged and desperate with mounting want, then shallow and quick as autumn leaves before the killing frost. Mothers stripped the final precious cloth from treasured wedding shawls—not for witness or ceremony now, but for the desperate alchemy of boiling fabric fibers into a broth too thin to sustain life, yet far too precious to waste.

THE TRIBUNAL, stripped naked of banners and functional authority, offered only the hollow, mocking echo of meaningless words. Their marble chambers rang with empty decrees that filled no bellies, with elaborate promises that dissolved on parched tongues like frost touched by dawn's first light.

GROUNDED and Untethered alike pressed cracked lips to cold stone, whispering desperate prayers for crusts that would never materialize, for scraps that survived now only in memory's most cruel theater.

HUNGER BECAME the city's new shared dialect—spoken fluently in the pause between one breath and the next. A shallow, careful inhale. A trembling, reluctant exhale. A silence grown too heavy for human speech. People no longer counted steps through familiar streets, nor catalogued scars from old battles and victories, but measured only the ever-widening distance between sustenance and mouth, between flickering hope and echoing hollow.

WHEN DAWN finally broke over the starving stones of Threshold, no grand decree shattered the suffocating silence. Only ribs outlined sharp and clear against skin stretched thin as parchment. Only eyes grown too weary to close properly, too empty of tears to weep.

THE CITY HAD DISCOVERED its new constitution at last, written in the most universal script ever devised: pure, undiluted want. Hunger inscribed its absolute law across every protruding chest, every hollowed cheek, every hand that trembled with more than age or fear—and before its final, impartial authority, no living soul could claim to stand beyond its hungry reach.

Chapter 49

Cascades of Consequence

"Every silence leaves a mark."

THE SHAWL SURRENDERED its final strip that night, unraveling in Salliwith's weathered lap like the last thread of memory itself. She tore without prayer, without ceremony—only the habit of giving worn smooth by endless repetition. When her hands reached again, they found nothing but empty air, fingers still trembling in the familiar shape of generosity long after the fabric had vanished completely.

Kess watched from her place beside the shrine, her builder's gloves blackened with accumulated soot, her rope sling folded carefully across her knees. She did not reach for cloth—her hands had always spoken their truth in fiber and frame, in knot and tension. "Straps are not endless," she said quietly, her voice rasped raw from exhaustion and smoke. "Neither are shoulders strong enough to bear everything. The weight must be shared, or it will break us all." Children leaned close to catch every word, knot-binders repeating her wisdom like sacred lessons, learning that witness was not just cloth and ceremony but method itself—that survival could be bound into covenant, woven into practice, made stronger through sharing.

Above them on the marble stairs, the Guards stood hollow as empty armor, their staves drooping like dead winter branches, their oppressive silence somehow heavier than any threat they had ever made. Once they had been feared throughout Threshold. Now they were only seen clearly—revealed as Grounded men who could rise no higher than the very children who laughed openly at their powerless posturing. That laughter rang through the Crawlways sharp as breaking glass, cruel in its perfect beauty, undeniable in its final judgment.

Mira opened her precious ledger with trembling hands, pen hovering uncertain above unmarked parchment like a bird afraid to land. Then she closed it again with deliberate force, pressing her ink-stained thumb deep into the margin instead. The dark smear became silence made visible— louder than any script, more eloquent than words. She did not need flowing sentences to bear testimony when refusal itself carried such devastating weight.

Rael's whispered vow spilled outward like water from a cracked vessel, unstoppable and pure. His rhythm—*seventeen, four, two*—began as breath beneath the stairs, whispered against cold stone, then multiplied and spread through the Crawlways until hundreds of lungs carried it like sacred chant. One fragile vow had shattered into countless echoes. The delicate thread of one man's breath had become a rope so strong that no decree could ever sever it.

The Tribunal remained fixed on their raised dais, but only as hollow husks now—robes sagging like empty skin, decrees falling forgotten like autumn leaves, no longer feared by anyone, no longer binding anything to their will. Their proud banners had already sagged into complete irrelevance, their commanding words stretched so thin in air that would no longer carry them that they dissolved before reaching any ear.

By dawn's pale light, Threshold bore scars carved not by imperial decree but by the weight of consequence itself. Cloth had been unraveled to nothing, given until there was nothing left to give. Guards stood hollowed out, revealed as powerless. Children carried both received cruelty and chosen compassion in their shared, defiant play. Ledgers closed themselves in eloquent silence that spoke volumes louder than flowing ink. Individual vows had multiplied into a breathing chorus of collective will.

And Kess's rope straps, bound tight against the bridge rail, still bore their essential weight—not only of physical bodies but of accumulated meaning, of promises kept and burdens shared. "Fiber tells the only truth that matters," she murmured, her calloused palms resting gentle on her sling. "It frays when strained beyond bearing, but binds strong when the load is shared." Around her, children repeated the phrase with growing understanding until it settled deep in the stones like natural law, like something that had always been true.

These were the cascades—not thunder or earthquake, not riot or sudden collapse, but the slow, inevitable reshaping that comes when power finally exhausts itself completely. Not revolution imposed from above, but evolution grown from within. Not verdict handed down, but consequence earned and witnessed—woven by those who saw clearly, sealed in silence that spoke truth, carried forward in the simple strength of straps and shawls, in shared vows and collective breath.

UR-IV: The Price of Up

(Upper Registers — Depositions of the Untethered)

THE MARKET at Threshold was louder than prayer.

Grounded traders sprawled low, jars glowing faintly with firefly light, chalk tokens marked with spirals and circles. Untethered merchants stood tall behind tables stacked with coins, scales, and ledgers balanced at eye level.

For weeks they had tolerated barter — a strip of cloth for a loaf, a jar for a tool. But then the council declared the *upper coin* official tender again. Exchange rates were posted on banners strung far above the thirty-six–inch line: *Three jars for one coin. Five cloth strips for half a loaf.*

The Grounded could not see the numbers. They asked, pleaded, argued. Children clambered to read the banners down, but Guards shoved them back.

One Untethered clerk began to skim. He accepted jars, recorded fewer than he received, then sold the extras back across the line. His profit grew faster than the chalk could trace.

That morning a jar cracked. Its light spilled out, wings frantic, scattering across the stair. The crowd surged. Cloth flew. Coins clattered down into the crawl. Shouts turned into a chant: *"Bring it down! Bring it down!"*

The Police raised staves but dared not strike. The Guards crouched with blades drawn, but the tide pressed too hard. Violence stood openly now, no longer disguised — her hand was in every push, every grab, every scream.

And the city learned: the *price of up* was not measured in coins. It was measured in how far a people would kneel before they pulled the banners down.

Chapter 50

Children's Oath

"What is too fragile for ink endures longer than marble; small vows, repeated, outlive decrees."

THEY GATHERED beneath the fallen banners like pilgrims at a new altar, young knees pressed against unforgiving stone, stolen firefly jars arranged in a trembling ring of amber light that pushed back the darkness. No elder had summoned them. No council had granted permission for their assembly. This circle belonged to children alone—the forgotten, the overlooked, the ones who had learned to see with perfect clarity in places where adults stumbled blind.

One by one, they spoke their truth—not in the pompous rhetoric of law or the hollow grandeur of decree, but in fragments small enough for hungry hearts to carry without breaking:

• "I will hold what others drop."

• "I will not rise above the breath beside mine."

• "I will keep the cracks named and mapped."

• "I will remember the weight of empty hands and the ache of hollow bellies."

No official parchment preserved their sacred vows. No ledger bound their precious words to permanent ink. Their covenant was scrawled in chalk dust and shifting shadow, written in a script so fragile that the night's rain might wash it completely away. Yet the sound lingered in the hollow spaces between ancient stones—thin voices weaving together into something far heavier than any decree, more binding than laws carved deep in marble.

From the circle's edge, the adults bore witness in their own ways. Mira watched with her ledger sealed deliberately tight, knowing instinctively that some truths are too sacred for ink, too pure for recording. Nessa touched the silver coins at her ears but did not speak aloud, recognizing a currency more valuable than gold or power. Rael counted the measured pauses between each whispered promise, measuring a new rhythm born of chosen vow instead of inherited fear. Karine traced delicate chalk patterns through her cracked lens, catching each child's solemn reflection in fractured light.

Kess crouched low among them like a protective guardian, her rope sling folded carefully across her knees, work gloves blackened from honest labor. She nodded approval as knot-binders repeated the sacred oaths, tying cloth strips into an unbroken chain that no iron could sever, no decree could dissolve. "Fiber frays when it stands alone," she murmured, her voice carrying the wisdom of years, "but woven together, it holds against any storm." The children echoed her words as if they had always belonged to them, as if they had been born knowing this truth.

Salliwith pressed her bare, trembling shoulders against the cold stone rail, empty hands shaking where precious cloth had long since unraveled into memory. "Witness breathes here," she whispered into the gathered darkness, and the children's collective oath answered her with breath enough to fill the square, breath enough for everyone.

When the solemn circle finally dissolved and the children slipped back into concealing shadow, their oath did not scatter like leaves on the wind. It walked with them into the honeycomb maze of Crawlways, into the hollow markets where hunger gnawed relentlessly at hope, into the storm drains where despair flowed quiet and deep but never, ever final.

By morning's pale light, the Tribunal's grand halls stood empty as discarded shells, their polished marble echoing with nothing but the ghosts of memory. But in the square where truth had been spoken, children's breath still held visible shape in the sharp air—small clouds rising like prayers, like living proof, like law newly made by those who had inherited nothing but chose to create everything.

The old order had not fallen to riot or revolution, had not collapsed beneath the weight of violence or rage. It had simply been outlived—quietly, inevitably—by something smaller, quieter, and infinitely more enduring: the stubborn, unbreakable vow of those with nothing left to lose, and everything still worth protecting.

Chapter 51

The Ledger Closed

"Some truths survive only unwritten; silence can bind where ink betrays."

THE LEDGER LAY open across her lap like a judgment awaiting its final sentence, its virgin pages pale as skin drained of all warmth and life. Voices pressed against her from every direction—children whispering their fragile oath into the consuming dark, desperate elders urging the false permanence of ink, hollow Guards demanding words they could later twist into convenient decree.

Mira raised her ink-stained thumb to the pristine margin, her pen poised like an executioner's blade above the waiting parchment. But her hand would not move. The ledger—her father's final inheritance, filled with a lifetime of his careful script—suddenly weighed more than granite in her trembling grasp. Every word she had ever committed to these pages carried the terrible power to transform living witness into dead law, breathing memory into cold, manipulable decree.

And with crystalline, terrifying clarity she saw the danger: if she set this sacred oath down in permanent ink, it would belong not to the brave children who had spoken it, but to the corrupt Tribunal who would dissect it, corrupt its meaning, and claim it as their own.

She closed the leather cover with one slow, deliberate breath.

The soft sound cracked the expectant silence like thunder over still water. Faces turned toward her, startled and disbelieving. Some would call her choice cowardice, others rebellion. Only Mira knew the deeper truth: this refusal was not absence but the most profound presence. Not weakness, but concentrated strength.

Her inked thumb pressed too hard as she sealed the ledger shut, leaving a single black smear across the page's pristine edge—not crafted words, only an honest stain. Yet that mute, wordless mark bore more genuine weight than a thousand lines could carry—living proof that some truths are too alive to be trapped in lifeless script.

"Let it live in breath alone," she whispered, her voice so low that only Rael—leaning patient against his familiar wall, still counting the rhythm of lungs around him—heard. His scarred cheek lifted in what might have been approval, might have been understanding.

The ledger remained closed, sealed by choice. The children's covenant belonged to no archive, no marble decree, no tower shelf. It traveled instead in the living lungs of those who had sworn it with fierce determination—moving chest to chest, breath to breath, soul to soul—impossible for distant towers to seize or silence.

For the first time in her life as Recorder, Mira chose not to write. And in that refusal, she discovered the most enduring record of all: words that survive in protective silence, kept safe from every grasping hand that would bind them, twist them, or claim them as something other than what they truly are.

Chapter 52

Cloth as Covenant

"What knots hold endures longer than banners; covenant stitched low outlasts stone."

THE SQUARE BORE its battle scars like an old soldier: straps snapped and fraying, glass jars shattered into glittering fragments, sacred vows cracked into stunned silence. Yet by morning's pale light, one thing remained unbroken—cloth tied wherever desperate hands could reach, stubborn as ivy creeping along ancient weathered stone, impossible to kill or silence.

Knot-binders moved through the wreckage with quiet reverence, their fingers fastening ribbons rinsed clean in the cold river water, colors bright as hope against ash-stained rails. No decree commanded their devotion; no ledger would preserve their names. Each strip of fabric was a living oath— sometimes whispered aloud in trembling words, more often sealed in silence.

The shrine at the square's heart swelled with offerings: worn straps layered upon weathered straps, precious cloth upon salvaged cloth, until Kess's broken sling was transformed from tool into sacred tapestry. Witness had hardened into covenant.

Salliwith pressed her bare palm against the intricate knots, skin brushing fabric touched by hundreds of hands, each carrying its own story. Her voice cracked but held: "No law stands higher than cloth that holds us together."

Karine bent low with her cracked lens, tracing the pattern of new knots onto her map. She named them with the same precision she once used for fractures: **Witness. Burden. Hold. Accord.**

Mira kept her father's ledger sealed shut, thumb blackened against its spine like a badge of honor. She whispered her truth into the morning air: "This record belongs to cloth and human hands, not to ink that fades."

Nessa's laughter rang sharp as breaking glass, her earrings flaring in the dawn. "Look at them," she cried toward the Guards slumped defeated on the stairs, "clutching their rotting banners while we bind eternal truth with rags torn from our own backs."

Rael pressed his scarred cheek to the wall and exhaled one word: *Hold.* The cloth strips stirred as if they had caught his breath, carrying that vow from rail to rail, promise woven into fabric.

On their raised dais, the Tribunal sagged in heavy silence, their banners drooping like shed skin. No decree could outlast strips tied patiently by children's fingers. No proclamation outweighed a single knot pulled tight in darkness by hands that refused surrender.

By evening's light, the shrine was no longer an altar to one failure, one broken sling, one life bent low beneath strain. It had become something larger—woven by a hundred hands, binding Grounded and Untethered alike into something Threshold had never known before.

Not verdict handed down.

Not decree carved in marble.

Only covenant—stitched low, humble, and strong enough to outlast stone itself.

Chapter 53

Ash Accord

"What burns still binds."

THE BRAZIER HAD long since gone cold, its coals grey as bone, but the ash remained. Wind scattered it across the square in thin trails, dusting rails and stairs, seeping into cracks already carrying names. Every witness who passed dragged palms through it, streaking grey across skin and stone. What had been meant as branding had become covenant instead.

The children led first. They pressed fingers into the soot and drew spirals on their arms, mocking the Tribunal's word. "Irreparable," one scrawled crookedly. "If they call us that, let it be ours." Laughter answered—bitter, but alive.

Salliwith let the dust sift through trembling palms. "Witness does not vanish," she whispered. "It changes shape." She smeared what remained across the rail where her shawl once hung.

Kess leaned close, gloves blackened, testing grit between her fingers. "Even ash finds the weave," she murmured, working the powder into the strap's grain until the knot bit.

Karine charted the scatter like a tide. "Ash has direction," she said. Her chalk named the deposits: Drift. Settle. Bind.

Mira pressed her ink-black thumb into the margin of her ledger, then dragged it through ash. She closed the cover without a word. "Enough."

Nessa raised a soot-marked hand, earrings blazing above the grey. "This is the only decree that holds. One smear, and every hand is equal."

From his wall, Rael exhaled: "Hold." His breath lifted a low cloud that settled on every shoulder, every brow, every child.

Above, the Tribunal sagged like statues weathered to ruin. Their banners hung limp, streaked with the same soot that now marked the crowd. The Canonister coughed dust. The Arbiter touched trembling fingers to his mouth and found them grey. The Magistrate prayed into hands no different from any other. The ash did not discriminate. It settled on all alike.

By nightfall, Threshold wore a single color—not the Tribunal's silks, not painted banners, but the residue of a fire that failed to scar. A law drawn low, shared by every breath, binding not by decree but by dust that kept returning to every hand that touched the city.

Chapter 54

Tribunal Husked

"Authority emptied leaves only costume."

THE DAIS still stood at the stair's crown, marble veined with cracks and stained by ash. But what perched upon it no longer resembled power.

The Chief Arbiter hunched over his scrolls, his cough rattling louder than any decree. Spittle smeared ink until letters bled into meaningless blotches. He no longer read the words—he clutched parchment like driftwood, a drowning man gripping scraps of a ship already sunk. The Defender Magistrate pressed her palms together, lips shaping the same phrase in endless repetition: *for the people, for the people.* But her voice never carried beyond her own ears. Prayers that once thundered like commandments had withered into private confessions, whispered to empty air.

The Canonister had screamed himself hollow. His throat gaped raw and silent, no sound emerging when his mouth moved. His banner—once raised like a war cry—hung limp across his shoulders, shroud instead of symbol. He clutched the fabric close like a blanket against the chill of so many watching eyes.

Below, the square did not rage or scatter. It only watched, patient as stone.

Children leaned against soot-smudged rails, palms grey with ash and chalk dust. Knot-binders tugged at strips tied tight around the shrine posts, testing bonds that refused to come undone. Spiral-chalkers traced new rings around the dais base, each circle binding tighter than the last, drawing the marble into their geometry. Jar-bearers crouched low, their vessels climbing step by step toward the platform, firefly glow advancing with patient inevitability.

Mira pressed her ledger tight against her chest, thumb black against its leather spine. "This is no record," she whispered to the ash-laden air. "This is only husk." Nessa laughed into the silence, earrings catching the jar-light like captured stars. "See them now? Not judges. Not rulers. Just robes draped on bones." Salliwith leaned her bare shoulders into the shrine's rough wood, voice emerging soft but certain: "Witness costs. They have nothing left to pay."

Karine bent close to the marble, her cracked lens fogging from breath that came quick with purpose. Her chalk scratched across the dais itself, bold and plain: *Husk*. The word etched white against grey stone, claiming the platform for simpler truths.

Rael, weak against his wall, exhaled his vow one more time: "Hold." It carried no command, no plea—only the weight of truth spoken. The word filled the silence where Tribunal voices had failed, sealing the air with the authority of breath itself.

The Guards did not move from their posts. Their ceremonial staves sagged like dead weight, knees bruised from crawling through ash to reach their stations. They no longer defended anything. They simply endured, part of the furniture now.

When the wind shifted, it pulled the Tribunal's banners earthward. No one moved to raise them back. Cloth sagged until it brushed the stairs, too heavy with soot and failure to fly. The fabric pooled like spilled wine, soaking up the ash of its own ceremony.

The square had outlived its theater. What remained above was mere costume, empty performance played to an audience that had stopped believing. What remained below was law itself—unwritten, shared, breathing with the rhythm of common hearts.

The ash settled deeper with each passing hour, and the watching continued.

Codex X– The Persistence of Evil

"A law written is not a law kept."

THE PULSE DID NOT unmake cruelty; it only stripped away excuses.

Evil does not vanish when knees touch stone, nor when spires touch sky. It changes mask.

Above, it wears coin, decree, silence.

Below, it wears knife, fist, hunger.

Both are Violence's children.

Both are seen.

Neither escapes the measure.

So ask: why do the Grounded not rule from below?

Because terror cannot govern those already broken by tether.

A bullet may fly upward, but it cannot hold a stair.

A blade may slice at a knee, but it cannot climb to claim a throne.

Violence devours those who hoard her.

She permits no kingdom, only consequence.

Chapter 55

Night of Quiet Banners

"Even silence has weight when cloth remembers."

When dusk settled over Threshold, no decree was spoken. No gavel cracked the air. No banner snapped in triumph.

Instead, the people gathered beneath rails and shrine, the square glowing with jars placed one by one in patient vigil. Their light pulsed steady as heartbeats, weaving constellations low to the ground. Above them, the Tribunal's banners sagged like funeral cloth, their gilded letters unreadable in the gathering dim.

Children climbed the steps with careful hands. They did not tear the banners down—they tied ribbons to the fraying edges, bright scraps fluttering like veins stitched into a failing body. Where silk rotted, new cloth held. Where golden thread unraveled, chalk circled to claim the ground beneath.

At the square's center, Kess's shrine bore fresh weight. Straps once stiff with ash now carried ribbons soaked in river water, their knots swelling against worn leather. Her broken sling—once mocked as failure—had become the truest banner, still holding when silk had withered to dust. People pressed their palms to its frame, whispering oaths not to power above, but to the covenant below.

Mira pressed her closed ledger to her chest, thumb black against its spine. "Let the cloth keep its own record," she whispered. She would not open her book tonight. The night belonged to silence, and silence could not be trapped in ink.

Nessa's laughter rang sharp as glass, but it carried no cruelty—only defiance. Her earrings glinted in jar-light as she tilted her chin toward the dais. "See how heavy they hang? Higher law doesn't rise. It sags."

Salliwith pressed her bare palm to the shrine's rough wood, shoulders bowed with weariness but unbroken. "Cloth keeps vigil longer than any tongue," she murmured.

Karine crouched with her cracked lens, sketching the limp banners into her map, chalk dust thick on her fingertips. She marked them not as symbols of rule but as fractures named *Ash*.

Rael exhaled into the dark: "Hold." His whisper threaded through the hush until lungs across the square repeated it, weaving a rhythm low and patient as the light itself.

The Guards shifted on their bruised knees, silent, their staves lowered. They neither defended nor attacked. Their silence matched the banners' droop.

The Tribunal hunched in the dimness, robes sagging like the cloth above them. They did not rise. They did not speak. They did not command. They became shadows, outlived by the very fabric that once proclaimed their power.

By full nightfall, the square was transformed. Banners that had been tools of decree now hung as quiet witnesses, woven together with children's cloth, claimed not through force but through presence.

No trumpet announced the change. No proclamation sealed it.

Only silence. Only cloth. Only the shared weight of night.

And in that silence, Threshold breathed as one.

UR-V: The Lowered Pulpit

(Upper Registers — Depositions of the Untethered)

THE CATHEDRAL HAD SURVIVED the Pulse—its spire still pierced the sky, bells still hung high, pulpits still raised voices far above the crowd. But few came anymore.

The Grounded gathered at the base, straining upward, unable to see the preacher's face or catch more than broken syllables tumbling down like crumbs. Children squirmed in the aisles, chasing echoes rather than words.

At last one bishop commanded the carpenters: *"Lower it."*

The pulpit was unbolted, carved wood groaning as it came down step by step, until it stood flush with the new measure. Thirty-six inches. A place where Grounded and Untethered could both hear, both answer.

Half the council of clergy rejoiced. The other half recoiled. *"If we kneel to speak, who will believe we still carry height?"*

That night, during the first sermon from the lowered pulpit, the old archbishop refused to descend. He raised his voice from the spire, fist striking the air. The moment his anger became intent, his knees buckled. He fell before the altar, robes tangled in dust.

Silence followed, heavier than bells.

Violence bent low, brushing her hand across the wood. *"Even prayer can be sharpened into a blade,"* she whispered.

The city learned: faith, too, could fracture on the line.

Interlude V – Global Echo

"What begins in one square circles the globe."

In Manchester's mills, chalk rings glowed pale against soot-blackened brick. Children circled looms that would never spin again, tracing spirals onto iron frames, weaving witness into silence. Bits of cloth torn from uniforms were tied to beams—a patchwork of memory over machines that had devoured generations. Glowworms pulsed green and gold in jars, their rhythm fragile but stubborn, low light among hulks of rusted steel.

In Detroit's rust-red factories, silent as mausoleums, elders dragged weary bodies along assembly lines, tying ribbons to axles that would never turn. Chalk spirals spread across conveyor belts, white as bone dust. The vow *"Hold"* echoed through cavernous spaces once filled with engines and anthems of progress. It sounded different there—deeper, touched by diesel and grief—but it carried the same weight.

In Dhaka, seamstresses stitched spirals in red thread across cracked pillars, their lungs raw from lint but their voices steady. *"Breathe,"* they whispered with each pass of the needle. *"Share."* Children placed jars of fireflies from fields beyond the city, their wings beating in cadence that matched Rael's numbers, light shimmering against concrete walls stained by decades of labor.

In Lagos's oil fields, chalk spirals encircled rusting valves, cloth strips fluttered from ladders, and mechanics whispered vows into puddles slick with crude. Jars glowed along the rigs, carried on salt wind that mixed vow with ocean spray. *"Hold,"* they whispered. Waves answered with a crash, as if the sea itself had joined the covenant.

In Havana, jars of phosphorescent beetles glowed on the steps of old churches, spiral chalk drawn on salt-stained tiles. Fishermen tied nets in knots not for catch but for witness, saying each knot aloud like prayer: *"For the ones who came before. For the ones who come next."*

In Novosibirsk, snow dusted chalk spirals drawn onto frozen stone, breaths steaming white into night air. Children tied bright scarves to railings and marked their vow in footprints that filled with ice. Their words cracked with cold, but still they whispered: *"Hold."*

In Riyadh, desert wind scattered chalk as fast as it was drawn, yet hands traced circles again and again into sand and stone. Strips of cloth tied to iron fences snapped in hot wind, their flutter a vow too insistent to silence. Lanterns replaced jars, but the rhythm of flame carried the same covenant.

Everywhere, the grammar repeated: chalk rings, cloth knots, jars of patient light, breath bound into vow. No decree summoned it. No council commanded it. It spread through children's games and whispered numbers, through hands that refused to let silence mean nothing.

By the time dawn circled the globe, boardrooms and markets, temples and factories, oil rigs and frozen streets bore the same markings. Not uniform, not imposed, but recognizably kin—threads woven into a pattern only the ground itself could hold.

The vow had become law, not because it was written, but because it was lived.

Chapter 56

The Five Bites

"Hunger writes its own covenant."

THEY BEGAN AT DAWN, before the square's heat could sour temper or grain. No bell, no decree—only a slow unfurling of bodies toward the low tables: salvaged doors on bricks, boards planed to three hands' height, bowls nested like little moons. What had been riot and scramble was now choreography. Not law written high, but memory rehearsed until it held.

Spiral-chalkers drew the rings first: three white bands touching the edge of the Ash Market and the mouth of the Crawlways, each wide enough for a body to kneel without bumping another's shoulder. Knot-binders tied short lengths of ribbon to the outer rail—plain cloth, no colors for rank. Jar-bearers placed glass behind each server's left elbow, fireflies pulsing in slow cadence. Breath-counters listened for Rael's rhythm against the courthouse wall and set the pace: seventeen, four, two—scoop; hold; pass.

No lists. No names. No questions asked. The rules lived low and were easy to remember, because hunger made forgetting the most dangerous thing in the world.

First bowl to the breath that breaks. Children next, but paired with older mouths so one bite did not teach greed to another. Then those whose hands bore the night's work: damp sleeves from hauling water, vinegar stains from tending wounds, splinters from keeping vigil at Kess's shrine. Untethered came when the jar-light dimmed. The bowls did not care who knelt or stood.

Mira sat at the head of the middle ring with her ledger tied shut beneath her knee. She refused to let hunger become an entry for the Tribunal to twist. Instead she counted smooth pebbles from a cracked saucer—three to a palm before each bowl refilled. When the saucer emptied, the ladle rested. Pebble-count was witness, not decree.

Karine chalked faint hash marks on the table edge—pots drained, barrels saved—mapping flows instead of faces. Her cracked lens fogged with steam, and she smiled at usefulness that did not require naming pain.

Salliwith wore a child's hair tie around her wrist like a vow. Each time a bowl passed, she untied it and bound it to a spoon, reminding the carrier to lift their eyes once—to see a person, not just a portion. "Witness costs; witness pays," she murmured.

At the shrine, someone tied a cook's rag to one splintered board, knot firm as a promise: *we will bring the pot back.* Straps blackened by ash now bore this new tether, proof that even failure could become altar, even altar could become table. Kess's sling, though broken, still carried the city forward.

They called the day's shape the Five Bites. Each person took five measured mouthfuls. Leave one for the absent.

Show empty hands. Eat at the height you live. The rhythm held itself: scoop, swallow, set down, breathe.

Rael loaned them his numbers—threadbare but enduring. Children echoed softly, metronome of breath and spoon. When his cheek pressed too hard to stone, he tapped twice, and the square paused together: wiping mouths, waiting, remembering lungs. When he lifted his hand, the ladles moved again.

By midday, the ritual had grown muscle. Runners moved like veins, carrying news: cistern steady, clinic needing bowls saved. A crate of dried fish arrived from across the river, tied with the same plain knot the children used here. The square inhaled as one—relief and grief together. The Five Bites held.

No one called it charity. They called it return.

Mira burned her pebbles at dusk so no tally could become leash. Karine erased her hashes, leaving only chalk lines where runners had passed. Salliwith slept with her palm on a ribboned spoon. Nessa ate last with those who had carried wood. Rael fell asleep against the wall, numbers spent but alive in every breath around him.

By week's end, no one asked who invented the ritual. Hunger had. The city had shaped it into something survivable.

At sundown, a spoon tapped the pot five times, slow as a heartbeat, and palms met once in answer—soft applause for the absent, the anxious, the tomorrow that must come.

No trumpet blessed it. No dais sanctioned it. It lived where mouths lived, where cloth tied low, where jars burned steady. And because it survived three mornings and three nights without breaking, the people called it what they had begun to call all things that endured without permission.

Law.

Chapter 57

Voluntary Kneeling

"A posture commanded is bondage; a posture chosen is covenant."

It began not as proclamation but as accident. One child—half-asleep from hunger, too weary to climb the low bench—folded to his knees at the rail before the first ladle passed. No one corrected him. A jar flickered once, as if to mark the gesture. By dusk, three more had knelt of their own accord, not dragged down by decree, not bound by stave, but by choice.

The square noticed. The square remembered.

Spiral-chalkers circled their knees in thin white rings, not as command but as witness. Knot-binders tied no ribbons this time—only left the chalk bare, so the posture itself could speak. Jar-bearers lowered their vessels until the glow lit faces near the ground, not banners above.

By the third evening, the talk had spread: kneeling is not weakness when it is chosen. A grandmother lowered herself, bones creaking like old timbers, and stayed there through the ritual of Five Bites. When she rose again, tears streaked her face, but her smile was fierce. *"Now the ground knows me,"* she whispered.

Mira pressed her ledger shut, thumb black against the leather. *"If I record this,"* she murmured to Rael, *"they will twist it into decree. Better it remain breath."*

Rael's scar burned cold against stone, his vow frayed but steady: *"Hold."* For the first time, others answered not standing, not crawling, but kneeling beside him, their lungs matching his broken rhythm.

Salliwith bowed her bare shoulders to the shrine of straps, palms flat against splintered wood. *"Witness is lighter at this height,"* she said.

Karine crouched with her cracked lens, sketching a new mark—half-circle beneath a figure, symbol of choice. She named it Consent.

Kess's tools were there too, no longer husked into silence. Her repaired sling—lashed with fresh fiber, iron rings scavenged from carts—hung at the shrine beside the straps that had once failed. Those who knelt often placed their palms on its boards, whispering as though her hands still guided theirs: *"Even weight. Keep it level."* The sling became more than relic; it was remembered instruction, a craft turned covenant.

And Nessa—Untethered still, tall as defiance—watched it all with eyes bright as jar-light on metal. She bent only once, at dawn, not to erase her difference but to show that choice itself was power. When she rose, her earrings flashed like captured stars. *"This kneeling shames no one,"* she said. *"It shames only those who demanded it by force."*

On the dais, the Tribunal sagged into irrelevance. The Arbiter's cough drowned his decrees. The Magistrate's prayers evaporated in morning air. The Canonister shrieked that kneeling proved obedience, but his voice found no anchor. The square laughed—not cruel, but certain.

Because here, for the first time, kneeling was no longer theirs to command. It belonged to the people, who could rise again when they chose.

And that freedom—fragile as breath, strong as fiber— became ritual. Quiet. Voluntary. Unassailable.

Chapter 58

Jars Across Oceans

"Light travels farther than ships."

It began in whispers carried by sailors who could no longer stand straight on their rolling decks. They tied glass jars to weathered rails instead of proud banners, fireflies pulsing steady against the salt wind's fury. Their vessels moved heavy and low through dark waters, masts groaning under the weight of enforced silence—but still the jars burned on, tiny suns that refused to drown.

On distant shores, children saw them first.

Along Havana's crumbling seawalls, answering jars were raised in defiant chorus, glowworms pulsing emerald where fireflies could not survive the tropical heat. In Marseilles, chalk spirals bloomed on wet stone piers—white rings that smudged beneath relentless tides, yet were faithfully redrawn each dawn by trembling hands. In Port Said's sweltering harbor, fishermen nestled jars among nets drying under merciless sun, their captured light mingling with the silver scales of dying fish.

Everywhere the code spread like wildfire across water.

One jar at the masthead: safe entry. Two side by side along the gunwale: danger close. Three shattered at the dock: scatter, hide, survive at all costs. The sacred rhythm of Rael's vow—seventeen, four, two—echoed across endless waves in the haunting lilt of sailors' songs, carried farther than any parchment scroll or royal decree ever could.

Mira received the first reports from a salt-stained girl who had traded chalk for dried fish. She pressed her ledger closed with deliberate force, her thumb leaving a black smudge against its leather spine. *"If the sea has chosen to carry our message,"* she whispered, *"then let the water itself be archive enough."*

Salliwith stood at the shrine rail, her bare shoulders gleaming bronze in dawn light. She tied a child's frayed ribbon to a battered jar that had floated ashore, still glowing faint despite the night's storm. *"Witness crosses farther than maps can follow,"* she murmured into the wind.

Karine bent over her cracked lens, sketching new coastlines on her growing map, naming each place not for empire but for witness: *Port of Ash, Spiral Wharf, Oath Pier.* Chalk traced no borders—only connections, the glowing arteries of a world rediscovering itself.

Rael pressed his scar to cold stone, whispering *"Hold"* into salt air, his vow answered by the sea's thunder. Children on the shore echoed him, lungs shaping his rhythm into songs sailors carried from tide to tide.

Kess's shrine, lashed with the same leather that once bore impossible burdens, had become part of the ritual of departure. Pilgrims crawled to it before voyages, pressing rope into its straps as if asking her craft to steady their journey.

"Even weight, keep it level," they whispered—her words living on as law of sea as well as square.

And Nessa—her silver earrings flashing like coins hammered from captured stars—threw back her head and laughed when the Tribunal sneered at these "insects in glass." She raised her marked palm, streaked still with ash, and shouted across the square:

"Your decrees have never crossed an ocean. Our jars already circle the world."

Chapter 59

The Arithmetic of Lungs

"What survives the lungs survives the world."

THE NIGHT after jars were sighted on distant shores, Threshold itself gathered in profound stillness. No proclamation had summoned them. No banner demanded their presence. They came because breath itself had become a summons—urgent, undeniable, alive.

The shrine of broken straps glowed with scattered jars, ancient leather darkened by salt carried inland on the restless wind. Chalk circles sprawled wide as the entire square, layered upon layers like growth rings, until the weathered stone seemed less courthouse than ribcage—white lines marking lungs too vast to contain.

One by one, voices began to rise. Not speeches. Not decrees. Just the raw sound of breath measured aloud, caught and passed along like torches flickering in the dark.

"Seventeen." "Four." "Two." Hold.

The sacred numbers pulsed like a collective heartbeat through the winding Crawlways, through the smoke-choked Ash Market, down into the fetid Drains where stagnant water whispered back in echo. Parents pressed children close so the little ones could feel the rhythm thrumming chest against chest. Strangers leaned their foreheads together to share it skin to skin, pulse to pulse.

It was not ritual yet. It was not law. It was witness—naked, immediate, blazingly alive.

Mira clutched her ledger shut, her ink-stained thumb marking its leather cover like a blood seal. *"This record needs no ink,"* she murmured. For once the square did not clamor for her words. They only breathed, and listened, and breathed again.

Salliwith knelt bare-shouldered at the shrine's base and whispered the names of her lost daughters between each measured count. *"Fray. Ember. Song. Ash."* Her breath carried them farther than any funeral cloth ever could, lifted on the salt wind.

Karine pressed her cracked lens against cold stone, sketching nothing. Instead, she let her own lungs mist the glass, tracing inhale and exhale with one trembling finger. *"The truest map lives here,"* she said softly, tapping her chest.

Rael leaned heavily against the wall, scar pressed to plaster like a brand. His lips shaped the vow, but this time he did not voice it alone. Hundreds of throats carried it for him, multiplying his silence into strength that filled every lung.

At Kess's shrine, offerings accumulated like prayers made solid—scraps of rope, fragments of harness, precious cloth dyed dark with ash. Each piece was tied with a whispered breath before being bound to the leather straps she had once knotted with her living hands. Her craft had become lungs of its own, each tether a rib in the square's expanding chest.

And Nessa—silver earrings flashing with every exhale—stood upright above the breathing crowd, laughing not in mockery but in wonder. *"Look at us,"* she cried. *"They forced our heads down to breathe their dust. Now dust itself has become our law."*

The Tribunal watched from their dais, pale as bone in jar-light, powerless before the arithmetic of lungs. The Arbiter's cough vanished beneath the rhythm. The Magistrate's prayers evaporated into silence. The Canonister's shrill command shriveled when no one cared to hear.

The square did not need to shout them down.

It only breathed.

And in that breath—unbroken and undeniable—witness became permanence. Truth was no longer written in books or banners but in the lungs of the assembled, carried from body to body, night to night, until the world itself would learn to inhale their defiance.

Chapter 60

Tribunal Vanished

"Power vanishes; what hands have bound endures."

AT DAWN, the dais stood empty.

No rasping cough from the Arbiter.

No whispered plea from the Magistrate.

No shrill insult from the Canonister.

Only robes collapsed on cold marble, limp banners sagging overhead, staves abandoned like toys too heavy for their keepers.

The square did not gasp. It did not cry out. It only looked once—and then turned away.

For what endured was not the dais.

It was the shrine.

Kess's shrine—leather straps bound by her own bleeding hands, boards splintered yet mended, cloth layered knot upon knot until even air carried the weight of her labor. The people pressed close to it as if to a hearth in winter, laying scraps of rope, tying new strips of cloth, setting jars low so their light breathed steady as lungs.

Mira pressed her ledger to her chest, thumb blackened but pages sealed. "This is the record," she whispered—not marble, not robes, but straps that still held.

Salliwith laid her bare palms against the shrine's wood. "Witness paid," she murmured, voice trembling but unbroken.

Karine traced the bindings with her cracked chalk, naming them as she had named fractures: *Burden. Hold. Accord.* Her word for the dais was different, scratched once on the marble step and left to crumble: *Ash.*

Rael leaned against stone worn smooth by his scar, whispering his vow—"Hold"—and the shrine seemed to answer, its leather breathing with him, its knots tightening in the dawn wind.

Nessa laughed sharp and fierce, her silver charm flashing like a small sun. She pointed toward the empty dais, then toward the shrine. "There's your law," she called. "Not robes. Not banners. This."

The children understood first. They swarmed not to the dais but to the shrine, tying their ribbons low, pressing their cheeks to straps that smelled of sweat and salt, tracing chalk spirals around its base. One child climbed the marble steps only to drape the Tribunal's abandoned robe across the shrine's wood, transforming costume into offering.

By full daylight, Threshold had chosen its altar.

The dais became backdrop, a hollow stage remembered only for absence.

The shrine became covenant, the true high place of the Grounded, built not of stone or decree but of fiber that frayed, held, and outlived those who mocked it.

And in the hush of that morning, the city discovered a final truth:

Power vanishes.

But what one woman's hands have bound—what her straps have carried—can hold forever.

Chapter 61

Accord of Silence

"Some laws weigh heavier unwritten."

THE DAY after the dais stood empty, the square filled again —not with triumphant shouts or defiant banners, but with something far more profound: quiet.

Word had spread like smoke through the Crawlways and markets: the Tribunal had vanished. Some arrived expecting riot, others fearing trap. Yet when they gathered beneath the sagging banners and shrine, no one dared lift their voice above a whisper.

It was Rael who gave sacred shape to the hush.

Scar pressed to familiar plaster, lips moving in the ghost of speech, no sound escaping. He had spoken *Hold* too many times, worn his voice thin as paper. Now his refusal to speak bore the weight of every vow he had carried. Children saw and understood. They pressed their own cheeks to stone, and silence multiplied like ripples across still water.

Mira opened her ledger as though to inscribe, then pressed her blackened thumb to the page and shut it again, leaving no line but the smudge itself. She set the sealed book on the steps for all to see. "This too is record," she whispered, and even the whisper seemed heavy as iron.

Salliwith rested her bare shoulders against the shrine of straps and boards, her palms flat to weathered wood. She breathed slow and steady, no words leaving her mouth, only presence. Her stillness drew others down, until heads bowed as if language itself had become unworthy of the moment.

Karine lifted her cracked lens, then let it fog with breath instead of tracing lines. "The map can wait," she murmured. "Today, absence is the path."

Children set their jars in a wide circle around the shrine, fireflies pulsing slow as heartbeats. No chants. No games. Only light and lungs, small wings beating in rhythm with the silence.

Nessa laughed once—sharp, startled, like flint struck in the dark. But even she lowered her voice to a murmur, earrings catching jar-light like twin stars. "Even our silence mocks them louder than our angriest words ever could."

The Guards did not speak. Knees bruised, staves lowered, they sank into the quiet as if it were judgment enough.

No decree was made. No parchment signed. Yet everyone knew the same bone-deep truth: the Tribunal's end would not be sealed by blood or riot, but by the stillness of a people who no longer required their voices to tell them what was law.

So the Accord was made—not written, not proclaimed, but lived in the breath between bodies. A vow carried only in silence: that the people themselves would decide when to speak, and when silence would weigh heavier than any decree.

By night, the crowd dispersed. Chalk spirals glowed faint as bone across the steps. Strips of cloth fluttered from Kess's shrine like prayers too stubborn to fade. The jars kept pulsing their patient light.

Nothing had been declared. Yet all who walked home understood: a covenant had been born. A law of silence, chosen and shared, enduring beyond words—stronger than any Tribunal that had ever dared to speak.

Chapter 62

Constellations Beyond Threshold

**"They promised us stars above; we made
our own close enough to carry."**

CHILDREN CARRIED THEM FIRST, as children always do
with precious things. They crawled through the narrow
Crawlways with glass pressed against their ribs, crossed the
ash-dusted marketplace on careful knees, descended into
the Drains where hope had long since drowned. Each vessel
pulsed with living wings, each circle of chalk renewed
where stone sagged under centuries of weight.

From the hillocks above the city, solitary watchers saw the
glow spreading outward in fragile threads of amber. These
were not the flames of conquest, nor the torches of war, but
constellations drawn impossibly low—stitched across the
night by determined hands too small to command, yet
strong enough to endure.

In the harbor quarter, fishermen lashed jars to masts scarred
by storm and neglect. Their boats drifted light-struck,
floating stars on tide's dark canvas. The nets hung empty,
but the glow carried farther than hunger, farther than fear.

In the tenements, mothers placed jars on broken sills, their glow falling soft across faces hollowed by want. Children slept counting points of light instead of missing bread. Even a single pulse in a cracked jar became a promise to endure until morning.

Karine traced the expansion into her growing map, chalk dust scattering like seeds. Through her cracked lens the scattered dots shimmered as a new sky. She named the farthest sparks with reverence: *Hope. Distance. Return.*

Mira laid her sealed ledger at the shrine, thumb pressed black against its cover like a seal. "If it spreads without my words," she whispered, "then it is truer than anything I could bind in ink."

Salliwith pressed bare palms to the shrine's splintered boards, her voice low but steady. "Memory runs where cloth cannot follow."

Rael leaned against cold stone, lips shaping *Hold* without sound. His vow no longer depended on his fragile lungs. It traveled now in wings and breath, carried outward in the light.

Kess's shrine blazed brightest of all. Leather straps mended and retied with fresh cloth became anchors for dozens of jars, until the broken sling no longer looked like burden but like constellation itself—her work transformed into covenant, her absence burning into presence.

And Nessa—silver earrings catching fire in every flicker— tilted her chin toward the low sky. "Look at what we've done," she laughed, fierce and awed. "They promised us stars we could never touch. We've made our own—close enough to carry."

Threshold no longer stood alone. From its wounded heart, constellations radiated outward—across stone and stair, across river and sea, across horizon after horizon.

A sky remade not above, but here below: written in jars and cloth, in chalk and breath, in the stubborn miracle of light kept low enough for every hand to hold.

Chapter 63

Circle Unbroken

"What holds once can hold again."

THE SQUARE GATHERED as it had on that first transformative night—cloth tied with reverent care, chalk circling ancient cracks like prayers, jars pulsing steady light into the dusk. But now the dais stood empty, the Tribunal vanished, their Guards absent. Only the people remained, returning to the shape that had carried them through riot, hunger, and grief: a circle breathing low and unbroken.

Rael leaned against his familiar wall, his scar pressed deep into stone. His voice was gone, worn thin by years of vow, yet the rhythm he had once carried alone now lived fully in others. Children breathed his sacred numbers for him— seventeen, four, two—carrying the count as naturally as their own heartbeats. The vow was no longer his solitary burden. It had become marrow in the lungs of the many.

Mira sat cross-legged with her ledger shut, thumb black against its spine. No ink passed tonight. Her refusal itself had become record, every sealed page a covenant of silence that could never be bent into decree.

Salliwith pressed her bare shoulders to the shrine's wood, her weathered palms spread wide. "Witness forms its own circle," she whispered, and though her voice cracked, the people received it as oath.

Karine knelt with her cracked lens, sketching the ring of bodies around her. Chalk moved soft and certain, tracing human forms like newly discovered constellations. She named the shape they made with one word: *Endure.*

At the heart of it all, Kess herself knelt by the shrine, gloves still on, her ribs bound but her hands steady. She tightened straps where children's knots wavered, tested the leather with her weight until it sang true. Straps mended and re-mended, cloth layered thick as bark, jars tied with knots of gratitude—every offering bound her sling tighter, transforming it from monument to failure into proof that what frays alone can still hold when joined by many hands. Her presence guided the work, her breath steady as the straps she bound. Living covenant, not relic.

And Nessa—Untethered, defiant—stood at the circle's edge where darkness pressed close. Her earrings caught jar-light like twin captured suns. She laughed once, sharp as struck flint. "Do you see what we've become?" she called. "They thought silence would scatter us. Instead it bound us tighter than chains."

Hands reached across the square—scarred palms clasping scarred palms, ink-stained thumbs grasping weathered fingers, children's fists nestled safe in larger hands. Breath rose and fell as one vast body, the circle expanding and contracting like a lung drawing life from shared air.

No leader spoke. No decree was proclaimed. No banner flew. Only the circle remained, beautifully unbroken. And in its shape the city remembered what collapse had tried to erase: that survival was never solitary, but always shared. That every vow, every act of witness, every broken fragment bound by love could become whole once more.

The circle breathed. The circle held.

And it would hold again, and again, and again—

as long as there were hands to join, lungs to share the sacred count, jars to light the darkness, and voices brave enough to choose silence over surrender.

Chapter 64

Breathing City

"A city alive is not its walls, but its lungs."

Dawn spilled over Threshold not with decree or mockery, but with breath.

The narrow streets, once echo chambers for Tribunal proclamations, now exhaled like living corridors, pulsing their own steady rhythm. Crawlways, markets, gathering halls, forgotten drains—each carried the same tide, low and patient as a heart that refused to stop.

At the square's center, the shrine of Kess stood transformed. Straps and cloth layered thick as bark, glowing jars set in concentric rings like prayer wheels of light. Karine's ever-sprawling map stretched across worn stone, its chalk lines blurred each night, retraced each dawn by eager hands. Mira's ledger lay sealed at the rail, her black thumbprint pressed into its cover like scripture written in flesh instead of ink.

Fragments had gathered into one breathing organism. Not law carved into marble, not banners raised above, but lungs shared generously across living bodies:

—Rael's vow carried in children's whispers.

—Salliwith's witness etched in shoulders bared to morning air.

—Nessa's defiance flashing from her single charm, silver bright, mocking the sky.

—Mira's chosen silence heavy as testimony.

—Karine's names pressed into every fracture until stone itself spoke.

—Kess's labor sanctified in the shrine, her hands still guiding straps that bore her strength beyond exhaustion.

Children darted through the Crawlways, jars clutched like captured suns, shouting rules of play as if proclaiming edicts: one jar—safe. Two jars—danger. A broken jar—scatter. Their laughter rang wild—cruel at its edges where hunger lingered, fierce at its heart where hope lived. They had inherited not decrees, but games remade as law of survival.

From rooftops and drains, from stair and square, the city pulsed with new life. Cloth strips fluttered like veins through stone arteries. Chalk spirals glowed faint but stubborn in the early light. Fireflies beat their fragile wings against glass, their small heartbeats stitched into the greater rhythm of the people.

Above, the Tribunal's banners sagged in the salt air. Their dais stood hollow, thrones abandoned to dust. Authority had shriveled to costume and memory.

Below, the city breathed.

And in that breath—low, unbroken, patient as stone worn smooth by tide—the people found what no verdict had ever given: a law they could live within, a rhythm they could trust, a city remade not in conquest or blood, but in the miracle of lungs drawing the same air.

The Breathing City endured, as breathing cities always do.

And with each slow inhalation, each steady exhale, it whispered its covenant to tomorrow:

We continue. We remember. We hold.

Breathmark — After the Drop

"An ending is only breath held between."

THE CITY HAS NOT RISEN from its ashes like some mythical phoenix.

It has done something far more profound: it has endured.

Through strips of memorial cloth and spirals of chalk, through the patient glow of jar-light and the sacred weight of whispered vows, Threshold has become what no Tribunal could ever decree by force: a breathing city, alive in ways stone and marble could never be.

But breath, by its nature, does not stand still.

It carries forward, outward, onward.

The vows that once circled a single square now cross oceans on salt wind. The witness that cost Salliwith her shawl and Kess the marrow of her strength now seeks new vessels to carry its light. The silence that husked the Tribunal into dust waits patiently to be tested against hungers larger than stone monuments, against fears greater than any banner raised in dominance.

The circle holds—beautifully unbroken, exactly as it promised.

Yet every circle is also a door.

And every ending, a beginning.

Here ends **Book I — *The Drop***.

Next comes the crossing into distances where witness must travel farther than captured light can reach, where laws written in lungs will be tested not by marble halls but by the vast spaces between them, and where every sacred vow whispers its eternal question into the waiting dark:

Will you hold?

Breathnote – Epilogue

"What holds in silence becomes the city's breath."

Mira — Ledger of Silence

She bore the ledger, but when she shielded her sister she was Grounded.

Her silence became heavier than ink.

Not verdict. Not decree. Only refusal that endured.

Nessa — Demon of Intent

She stood Untethered, marked by ash and laughter.

Her demon was not the Tribunal's iron, but her own memory of harm.

She turned intent into shield, though it left her alone.

Rael — Silent Vow

He counted when nothing else held.

Seventeen. Four. Two.

His vow cracked, but it multiplied, carried in lungs beyond his own.

Salliwith — Cloth Witness

Her shawl unraveled strip by strip until her shoulders were bare.

Exhaustion bent her low, but cloth carried witness forward in children's hands.

She endured in fragments, her giving scattered yet unforgotten.

Kess — Straps of Invention

Her sling failed and her straps frayed, but she rose each time to bind them tighter.

She lived in the stubborn fiber that would not surrender.

Leather and cloth endured with her hands still working, turning burden into shrine.

Karine — Maps of Fracture

Her cracked lens saw the world's weakness and named it.

She mapped not empires but the fault lines of witness—each mark a reckoning, each name a vow.

Her maps widened until oceans glowed, though one fracture she never charted was her own.

The Braid

Six threads woven low:

• Ledger

• Intent

- Vow

- Cloth

- Straps

- Maps

Together they form *The Shape Between*.

Not a council. Not a decree.

But a braid that held the city when nothing else did.

Part Two

Book II - The Shape Between

Where fracture became covenant, and children marked the scar.

Law bends at the scar, not above it.

Those who kneel learn faster that those who stand.

Chapter 65

The Half-Height Walk

"A bridge is not built of stone, but of bodies willing to meet in the middle."

AT DUSK, jars crowned the bench-bridge, their captive fireflies pulsing steady as breath. Cloth strips fluttered in the cooling air while chalk rings glowed pale against worn stone. The Half-Height Walk had not ended—it had transformed.

Children came first, their small voices weaving covenant from play. One girl pressed her palm flat against the bench, whispering, "I will carry light across." Another laughed, declaring, "I will not rise higher than the breath beside me." Each vow emerged in fragments small enough for fragile lungs to hold, yet strong enough to span the divide.

The crowd stirred and answered. Knot-binders abandoned the rails, tying ribbons instead to wrists, linking neighbors hand to hand. Spiral-chalkers traced rings that enclosed not one side or the other, but both together. Jar-bearers lifted glass vessels high, passing them from Untethered to Grounded—each exchange a wordless pledge that no one would face the darkness alone.

Mira settled her ledger on her knees and opened to a waiting page, pen poised. But when she lifted her eyes, she watched the crossings shimmer in jar-light, moving from mouth to mouth, hand to hand. She closed the book without marking a single word. "It lives better in breath," she whispered.

Rael leaned against the stone wall, his careful numbers now carried by children's chant, no longer his burden alone. Seventeen, four, two became rhythm, became song, became bridge itself.

Salliwith raised her bare palm in witness. Her shawl had been stripped to nothing, yet her hand—empty, trembling—was enough. "Even without cloth, we bind each other."

Karine's cracked lens caught the glow of jars in motion. She mapped each crossing, naming not fractures this time but promises: *Carry. Share. Endure.*

Kess pushed forward through the crowd with a coil of worn straps in her lap. She tied them into a loop and lifted it high. "If cloth and chalk can bind us, so can what remains," she said. She passed the loop to a child, who threaded it with ribbon and held it taut between them like a bridge remade in leather and thread.

On the bench-bridge, Nessa stood with the ash-mark still dark against her wrist. Her voice cut sharp through the gathering night: "If fireflies can survive the jar, then so can we. Pass the light."

And so they did.

The jars moved like captured stars, hand to hand across the

span. Each crossing forged a bond. Each breath held steady as the final vessel reached the far side.

The square exhaled as one—quiet, waiting, expectant.

The Half-Height Walk was complete.

UR-VI: The Teacher's Desk

(Upper Registers – Depositions of the Untethered)

THE WOOD GROANED when I sawed through the legs. Each desk shrank, splinters scattered like pencil shavings. I cut them all—thirty in a row—until every surface stood no higher than a child's waist.

The Grounded children dragged themselves in at dawn, their straps and carts squealing. Before, they sat in shadow under tall desks, looking up, necks bent, shame folded into their posture. But today, when they pulled close, their chins cleared the tabletops.

When the Pulse came, I stayed on my feet. I had never raised a weapon. I had never meant harm, never sworn it, never carried it in readiness. Only my voice—sharp, too sharp at times. But words alone, not bent to wound.

Standing felt like theft. So I lowered the desks until the room itself was honest.

They looked up at me, waiting for a lesson. I could have stayed tall, but I slid to the floor beside them, chalk in hand. I traced letters across wood now level with my heart.

For the first time since the Pulse, they smiled. Not because I stood. Because I chose not to.

Chapter 66

The Firefly Oath

"Light carried across is promise kept."

THE JARS HAD CROSSED. What began as play and fragments now lingered in trembling hands, their glow circling the square like stars gathered low enough to touch. The Half-Height Walk was finished—but something greater pressed close, waiting to be named.

No one commanded it. No decree summoned it. It rose in breath.

Children whispered first, voices fragile but certain: *Carry. Share. Endure.* Their vows flickered in firefly light, each syllable echoing wider until the whole square seemed to inhale together.

Rael leaned against the wall, his cheek pressed to stone. His voice was nearly gone, but his rhythm was not. Seventeen. Four. Two. The children answered for him, carrying the numbers as chant, as song, as living law.

Mira opened her ledger as if to record, pen trembling. But she watched the vow flow mouth to mouth, hand to hand, shimmering brighter than ink could hold. She closed the book without marking it. "It lives better in breath," she whispered.

Salliwith raised her bare palm in witness. No shawl, no cloth left, only her trembling hand lifted steady into the night. "Even empty, we bind each other."

Karine's cracked lens fogged as she mapped the pattern of passing jars—not fractures this time, but promises. She named them aloud as chalk scratched: *Carry. Share. Endure.*

At the bridge's center, Nessa lifted her ash-marked wrist. The firefly light caught her earrings until they blazed like twin stars. "If they can survive the jar," she called, her voice cutting sharp as glass, "then so can we. Pass the light—and swear with it."

And so they did.

One jar, then another, fireflies glowing steady as they moved hand to hand. Each vessel no longer a container but a covenant. Each breath exhaled no longer witness, but oath.

When the last jar reached the far side, silence fell—not empty, but full, heavy as stone. Then lungs released together, a tide loosed into the night.

The Firefly Oath was sealed.

Not written. Not decreed. Not bound to any parchment high above. It was sworn in the low places, in breath and silence, in the fragile glow of wings beating against glass.

And for the first time since the Pulse, Threshold did not only remember.

It promised.

Chapter 67

The Ash Feast

"Even hunger becomes ritual when nothing else remains."

THE BRIDGE of arms had dissolved back into bodies, but its memory lingered in breath and bruised shoulders. Morning brought no triumph—only hollow stomachs and the smell of ash rising from cook fires that offered no food.

The crowd gathered in the square, not summoned by decree but drawn by the ache they all carried. Children set empty jars on the rail, fireflies long fled, glass catching pale dawn as if it too hungered for light. Knot-binders tied strips of cloth not to mark abundance, but to name absence: None. Little. Less.

Women bent low over pots filled with nothing but boiled rags, broth thin as memory. They passed the steaming bowls as if sacred, each sip more witness than sustenance. A boy chewed leather from his sandal strap, eyes fixed on the shrine where Kess's broken sling still hung, as though it might yield bread if he stared long enough.

Mira opened her ledger, but the page resisted her pen. What could she record? Hunger again. Want again.

Instead, she pressed her thumb into the margin and left only a black smudge—the mark of silence that said more than words.

Rael whispered his count against stone, but the rhythm faltered between breaths that wheezed with emptiness. Children picked it up, not as vow this time but as measure: seventeen days since bread. Four days since broth. Two since anyone laughed.

Salliwith knelt by the empty pots, shoulders bare, hands trembling as she lifted an invisible ladle. "Even nothing can be shared," she whispered, and those around her bowed their heads to honor the gesture.

Karine scratched circles onto the square's stones, chalk faint against grit, naming each spiral after what they lacked: Bread. Salt. Oil. The map of hunger spread outward until the whole plaza seemed etched with appetite.

Kess herself bent low before her shrine, calloused fingers touching the stiffened straps. She tore one fragment free— no longer strong enough to bear weight, but still thread enough to bind. With slow care she tied it around a cracked bowl, holding its emptiness together as though mending hunger itself. "Even scraps can hold," she murmured, and a child pressed his palm to hers, sealing the knot.

Nessa stood upright among them, her ash-marked wrist raised high. "If the Tribunal could starve us, they already would have," she said. "Their hunger is louder than ours now. So we feast—not on what we lack, but on what they cannot take." She slapped her palm against her chest. "Breath. Witness. Each other."

The crowd answered not with cheer, but with the long, slow exhale of a hundred lungs that had learned the shape of scarcity.

It was ritual.

It was oath.

It was feast enough to carry them into the next day.

Chapter 68

The Quiet Market

"Trade bends when weight itself becomes currency."

THE ASH MARKET REOPENED, not with goods but with gestures. Stalls once stacked with bread and grain now bore tokens laid out like offerings: a strip of cloth frayed at both ends, a jar cracked but still capable of holding light, a piece of chalk worn to a nub.

Buyers and sellers met on equal ground—knees to stone, shoulders brushing as they bent to examine what scraps of worth remained. No coin passed hand to hand. Coin was metal, metal was weapon, weapon was memory of height. All such relics had been grounded long ago.

A woman offered a ribbon dyed deep blue, threadbare but whole. In exchange, she received three whispered breaths from an elder who promised to remember her son's name for as long as he drew breath. The bargain sealed itself with shared exhale.

Children turned trading into play. One placed a feather on the rail and demanded two stories in return. Another knelt with a shard of broken jar, asking for chalk marks on her palm so she might carry constellations on skin. The trades were absurd by the old world's measure, yet binding in the new.

Mira walked among the stalls with her ledger closed. Each black thumbprint she carried across its cover became her currency—witness offered in exchange for cloth or silence. She recorded nothing; the Market itself was record enough.

Rael traced his sequence into the dust with trembling fingers: 17—4—2. A boy read the numbers aloud and traded him half a bowl of rag broth for the right to carry the pattern away, as if mathematics itself could nourish.

Salliwith pressed both hands flat on a stall's wooden slats, bare shoulders bent low. "Witness cannot be hoarded," she murmured, and a girl with sharp eyes tied a knot of string around her wrist in payment for the truth.

Karine crouched with her cracked lens, sketching the shifting stalls into her map. She marked each corner not with goods but with the words traded there: Name. Story. Breath. Witness. Her map became less geography than a ledger of promises.

Kess sat cross-legged on the stones, her lap filled with worn straps and broken buckles salvaged from her dismantled shrine. She cut one strip free and laid it gently on a mat. A child offered in return a single breath—slow, deliberate, solemn—and knotted the strap to his own wrist. Others followed, taking her frayed remnants and weaving them into new ties across bowls, jars, and even each other's hands. What had once been tools of burden became tokens of covenant, scarce leather transformed into a market of binding.

Nessa moved upright through the kneeling crowd, silver studs and coin-charms glinting with defiance. "Look well," she called. "The old Market sold hunger. This one trades in what we already are."

The Guards stood apart, staves slack in their hands, watching as the people bartered without coin, without decree, without law. Their silence was its own kind of currency—the only thing they had left to spend.

By dusk, the rails were wrapped in cloth, the stalls dusted white with chalk, the jars glowing faint with captured light. Nothing had been bought or sold, yet everyone carried more than they had brought.

The Quiet Market had spoken. In the world remade, value no longer rose from what could be owned, but from what could be shared.

Chapter 69

The Scar Council

"Scars speak when voices cannot agree."

THEY GATHERED NOT in chambers raised too tall but at the stair itself, where cracks ran wide and deep as memory. No dais lifted anyone above another. The council formed in the hollow between rail and crawlway, each member marked not by title but by scar.

Rael pressed his cheek to the wall, the half-moon cut that had once bled him now a seal of witness. "Stone remembers what flesh forgets," he whispered, beginning the rhythm: seventeen, four, two. The sequence circled like breath until the meeting could begin.

Mira laid her ledger on her knees but did not open it. Her thumb left a black stain across the cover, an unspoken reminder that silence could be record enough.

Salliwith bared her shoulders, skin pale where cloth once clung. Her voice trembled but carried: "Every strip I gave still speaks. Cloth is council, whether tied or torn."

Karine set her cracked lens across the stair, light splitting through it into fragments. She named each fissure aloud as if calling roll: Ash. Oath. Burden. Hunger. Each name stood as a seat at the council's circle.

Kess lowered herself onto the stone with a slow exhale, ribs bound beneath her patched tunic, gloves tugged snug over hands scarred from years of strain. The shrine still stood nearby, but tonight her body spoke louder than leather or wood. She uncoiled a strap across her lap, running her fingers along its frayed edge. "Not shrine alone," she said, her voice hoarse but firm. "My scars sit here with yours. Fiber still binds because hands still tie." She tapped her chest once, then the strap, as if stitching the two together.

And Nessa—untethered, upright—let her earrings catch the jar-light until they glowed like twin stars. "Scars mark us all," she said, her tone sharp as winter air. "But let them mark us equal. No scar is higher, no wound holier than another."

The crowd answered by revealing their own: knees calloused raw from crawling, palms split by rope, backs bent from carrying too much weight. Each mark became argument, each wound testimony.

Disagreement flared. One elder demanded order, another cried for bread first, a third called for vengeance against the husked Tribunal. The voices tangled, rising to shouts that no breath-counter could steady.

It was the children who settled the noise. They pressed chalk to stone and traced their own small scars—scrapes, bruises, the thin lines where play had turned to accident. Around each they drew bright spirals, marking them into permanence. The square hushed, watching the smallest claim their seats at the council table of stone.

Mira closed her ledger with finality. "This is enough," she said. "Scars hold what voices cannot."

No decree was issued. No vote was tallied. But the Scar Council had spoken: governance would not rise from banners or benches, but from the marks carried on bodies that had survived.

Chapter 70

Ledger of Ash

"What burns away still leaves its mark."

MIRA SAT BEFORE THE SHRINE, ledger closed in her lap. The straps and boards above her head whispered in the night breeze, creaking like a tongue too tired to form words. She touched her thumb to the spine—ink already blackened there—and pressed down as though sealing the book forever.

"I will not write hunger again," she said softly. "The stone has already written it."

But the crowd insisted. Children pulled at her sleeve, begging her to mark their games. Elders pressed coins or scraps of cloth into her hands, tokens of promises they had made. Even Guards, stripped of staves and shame, muttered that a record might prove they had not vanished without meaning.

Mira lifted her gaze to the scarred stair. Chalk spirals still shone pale against granite. Strips of fabric fluttered like prayers too numerous to bind. Jars flickered in rhythm with

Rael's sequence, their captive fireflies carrying law more durable than any script.

"What do you want recorded?" she asked, not unkind.

Silence answered. The hunger ritual had already consumed itself. Kneeling had already spoken louder than parchment. Ashes carried more truth than any pen could scratch.

She opened the ledger once—one page, one final chance—and lifted a charred stick pulled from the brazier. No ink, only ash. The marks smeared as she wrote, the words dissolving even as they formed: *We breathed. We endured.*

When she closed the book, the black dust fell across her palms, staining them darker than any ink. "This ledger belongs to the fire now," she whispered, and set it at the shrine's base.

Children knelt around it, tracing the ash-flecked cover with reverent fingers. "It breathes," one said. "Even when shut."

From his place against the wall, Rael whispered *hold,* and the sequence lifted the ash like incense, scattering it into the night.

Kess stepped forward then, her hands raw from labor. She touched the broken sling that still hung across the shrine, its leather straps stiff with ash and memory. With slow care she tied one strip into a knot above Mira's blackened ledger. "Fiber remembers what flesh forgets," she murmured. "Even burned, it binds."

Nessa raised her branded wrist into the jar-light, scar bright as any ribbon. "And some marks the fire gives back to us," she said. "Scars that cannot be erased, even when every word burns away."

The Ledger of Ash had been written—not in words but in the silence between them, not in ink but in the breath, the straps, and the scars that kept its memory alive.

Chapter 71

Breath of Children

"The smallest lungs keep the largest law alive."

NIGHT POOLED heavy in the Crawlways, but children gathered where light still pulsed in jars and chalk still clung to stone. No Tribunal summoned them. No elder called them forward. They came because silence itself demanded their answer.

One child pressed her palm to the stair, ribs sharp beneath thin skin, and whispered, "Seventeen." Another took the pause, breath shaky with hunger: "Four." A third exhaled the final number, voice no louder than a moth's wing: "Two."

The rhythm circled outward, multiplying in every chest, until the whole square breathed as one great organism. Breath-counters took their places, but they did not lead— they only listened, measuring the pulse of lungs too small to be silenced.

Mira stood apart, hands still dark with ash, ledger sealed and abandoned at the shrine. "This is the only record that matters now," she murmured. "Not my words. Their breath."

Salliwith pressed her bare palm against the stair, shoulders trembling with exhaustion, and wept quietly as the children carried her vow when she no longer could.

Karine leaned on her cracked lens, mapping the cadence in quick strokes of chalk—dots for inhalation, lines for exhalation—until the rhythm itself became charted like constellations across stone.

Rael, half-collapsed against the wall, mouthed the numbers with them. His scarred cheek pressed hard to stone, he no longer carried the sequence alone. The children had lifted it from him, multiplied it, transformed his fracture into chorus.

Kess knelt among the smallest, gloves creased and raw from labor, her sling straps looped across her lap. She tied one strip into a child's hands, guiding his fingers knot by knot. "Level. Cross. Lock. Test. Check," she whispered, syncing her cadence to their breath. The children echoed her, their lungs keeping time with her knots until fiber and breath held the same rhythm.

A boy reached to steady her fraying strap, and Kess let him tie it, her hand resting over his. The leather trembled not with age but with life, breathing as they breathed. Around her, children followed suit—threading fingers through straps, tugging them taut, proving that even worn fiber could sing when carried by many lungs together.

And Nessa stood upright, her mother's silver studs catching the jar-light, her father's hammered charms glinting as she tilted her chin toward the dark sky. "They're louder than any banner," she said, sharp with pride. "And they don't even need words."

Above, the Guards kept their distance, staves slack, eyes hollow. On the dais, the Tribunal seats stood empty, shadows curling over them like shrouds. Power had abandoned those heights forever.

The law now moved only in breath—small lungs, fragile ribs, children who had nothing but air to give and gave it freely.

And with every inhale, every exhale, the city found itself bound tighter than parchment could hold, steadier than stone could last.

Chapter 72

Ash Market Accord

"Trade bends when hunger teaches it new law."

THE ASH MARKET had once been barter laid flat on stone —bread for cloth, jars for grain, labor for survival. Now its stalls were hollow frames, their planks gnawed thin by years of want. The air smelled of soot, of hunger cooked down to nothing.

Yet still, the people gathered.

They came not to sell, not to buy, but to witness. Children knelt at the market's center, placing jars in a wide ring. Fireflies pulsed like slow embers, each flicker a reminder that even ash could hold light. Chalk spirals bloomed outward, thin and wavering, but clear enough to mark the circle where voices would meet.

The first offer was not grain or meat, but a strip of cloth— torn from a mother's sleeve, tied to the rail as pledge. Another followed: a cracked lens shard laid gently beside the jar-light. Then came an iron nail, bent but unbroken, placed as if it were treasure.

"What do you ask in return?" Mira whispered, black-stained hands folded around her sealed ledger.

"Nothing," the woman answered. "Only witness."

Others followed—handfuls of soil, a ribbon, a broken stave surrendered without shame. Each offering was ordinary, even useless by the old market's measure. But in the circle of jars and chalk, each object became weight, became law.

Salliwith pressed her palm to the pile, bare shoulder trembling. "These are not trades," she said. "They are accords."

Karine marked the moment on her map, writing a single word beside the sketch of stalls and rail: *Accord*.

Rael whispered *hold* against the stair, and the sequence carried across the circle, catching in lungs that had known too much emptiness.

Kess stepped forward then, straps draped across her shoulders, her gloves blackened from weeks of work. She placed one frayed length of leather on the pile—not to sell, not to bargain, but to bind. "Fiber holds what words forget," she said, her voice hoarse but steady. She tied the strip around the bent iron nail, knotting ruin to ruin until both stood stronger. Children leaned in, learning the pattern of her knots, repeating the cadence with their breath.

Nessa laughed—sharp, bright, Untethered still. "Look at them," she called, earrings flashing in jar-light. "Trading scars and scraps as if they were gold—and somehow making them worth more than coin."

The crowd's murmur answered her—not mocking, not desperate, but solemn.

The Ash Market had shed its hunger and become something else: a place where value was not measured in bread, but in witness, in breath, in the stubborn dignity of offering what little remained.

The accord was sealed not by signatures, not by ledgers, but by silence—heavy, unanimous, unbreakable.

The Ash Market, once named for soot and failure, had become altar.

Chapter 73

Silence Courts

"Where no verdict is spoken, breath becomes judgment."

THE TRIBUNAL's halls stood hollow, banners rotted to rags, marble dais crumbling under the weight of abandonment. Yet people still came—not to bow, not to beg, but to sit.

They gathered on the cold stone in concentric rings, Grounded and Untethered side by side. No guards barred the door. No heralds announced decrees. Only silence filled the air, thick as smoke.

One by one, disputes were carried in.

—A broken jar: two children argued over who had dropped it.

—A torn cloth: two mothers whispered blame, their voices fraying like the fabric itself.

—An empty pot: neighbors accused each other of taking what had never been enough to share.

But no judge rose to preside. No gavel split the hush.

Instead, the circle waited. Breath by breath, the noise fell away until only the sound of lungs remained—inhale, exhale, the rhythm steady as tide. The quarrels faded, not solved but absorbed, drawn down into the quiet until words lost their teeth.

Mira sat near the outer ring, ledger closed. Her blackened thumb traced the leather spine, but she made no mark. "This silence writes louder than ink," she whispered.

Salliwith leaned against the rail, her bare shoulder pressed to stone. "Witness weighs heavier than verdict."

Karine set her cracked lens on the ground, watching how jar-light fractured across it, scattering patterns like invisible chalk. "The map expands here," she murmured. "But with no boundaries."

Kess shifted forward from her place at the shrine's edge, raw hands folded in her lap. Straps were looped across her shoulders, not as burden but as reminder. "Fiber holds only if it rests," she said quietly. She laid one strap between disputing children and let it lie slack. "See? Nothing breaks if no one pulls." The lesson spread like breath, not command but demonstration.

Children were the first to understand. They mimicked the hush, giggles caught in throats until even laughter softened to breath. They learned that judgment was not thunder from a dais but the patience of sitting still together until anger tired of itself.

Rael pressed his scarred cheek to the wall, whispering *hold*. The word carried like a seed, planted in lungs that had no fuel to feed their rage without breath to carry it.

Nessa tilted her chin high, earrings flashing faintly in the dim light, ash-mark still dark on her wrist. "Imagine that," she said, her voice sharp but not mocking. "Justice through nothing but silence. No banners, no brands—just the weight of waiting until even fury grows bored."

And it was true. By dawn, no verdict had been pronounced, yet quarrels had dissolved, frictions dulled, and the circle remained unbroken.

The Silence Courts endured—not as law written in ledgers, not as decree carved in stone, but as breath made visible. Where no voice could stand above another, silence itself had claimed its place.

Codex XI – The Law of Broken Accords

"Every promise in this time was unstable."

EVERY MARKET, every council, every oath in this time was unstable.

• The Ash Market promised order, but each trade carried betrayal.

• The Silence Courts demanded justice, but judgment was uneven.

• The Scar Council claimed authority, but their words carried no weight.

The lesson was clear:

• No accord survives if built only on fear.

• No promise endures if not carried together.

This law defined the Shape Between:

Accords could be made, but none could fully hold.

Chapter 74

Witness Fires

"Flame remembers what ink cannot."

CHILDREN CARRIED jars not with fireflies but with kindled flames—tiny cloth wicks dipped in rendered fat, balanced in clay bowls scavenged from abandoned homes. Their light was harsher than the patient pulse of insects, yet steadier against wind and cold.

They placed them on rails, in cracks, at the shrine's edge— each fire a small oath against forgetting.

Mira stood closest, her palms still black with ash from the ledger she had surrendered. She whispered to the flames as if they were pages: "Do not let the silence erase us."

Salliwith tore the last usable scrap from her daughter's ribbon and fed it to the fire. It curled, smoked, then burned away. "Witness always costs," she murmured. "Even when the price is memory itself."

Karine crouched with her cracked lens, tilting it until fire-light scattered into jagged constellations across stone. She mapped them as she always had—lines of heat traced like scars across the ground. "The map must include fire," she said. "Because fire, too, is law."

Rael leaned against the wall, the scar along his cheek glowing red in reflected light. His lips shaped the sequence —*hold*—and the flames seemed to answer with their low crackle, alive and fragile.

Kess stepped forward from the shadows, straps looped over her shoulders, her raw hands blackened from smoke. She knelt beside the children and steadied one flickering wick with leather stretched between her palms. "Even fire needs a brace," she said softly. She lashed her strap to the clay bowl so it would not tip, showing them how to bind flame as they once bound bodies. "Level. Cross. Lock. Test. Check." The children repeated the litany, and the fires steadied, small suns woven into order.

Nessa stood upright at the circle's edge, her mother's studs glinting, her father's hammered charms warmed by firelight. She lifted her hand over one of the flames, letting the heat lick her palm. "This," she said, voice sharp as flint on steel, "is warmer than any decree. And it burns longer."

The crowd echoed her not in words but in action. One by one, they brought scraps of cloth, splinters of broken tools, fragments of paper too damaged for ledgers. Each offering burned, each flame joined the others until the square itself glowed like a field of stars pulled down to earth.

The Guards—those who still lingered—watched from the shadows, their staves lowered, their eyes wide with awe and unease. The Tribunal seats stood empty, blackened by soot drifting down from above.

By midnight, smoke clung to every lung, every garment. The fires smoldered low but did not vanish. They remained, small and stubborn, marking the night with the truth that witness could no longer be confined to ink, to cloth, or to silence.

Witness now burned—alive, visible, untamable.

Chapter 75

Ribbons Across the Scar

"Where stone breaks, cloth remembers."

THE SCAR that split Threshold had never closed. Cracks in marble widened with each passing season, jagged reminders of collapse running like veins from stair to market square, from shrine to rail. Once the Tribunal tried to cover them— first with silk banners, then with decrees, then with silence. All had failed.

It was the children who first tied bright ribbons into the stone's wounds—strips torn from skirts, scavenged from abandoned stalls, dyed with ash and river water until they bloomed in rust and amber. At first it looked like play— small hands stitching a broken city as if mending a beloved garment. But the gesture spread like fire in dry grass.

Mothers knelt beside their daughters, binding threads into fissures. Old men, hands trembling, knotted scraps where pride had once split. Even the Untethered bent stiff backs to lay their offerings in the cracks. The scar became not something to hide but something to honor—a seam of shared memory, undeniable, strangely beautiful.

The six witnesses bent close:

• **Mira** pressed her ink-black thumb into the ledger's cover, refusing to reduce these ribbons to ink. "The color speaks more eloquently than I could," she murmured.

• **Nessa's** silver studs caught the jar-light as she tilted her chin, her ash-scar visible in the glow. "Better ribbons than banners," she said, voice edged with triumph.

• **Rael** whispered his count—seventeen, four, two—and each number landed like another knot pulled tight against silence.

• **Karine** peered through her cracked lens, sketching fractures transformed into woven seams. She whispered each name as if calling roll: Ash. Oath. Burden. Hunger. Now ribbon joined those names.

• **Kess** pressed her palm to the shrine's wood as a boy tied a strip directly to her sling's strap. Her hands were raw from labor, her voice steady as stone: "Straps can fail, but cloth binds even what breaks." Her words braided shrine and scar into one tapestry.

• **Salliwith**, shoulders bare where cloth had once clung, laid her hand against the stone itself. "Every strip I gave still speaks," she whispered. "Now your hands carry it forward."

By evening's shadow, the scar shimmered like a river—not banners of empire, but ribbons of witness. Each thread a vow that collapse would not remain wound, that fracture could be bound into grace.

No decree declared this act law. No vote ratified it. But from that day forward, every ritual ended at the ribboned scar. Every procession paused to tie cloth. Every oath fluttered low enough for even a child to reach.

And so the scar held—not as weakness, but as living proof that what breaks may also bind, and what collapses may yet endure.

Codex XII – The Law of Witness

"Survival depended on what others could see and remember."

WHEN WORDS FAILED, people turned to witness.

- Ribbons stretched across scars.

- Fires were lit in memory.

- Children spoke when elders would not.

These acts were not decoration.

They were proof that survival required memory.

The lesson was clear:

- Bonds without witness collapse.

- Silence without witness becomes emptiness.

This law defined the Shape Between:

Survival was not secured by power, but by what others could see and remember.

Chapter 76

Ledger of Silence

"What is unwritten sometimes speaks the loudest."

THE LEDGER SAT UNOPENED at Mira's side, its leather still dusted with soot from the brazier. She traced the spine with her thumb but did not untie the cord, did not let the pages breathe. The square hushed, as though her refusal itself had become law.

"Will you not write the Accord?" a child asked, ash streaked across her cheek like a second birthmark.

Mira shook her head. "It does not belong to paper. It belongs to lungs."

The crowd leaned closer, listening not for words but for the silence between them. Where once they had demanded her pen, now they felt the weight of what remained unwritten. Each breath filled the gap the ledger refused to hold.

Salliwith pressed both bare palms to the closed book, her shoulders trembling. "This silence costs more than ink," she said softly. "It forces us to remember with our own bodies."

Karine lifted her cracked lens, but instead of mapping, she held it high so light fractured into the gathered air. "Even the map cannot hold this," she whispered. "It is written only in what we breathe together."

Rael pressed his scarred cheek against stone, whispering one word only: "Hold." The rhythm carried outward until the whole circle echoed it back, proof that witness lived beyond pages.

At the shrine, Kess laid her own hand on the sling that still hung heavy there, its straps stiffened by ash and memory. A boy tied a bright ribbon to one strap, and she nodded once, her raw fingers brushing his. "Straps can fail," she murmured, "but silence binds stronger than any knot."

Nessa bent low, earrings catching jar-light, her ash-scar stark across her wrist. She tapped the ledger's cover with her finger and laughed sharp as flint. "This blank book screams louder than their banners ever did."

Mira smiled faintly, eyes wet but steady. She tied the cord tighter around the ledger and set it in the shrine's shadow. "This book is not dead. It is sleeping. And its silence will guard what ash cannot."

The people exhaled as one. Pages unwritten, vows un-penned, but held in lungs and in silence.

The Ledger of Silence was complete—not because it was filled, but because it was refused.

UR-VII: The Midwife's Hands

(Upper Registers – Depositions of the Untethered)

I HAVE CAUGHT sixty births since the ground changed.

Fathers grounded, mothers half-broken, rooms too narrow to hold all the crawling bodies. Yet babies come, wet with breath, fists clenched like they already know the weight of this world.

When the Pulse struck, I was alone, walking home. My bag of cloths spilled. I braced myself for the fall that never came. My knees bent—but I stayed standing.

I had never willed harm. These hands had pressed, stretched, cut when cutting meant life—but never once to kill, never once to injure in intent. The law knew. It passed me by.

Now I stand in rooms full of lowered bodies. I reach down, down, always down. They call me Untethered. I dislike the word. It makes me sound above. But I am only taller because I never chose harm.

When I wash my hands after birth, I whisper the same vow:

May these hands never close into fists.

Interlude VI – The Tower of Stolen Hours

"What begins in one square circles the globe."

THE TOWER HAD ONCE MEASURED the city's heartbeat. Its bells tolled the hours of labor and rest, its shadow carved the seasons into the streets below, its clock face glittering like a promise above markets that danced to its relentless rhythm.

When the Pulse came, its hands froze at 11:47—a meaningless minute that would stretch into forever. Guards collapsed mid-step on the winding stairwell, their bodies crumpling against stone, weapons clattering down like broken prayers. They lay piled like sandbags against time itself, unable to rise, unable to fall. The bells fell silent. The clock's commanding height no longer mattered.

Yet people still gathered at its base. Not to keep hours, but to steal them back.

Mothers brought threadbare shawls to cushion the cracked marble floors. Children traced chalk spirals where bronze gears had seized and rusted. Old men pressed weathered palms flat against the tower's stone skin, whispering *Hold,*

hold as if the structure itself could be taught to breathe again.

Inside, the great mechanism sat gutted and still. Brass wheels that had once devoured entire lifetimes in their endless rotation now held nothing but shadow and dust. The pendulum hung motionless, a golden tongue that would never again speak the language of seconds.

No one asked the tower for the hour anymore. Instead, they knelt on its steps and claimed what time had always stolen from them: a moment to rest without guilt, a pause to breathe without purpose, silence deep enough to count seventeen heartbeats, then four, then two—without interruption, without judgment, without the tyranny of what comes next.

The tower no longer measured life. It witnessed it.

And in its cathedral stillness, a truth spread through the city like dawn: hours were never meant to be kept in cages of brass and stone. They were meant to be shared, moment by precious moment, between hearts that beat in their own wild time.

Chapter 77

Quiet Exodus

"When breath no longer fits the square, it seeks new air."

THE SQUARE COULD NOT HOLD them forever. Ash clung too thick to the rails, jars burned low, cloth strips sagged in damp wind. The air itself had grown heavy, too saturated with witness to carry one more vow.

Families gathered what little they owned—blankets cut short, pots cracked but still serviceable, jars faint with firefly glow. They did not shout their departure, did not declare rebellion. They pressed palms to stone one last time, then moved outward through Crawlways, corridors, and fractured streets.

Mira walked among them with her sealed ledger bound tight against her chest. She did not call for order or record names. She simply touched shoulders as they passed, letting silence itself confirm their witness.

Salliwith leaned against the shrine, her body nearly spent. She tore one last strip—no longer from shawl, but from the hem of her own tunic—and tied it to the rail with trembling hands. "Go," she whispered. "Let the world see what was born here."

Karine crouched with her cracked lens, sketching hurried marks on scraps of cloth. Not full maps, only signs: arrows, spirals, circles. Enough to guide those leaving toward water, toward shelter, toward places where breath might still gather.

Rael pressed his cheek to the wall, lips barely moving: *hold*. Those who passed him bent close, repeating the word back, carrying it like an ember into the unknown.

Kess stood in the square's center, straps and sling draped across her shoulders. Her gloves were blackened, her hands raw from work, but she lifted one length of leather high and tied it across the rail herself. "Carry it outward," she said. "Straps can bind farther than walls." Children took her words like inheritance, tugging gently at the leather before walking on.

Nessa strode ahead of many, her studs flashing in the faint light, her father's hammered charms brushing her jaw. She laughed once—sharp, bright, startling even herself. "So the Tribunal thought to bind us in one square? Let them choke on the silence we leave behind."

The Guards did not stop them. Some even trailed at the edges, staves lowered, no longer enforcers but fellow wanderers.

By dusk, Threshold Square stood nearly empty. Only the shrine remained, bound in straps and ash. Only chalk rings and smeared vows lingered on stone. Only silence hummed, vast and enduring.

The Exodus was not a march of conquest, nor a flight of defeat. It was the quiet migration of a people who had remade law from breath and cloth, carrying it outward like seeds on wind.

Threshold did not end.

It multiplied.

Chapter 78

Circle of Ashes

"What scatters as dust can still bind as circle."

THE LAST FIREFLY JAR GUTTERED NEAR the shrine, wings beating until the glow dimmed to darkness. In its place, ash settled—fine grey powder from torches, from cloth burned too thin to save, from breath exhaled until it left nothing but residue.

At dawn, children returned—not many, only a handful. They knelt where the shrine's straps still hung and drew circles in the ash with their fingers. No chalk. No cloth. Only dust.

The circles held.

Mira watched from the steps, ledger unopened. She pressed her thumb into the ash and smeared it across the cover, black upon black. "Even what falls apart can still witness," she murmured.

Karine bent low, cracked lens fogging as she traced the dust with her stylus tip. "These rings will not last an hour," she said. "Yet they are maps nonetheless. Proof that even ash can orient us."

Salliwith lowered herself beside the children, her bare shoulders trembling. She pressed both palms into the powder until her skin turned grey. "So the circle remembers," she whispered. "So even after cloth and shawl are gone, I still give."

Kess knelt with them, her raw hands resting on the shrine's leather straps. She lifted one stiffened loop, then let it fall into the ash, binding the two together. "Straps fail," she said quietly, "but even dust can carry weight if we share it." A boy copied her, smearing his fingers across both leather and ash.

Rael breathed *hold* into the silence, his exhale stirring a faint cloud that swirled into the children's rings. They echoed the word, sealing the shapes with sound.

Nessa stepped boldly into one of the circles, her earrings flashing faint light. She lifted her ash-streaked hand high. "See?" she called. "Even dust carries louder than their decrees." Her grin broke sharp, almost cruel, but the children laughed, scattering the powder into new forms.

By midday, the wind swept much of it away. Yet when the people returned, they still saw the outlines—half-erased, half-reborn—proof that witness need not endure in permanence to endure in meaning.

The Circle of Ashes became both memorial and promise: what is burned is not gone, what is scattered is not silenced, what is dust can still bind.

Chapter 79

Children's Accord

"What the elders fear to sign, the young will swear without parchment."

EVENING FELL over the emptied square. Where ash circles had smeared and straps sagged, children gathered again—this time not in play, but in council. They dragged the short bench closer to the shrine, its legs sawn to the height of their crawling bodies, and crowned it with jars glowing faintly with borrowed flame.

One by one, they pressed palms to the scarred wood and spoke. Not decrees. Not verdicts. Only promises.

"I will carry your name when you cannot breathe it."

"I will tie cloth when your hands are too raw."

"I will laugh when hunger tries to steal the sound."

"I will remember the cracks Karine named."

Their voices trembled, some breaking with hunger, some bold with defiance. Yet each vow, fragile as moth-wing, hung in the night air like iron.

The six bent close to bear witness:

• **Mira** kept her ledger bound tight, thumb blackened on the spine. She did not write. She whispered only to herself: *"This is the first true accord."*

• **Karine** sketched not fractures in stone but the children's faces, caught through her cracked lens as if their vows were constellations.

• **Salliwith** pressed her ash-streaked palms flat to the bench, eyes closed. *"Witness lives longer in breath than in thread,"* she said, voice weary but steady.

• **Rael**, leaning against his wall, mouthed *hold*, and the children answered as one, lungs swelling, exhale scattering the last ash from the rails.

• **Kess** stood beside the shrine, hands raw, shoulders wrapped in patched cloth. She knelt to the bench and tied one of her straps through its leg, binding invention and vow into a single frame. *"Fiber holds,"* she said simply, *"because hands keep holding it."*

• **Nessa** stood tallest, her studs glinting, and the last coin-charm warm against her skin." She laughed once, sharp as flint, then declared: *"Then let this be our law—no Tribunal, no banners. Only this bench, these jars, and the breath we share."*

The Guards did not intervene. They watched from the shadows, staves lowered, some nodding with quiet assent.

By night's end, the bench bore more than vows. It bore handprints in ash, cloth tied at its corners, chalk spirals renewed on the ground beneath it.

The Children's Accord required no scroll, no ink, no decree.

It bound them nonetheless—stronger than iron, steadier than law, more enduring than fear.

Chapter 80

Ash Market Reborn

"What once sold survival can still trade in dignity."

At FIRST LIGHT, the old market groaned awake. Stalls long emptied of bread, beans, and grain were swept clean of ash by hands too stubborn to quit. Mats once soaked in oil and blood were shaken out, their fibers worn thin yet willing to hold one more gathering.

The square did not smell of yeast or meat—it smelled of stone rubbed raw, of cloth rinsed in river water, of jars glowing faintly in the pale dawn. Yet people came, carrying not goods but fragments.

One woman laid down a strip of shawl. Another placed a shard of broken glass, its edges smoothed by careful fingers. A boy dropped a chalk nub into the dust. A jar-bearer set down a vessel alive with two stubborn fireflies, pulsing like twin heartbeats.

The Ash Market was not reborn in plenty. It was reborn in witness.

• **Karine** traced new paths where stalls had once stood,

chalking the word *Trade* at each crossing. *"Not bread for coin,"* she said, *"but burden for breath."*

• **Salliwith** pressed her bare palms flat to the ground, shoulders trembling, voice frayed. *"Every offering costs, but the cost is what binds us."* Grey handprints spread across the stone like signatures written in ash.

• **Mira** opened her ledger for the first time in days. With a steady blackened thumb, she wrote a single line: *Ash Market Reborn — goods of memory, traded in witness.* Then she closed it again, as if one line was enough to hold the weight of an entire square.

• **Rael** whispered *hold* from his place by the wall. This time children carried the word into practice: one lifted jars for another, one shared cloth for bandages, one traced chalk paths while others swept the stone. The vow became economy.

• **Kess** bent at her shrine, raw hands tightening the stiffened straps into knots that groaned but held. She tied one fragment directly to a market stall, binding invention to exchange. *"Even markets need fiber,"* she murmured. *"Nothing holds without it."*

• **Nessa** leaned against a rail, her studs catching the weak light. *"Once they sold us bread,"* she said, grin sharp. *"Now we sell each other courage."* Her words sparked a ripple of relief, thin but undeniable.

The Guards lingered at the edges, staves dragging across stone. One knelt at last, laying down his iron stave on a mat like an offering. *"Take it,"* he murmured. *"Melt it, mark it, or break it. I have nothing else to give."*

The crowd did not cheer. They nodded, silent as law itself, and made room for him in the circle.

The Ash Market had been born in hunger. Reborn, it became a place to barter what the city still held: cloth, chalk, light, witness, and the fragile courage of those who refused to scatter.

It was not enough to feed the body. But it was enough to keep the city breathing.

Chapter 81

Rael's Silence Shared

"A vow breaks only when hoarded."

RAEL NO LONGER COUNTED ALOUD. The sequence that had once been his marrow—seventeen, four, two—dissolved into something quieter, almost invisible. He leaned against the wall as always, scar pressed to cold plaster, but his lips moved without sound.

Children noticed first. They always did.

One girl leaned close, her ear nearly brushing his mouth. She caught no numbers, only the tremor of breath.

"He's not saying it," she whispered.

"But he's still holding it," another replied, watching the faint rise and fall of Rael's shoulders.

They carried the silence away like contraband, sharing it with others who pressed near to listen. Soon dozens gathered—not to hear words, but to feel their absence. Silence became the new rhythm, a vow passed not in sound but in withheld breath, in lungs steady together.

• **Mira** rested her thumb against her sealed ledger. She did not open it. "Not every witness needs writing," she murmured. "Sometimes the gap itself speaks."

• **Karine** crouched close, chalk trembling in her hand. She traced only an empty circle, leaving it blank. "This fracture doesn't need a name," she said. "It already knows itself."

• **Salliwith** pressed both palms flat to the ground, her bare shoulders sagging. "Witness holds even when words fail," she whispered, her voice breaking into silence that others carried for her.

• From **Kess's shrine**, the stiffened straps gave a low groan in the breeze, leather pulling taut as if the vow itself were being carried by fiber long past breaking.

• **Nessa** tilted her chin, her mother's studs flashing, her father's last charm trembling faintly. "He's teaching us without trying," she said, her grin sharp but not cruel. "Even silence can't be hoarded—it leaks into every ear."

The Guards shifted uneasily at the square's edge. "He says nothing," one muttered, but his voice shook, unsettled by how nothing commanded more than their decrees ever had.

Children scaled their lips with chalk dust, faces pale as moonlight. Adults matched Rael's rhythm in shared lungs: inhale, hold, exhale, nothing spoken.

Seventeen. Four. Two.

The numbers were gone, but the pattern endured.

The vow was no longer Rael's alone. It had become theirs.

Chapter 82

Mira's Ledger Closed Again

"Refusal can be record enough."

THE LEDGER WAITED on Mira's knees, spine worn smooth by years of her thumb pressing the same anxious groove. The blank page stared up at her like a wound, luminous in the jar-light, daring her to trap Rael's silence in ink.

Her pen hovered. A smear of black trembled at its tip. She could have written absence: *Rael spoke nothing, yet all heard.*She could have fixed silence like an insect pinned to glass.

Instead, she snapped the book shut. The sound cracked sharp across the square, louder than any decree.

Children gasped. The Guards on the dais leaned forward, startled by how a gesture so small could drown out their tired authority.

Mira wound the leather cord twice around the ledger and pressed her thumb to its cover. The familiar crescent of ink bloomed black against brown. A seal—not of writing, but of refusal.

"Why won't you keep it?" a child asked, voice thin as reed-flute.

"Because some truths are stronger unwritten," Mira said, her words cutting the night clean. "If I claim this silence with ink, it becomes mine alone. Closed, it belongs to all of us."

• **Salliwith** bowed her bare head, palms folded in witness. "A sealed ledger speaks louder than an open one."

• **Karine** brushed chalk dust from her cracked lens and drew a hollow box on stone. She left it empty, labeling it simply: *Unwritten.*

• **Kess's shrine** loomed at the edge, straps stiffened, leather creaking faintly as if approving her refusal.

• **Nessa** laughed low, her earrings catching the glow. "Careful, sister. You'll turn silence into scripture."

Mira clutched the ledger tight against her chest and looked toward Rael. His lips still shaped nothing, but the silence had multiplied. It filled the square, pressed into lungs, bound bodies closer than words ever had.

The ledger stayed shut. And in that deliberate closing, every breath became archive.

Chapter 83

Karine's Map Fractured Further

"Every map breaks before it holds."

KARINE CROUCHED at the stair's base, chalk trembling in her hand, cracked lens crooked against one eye. The map sprawled before her—fractures already named, paths already bound with cloth. Yet tonight new lines had opened, fine as hair, sharp as lightning veins caught mid-strike.

They crossed her old borders without mercy. **Ash** forked into two paths, **Oath** bent toward silence, **Hold** split into tributaries like rivers breaking apart. Each new crack undid her certainty.

Children clustered at her elbows, knees white with dust. "What's this one?" one asked, pointing to a fresh fracture threading outward.

Karine pressed her chalk deep, naming aloud: "Division."

Another child tugged her sleeve, showing where two cracks curved back toward each other, meeting like hands across an impossible gulf. Karine circled it slowly, reverently. "Reunion."

Her lens fogged, every flaw multiplying the breaks until each line seemed doubled, every path uncertain. Terror gripped her—that her map would collapse, her names swallowed by too much chaos.

A bare palm steadied her back. **Salliwith**, shoulders trembling but voice steady, whispered: "Fray still remembers. Even when cloth unravels, the weave tells its story."

Mira leaned near, ledger bound tight against her chest. "Not every fracture needs ink. Some truths survive in silence."

At the shrine, the **stiffened straps of Kess's sling creaked in the night air**, reminding all that broken fiber could still bear weight.

Nessa laughed softly, her studs catching jar-light like cold stars. "Careful, cartographer—you'll name cracks faster than the city can make them. One day the ground might answer back."

Karine smiled faintly, pressing chalk to stone again. "Then let it. If it speaks, we'll learn its tongue."

She worked until her fingers bled dust, until the stair was covered with chalk rivers, spirals, and circles—fractured, yes, but alive. When her chalk finally dropped, the children scrambled to claim the nubs, whispering her new names into memory as they carried them away like seeds.

The map was broken. And only in breaking did it begin to hold.

Chapter 84

Salliwith Bare Shoulders

"Witness costs the body first."

THE SHRINE glowed dim in the failing light—straps bound tight, jars flickering steady, chalk rings breathing pale across worn stone. Yet Salliwith herself was stripped nearly bare.

Her shawl was gone, unraveled strip by strip to tether jars, to bind wounds, to mark cracks. Now only skin remained— pale shoulders mapped with the shadows of cloth once tied there, a ghost-weave only she could feel.

She sat low against the shrine, her back bowed not in surrender but in an exhaustion that had no fabric left to mask it. Every breath rattled thin as parchment. Still, she gave.

A knot-binder child approached quietly, carrying a ribbon pulled from her own dark hair. She placed it in Salliwith's trembling hands without a word.

"Take mine," she whispered.

Salliwith's eyes burned. Gratitude and shame warred in her chest. Yet her fingers tied the ribbon with steady care to the cracked wood of the shrine. The knot held, bright against the night. "Witness doesn't end with me," she whispered. "It multiplies."

Mira, ledger bound shut against her chest, murmured, "Sometimes the record lives in bodies alone—written in what we surrender."

Karine raised her cracked lens, scattering jar-light across Salliwith's bare skin until it shimmered as if woven once more in unseen threads. "The pattern remains," she said. "Even when the cloth is gone."

Rael pressed his scarred cheek to the wall, whispering *hold*. The word lingered between her shallow breaths, a prayer stronger than lungs.

At the shrine's edge, Kess placed her work-scarred hand on the rail beside Salliwith's arm, palm against skin. "Fiber never lies," she said. "It frays when it must. So do we. And in the breaking there is beauty."

Nessa stood tall, silver studs flashing, coin-charms trembling faintly in the still air. Her voice carried clear, for once without edge: "Even bare, she carries more than any of us."

Salliwith pressed her palms flat to stone, feeling straps, rails, and chalk dust beneath her fingers. Her shoulders sagged, naked against the cooling wind, but her voice remained steady. "Witness costs until nothing is left," she said. "And still it asks for more."

The words echoed through the square. The children saw her emptiness and understood it as fullness. In that paradox lay something sacred—the knowledge that even stripped to nothing, a body could bind others closer than cloth ever had.

The shrine flickered in jar-light, straps stiffened, flames low. And Salliwith, bare as the truth she carried, became the most eloquent witness of all.

UR-VIII:The Mason's Level

(Upper Registers – Depositions of the Untethered)

THE OLD LEVEL lay across my palm, bubble frozen in its glass tube. I had carried it since apprenticeship, measuring every wall, every span of stone.

When the Pulse struck, I did not fall. My brothers did—masons who once brawled, who once swore harm in fury or drink. They crawled home that night, dragging tools they could never raise again.

I stood, ashamed. I had never struck with intent. Never built walls to cage or crush. Stone was my craft, not my weapon.

Now every line I mark, I draw low. Thirty-six inches is the measure. No higher. No arches lifting skyward, no door-frames meant to tower.

I took my level to the quarry and struck it against stone until the glass burst. The bubble ran like a tiny soul escaping.

I can still stand, but I will not build what others must crawl beneath.

Interlude VII– The Architect of Downward Homes

"Shelter bends to the height of those who must live in it."

HE WAS NEVER CALLED architect in the old sense. No guild bore his name, no plaque gilded his work. But in Crawlways and hollow courts they whispered of him with reverence: the builder who designed for knees and palms, not for spires.

He had watched families perish behind doors set too high for crawling hands to reach, stairwells that became death-traps when legs failed, rooms that mocked survival with ceilings beyond touch. He had seen hunger carve more than bodies—it carved dignity from homes that refused to bend.

So he began again. This time, low.

Doorframes cut to three feet, tops smoothed by patient hands. Windows dropped to elbow height, where even the smallest child could rest a jar and see the light. Beds bound flat to the floor with salvaged straps and rope, things that could not betray by falling. Tables made as wide circles set at ground level, where no one needed to strain upward to eat, to share, to touch.

He drew no blueprints—only chalk lines traced across broken walls. He measured not with steel rods but with the span of a forearm, the width of a palm pressed flat. Every mark was both design and vow: here life can continue, here breath can still belong.

At first the Untethered sneered. *Rat-nests,* they called the rooms cut so low children had to bow to enter. But when winter pressed cruel and long, it was those "rat-nests" that held warmth. It was those low ceilings that gathered laughter where once wind had only howled.

The builder never gloated. He simply tied one strip of bright ribbon into each new rafter and whispered the word that had become his prayer: *Hold.*

Others learned. Crawlways bloomed into neighborhoods of low rooms, each ribboned beam a quiet refusal to abandon the grounded. Markets lowered their stalls. Even shrines bent their altars so children could lay witness with their own hands.

It was said Salliwith passed through one such home. She pressed her bare shoulders against its beams, tears stinging her eyes, whispering: *This remembers what cloth cannot.* She left with nothing but her palms dusted white, yet those who lived there spoke for years of how her witness had consecrated their dwelling.

No decree ever named the builder. No ledger recorded his plans. But the city itself became his testament: a breathing architecture of humility, where survival meant bending until the low became sacred, until stone itself remembered mercy.

The city bent. And in bending, it endured.

Chapter 85

Nessa Defiant

"Height is not privilege when it refuses to kneel."

THE SQUARE REMEMBERED TOO MUCH—ASH where branding irons had hissed, shawl strips unraveled to nothing, Rael's vow carried until his lungs frayed. The shrine stood steady with its straps and boards, bound by children's hands, pulsing in jar-light like a heart that would not stop.

And Nessa stood tallest.

She rose at the circle's edge, untethered, ash-mark still stark on her wrist. Silver studs glinted, her father's charm swayed faintly with breath. She said nothing at first, but silence bent around her like iron.

From the shadows a Guard hissed, "Sit down, girl. Crawl with the rest." His stave rattled weakly against the rail, hollow as a spent drum.

Nessa laughed—sharp as shattering glass, bright as sparks on stone. "If you want me down, you'll have to crawl here yourself. And when you do, every eye will see just how low you've fallen."

The crowd stirred, half afraid, half exultant. Mira pressed her sealed ledger tight to her chest, whispering, "She makes silence speak louder than ink ever could."

Karine lifted her cracked lens, chalking one word on the rail: *Defiance.*

Salliwith pressed both bare palms to the shrine's wood, shoulders trembling with exhaustion. "Even without cloth to bind her," she whispered, "witness stands in her bones."

From his place against the wall Rael breathed his sacred count—"Seventeen. Four. Two."—and the rhythm seemed to wrap itself around Nessa's upright frame until her very body became the vessel of the vow.

The Guards muttered but did not move. Their staves sagged. Authority bled away in the presence of one girl's refusal.

Nessa tilted her chin toward the shrine, toward the Tribunal's hollow dais, toward the memory of banners that no longer mattered. Her voice rang clear, each word like a bell:

"You call me irreparable. But I am whole enough to refuse you. Whole enough to stand when you cannot. Whole enough to laugh when you choke on your own silence."

Her laughter rang across rails and chalk rings, through firefly jars and ribboned cracks. And in that moment, defiance itself became law—upright, unbroken, unafraid.

Chapter 86

Karine's Cartography

"A fracture becomes a map the moment it is named."

KARINE CROUCHED low at the base of the stair, her cracked lens strapped crooked across one eye. The marble was no longer just stone—it was scarred flesh, a wounded body remembering every collapse. She set chalk to its surface with hands steady as vow.

"This one: Hunger." She circled the groove worn deep by knees that had crawled season after season for bread that never came.

"This one: Ash." She traced the jagged mark where a jar had shattered, soot still dark in its depths.

"This one: Oath." She touched the long scar where Rael had pressed his cheek and whispered the rhythm until even stone had learned to breathe with him.

Children leaned close, voices catching the names and repeating them aloud. Spiral-chalkers echoed each word, turning the act of mapping into liturgy. Knot-binders tied scraps of cloth into the fresh cracks, anchoring memory with fiber. Jar-bearers placed their vessels at the ends of each named line until fractures glowed like constellations spread across the stair.

Mira stood nearby, ledger unopened. She pressed her blackened thumb against the cover, whispering, "Some truths don't need lines of ink. They're already written in the ground."

Salliwith, pale shoulders trembling, pressed her palm to the mark called Hunger. "Witness begins where need is carved deepest," she murmured, her voice thin but resolute.

Kess shifted near her shrine. The stiffened straps of her broken sling swayed in the breeze, leather fraying at its edges. She laid one raw hand on the crack Karine had named Burden and whispered, "Truer than anything I ever built."

Nessa, still upright at the edge, laughed once, sharp and bright. "At least the stone tells the truth. Those banners never did." Her studs caught the jar-light, gleaming like tiny stars fallen low enough to be touched.

From his corner, Rael pressed his scar to the wall. Breath scraped his lungs as he whispered one word only: "Hold."

Karine circled the nearest crack with chalk and inscribed the word beside it. In the glow of jars and ribbons, the stair became a living atlas—not of empires or borders, but of scars, burdens, and vows too honest to be forgotten.

She leaned back at last, palms dusted white, lens fogging with her breath. "The city knows itself now," she whispered. "At last, it knows itself."

Interlude VIII– The Choir of Glass

"Even broken voices can sing."

It BEGAN with shards swept from the ruins of grander times. Windows shattered by desperate riots, jars cracked by trembling hands, bottles drained of their last precious oil and cast aside like promises. The children gathered these fragments—not for trade or repair, but for the secret music hidden in their jagged edges.

They discovered that each piece held its own voice. Shard struck against shard in careful experimentation, some crying out bright and sharp as winter air, others humming low and dull as heartache, still others trembling like voices caught on the edge of tears. Soon circles formed in the Crawlways— mason jars arranged in patient rows, window fragments balanced on worn stones, every edge tuned through accident and infinite patience.

At dusk, when the settlements filled with the day's last breathing and the first whispered prayers, the children played. Not with melody—that belonged to a world that could still stand upright—but with rhythm. The same sacred rhythm Rael had pressed into stone and hearts alike:

seventeen, four, two. Over and over, like a pulse made audible.

The sound drifted through markets and makeshift shrines, broken glass chiming like bells that had forgotten how to be whole but remembered how to sing. People paused mid-step in their daily struggles, grocery lists forgotten, grief momentarily lifted. Some wept at the beauty of it. Others laughed with unexpected joy. A few pressed scraps of cloth to nearby rails in wordless response, adding texture to the glass song.

Witness was shifting, evolving. No longer confined to silence, or cloth, or chalk marks on stone. Now sound itself —fragile, fractured, impossibly low to the ground—became testimony to what endured.

Mira closed her ledger at the first crystalline notes, her ink-stained fingers stilling above the page. "Let this music live only in air and memory," she murmured, unwilling to trap something so alive in the prison of written words. Across the courtyard, Nessa leaned against weathered stone, her silver studs catching the amber jar-light, and smiled her rare smile. "Even shattered glass mocks their grand decrees better than my sharpest tongue." Karine adjusted her cracked surveyor's lens, marking the circle of singing jars on her ever-growing map, the glass fogging with each vibration that reached her. In careful script, she labeled the spot simply: *Choir*.

And so the people learned a truth that no academy had ever taught: fragments, when gathered with intention and bound by shared rhythm, could create something more beautiful than anything that had never been broken.

The Choir of Glass became law—not written in books or carved in marble, not decreed from towers or enforced by guards, but heard. Each strike of shard against shard served as reminder and promise: broken things could still make beauty, and broken voices, singing together, could still shake the world.

Chapter 87

Salliwith's Last Thread

"Witness costs until nothing remains."

JAR-LIGHT WARMED the shrine's leather and boards, straps fluttering with cloth that was no longer hers. Karine's new names ringed the stair in white—each fracture circled, each wound at last spoken. Children laughed softly as they tied fresh ribbons to the rails, small hands anchoring memory with color.

But Salliwith's shoulders were bare.

Her shawl—winter-woven by a mother's patient hands, softened by years of storms and solace—was gone. Strip by strip it had become tether and bandage, vow and marker, thread spent into the square until nothing remained but skin, pale as first light.

She reached for the absent fringe on reflex. Her fingers met only air. The gesture was small, aching, human.

A child with uneven hair and bright, serious eyes pressed a red ribbon into Salliwith's trembling hands. No speech. No ceremony.

Salliwith tied it to the rail. The knot shook, then held.

"Fray remembers longer than decree," she whispered. "What we bind outlasts what we build."

Mira stood nearby with her ledger closed. She wrote one word in the margin before fixing the cord tight: **Emptied**.

Karine lifted her cracked lens and sketched not cloth but absence—the negative space where comfort had lived. On the stone she pressed chalk hard enough to snap the tip and named it: **Cost**.

At the shrine's edge, the stiffened straps of **Kess's** broken sling creaked in the night air. Kess laid a work-scarred palm beside Salliwith's arm, skin to skin.

"Fiber does not lie about its limits," she said. "It breaks when it must. So do we. And in the breaking there is use."

Nessa, untethered and upright, let her father's hammered charm brush her cheek. For once her voice carried no edge.

"We see you," she said simply. "All you have given. All you are."

From his place against the wall, **Rael** breathed the vow with what breath remained. "Hold." A dozen voices lifted it for him until the word moved through the square like a tide.

No daughters came. Untethered long ago, they did not return. The space they left did not close; the city filled it with witness.

Above, the husked Tribunal watched and could not speak. Their banners, long since rotted to thread, hung without meaning. Law had slipped their height and nested here, at the level of jar-light and stone.

Salliwith pressed both palms flat to the cold ground, feeling strap, grain, chalk dust beneath her hands. Her last inhale came thin; her last exhale long—as if surrender itself had weight and needed setting down.

The shrine flickered. Ribbons answered in a low rustle. Jars pulsed like patient hearts.

She had nothing left to give but the eloquence of emptiness —the testimony of bare shoulders held in light, the law of love spent completely.

And the square received it. What she set down, they lifted.

BREATHMARK (**ALL**): *We carry what she could not. Hold.*

Chapter 88

Threshold Fractured

"Every scar widens when carried by too many feet."

THE STAIR SPLIT the city in two, a marble scar dressed in chalk and cloth. By night it pulsed with firefly jars like a constellation fallen to earth, by day with the endless scraping of countless knees seeking witness. Memory had accumulated in its stone until the very marble seemed swollen with the weight of what it had been asked to bear.

But weight carries cost.

The cracks Karine had so carefully named—*Hunger, Ash, Oath, Cost*—spread under the relentless press of bodies. New fissures crept outward like blood vessels across pale marble, branching beneath weathered hands and worn knees, spidering toward the plazas above where power still pretended to reign.

Children traced each new break in chalk as quickly as it appeared, their small hands moving with the urgency of scribes racing against time. Each fresh line became geography, each fracture folded into the living map that grew beyond any single person's ability to contain. "This one: *Silence.*" "This one: *Bread.*" "This one: *Waiting.*" Their voices rose like liturgy, naming truth faster than any decree could erase it.

Mira crouched low beside the spreading network, her ledger clutched but unopened, thumb black with ink against the worn leather spine. "If I record every split, the book will never end," she whispered, voice thick with the weight of impossible documentation. Instead, she pressed her stained hand flat to the stone, leaving a palm-print that said more than volumes of careful script ever could.

Nessa leaned against the rail above, silver earrings catching morning light like tiny knives. Her grin was sharp as winter glass when she spoke: "Let it break completely. When it shatters, no one will be able to climb high enough to look down on us again."

Salliwith's absence ached like phantom pain at the edge of the gathering circle. Her last ribbon trembled on the rail—a scarlet ghost waving in the wind, the final witness to her complete surrender. Kess approached it with reverent fingers, touching the fabric as gently as she might touch a wound. "Stone is more honest than flesh," she murmured. "When it breaks, we'll finally know the truth it's been trying to tell us."

From his place against the wall, Rael pressed his weathered cheek to a widening crack where he had once whispered his sacred count. His breath came shallow but still carried the rhythm that had sustained him: "Seventeen. Four. Two." The words trembled into the fracture like water finding its natural level. Children heard and repeated them, their voices threading through the broken stair until the ancient rhythm became mortar binding the crumbling stone.

Karine's cracked lens revealed hairline fissures invisible to ordinary sight, a hidden network of weakness spreading through the foundation itself. She mapped them with desperate intensity, chalk dust clouding her dark hair, her trembling stylus racing to document what felt inevitable. "The stair is becoming atlas," she whispered to no one and everyone. "Not a map of where we might go, but of how we break."

Above them, the Tribunal sagged lower in their elevated seats, as if the stone's weakness had somehow infected their bones. Their silk banners drooped like dying flowers, golden letters flaking into dust that fell like snow on the witnesses below. The Arbiter's prepared decree crumbled in his manicured hands before a single word could be spoken. The Magistrate stared at the spreading cracks as if reading prophecy written in a language she had never learned. The Canonister opened his mouth to roar condemnation, but the sound caught and broke in his throat, emerging as something closer to pleading than power.

The entire square fell into hushed anticipation. Every eye turned to the stair, to the central fracture that grew wider with each passing heartbeat, each labored breath. The law of stone was writing itself in real time—wordless, merciless, utterly unchangeable by human decree or desire.

The threshold was no longer a stage for performance. It had become what it had always truly been: a wound in the city's heart.

And wounds, once split wide enough, demand a choice—healing or complete collapse.

Breathmark (all): The stair breaks, and so do we. Yet in the breaking, we are bound.

Interlude IX — The Boy Who Traded His Weapon for a Story

"Not every weapon must draw blood—some can be remade as breath."

THE BOY HAD BEEN GROUNDED EARLY—BARELY sixteen, with a knife gripped white-knuckled in his trembling fist during a market quarrel over moldy bread. He never struck a blow, never drew blood, but intent alone was enough. The Pulse read his heart's readiness and claimed him, dropping him to his knees mid-threat. From that moment forward, his world shrank to the height of crawling children and scraping stone.

He carried the blade still, tied to his belt with fraying kitchen twine. Not for protection—what good was a weapon to hands that could barely lift themselves?—but because grounding had welded it to him like a scar. The knife had become part of his shame, his reminder, his identity. Children pointed and whispered cruel names. Adults offered pitying glances and worried murmurs. Yet no one, not even the kindest souls, ever asked him to set it down.

One evening, beneath the great stair where shadows gathered like secrets, he did the unthinkable.

He placed the knife on a strip of faded cloth—gently, as if it were made of glass—and began to speak. Not of hunger gnawing at empty bellies, or riots that had torn families apart, or decrees that fell like hammers from the high places. Instead, he spoke of a fox with silver fur who outwitted three kings with nothing but cleverness and patience. Of a river that remembered every name whispered to its waters. Of a sky that grew lonely in its vastness and bent low just to hear the earth's secrets.

His words tumbled rough and uncertain at first, voice cracking like a boy's voice should. But then they steadied, grew sharper, more sure of themselves—cutting not flesh but the suffocating silence that had settled over the Crawl-ways like dust.

The children crept closer on silent hands and knees, eyes wide as coins. The adults stilled their evening tasks, bowls forgotten, mending set aside. Even the guards, shifting uneasily in the deeper shadows, found themselves leaning forward despite their duties, caught in the web of words.

By the time the last sentence fell soft as a prayer, the knife lay forgotten on its cloth. All anyone could remember was silver fur in moonlight, water singing names, the sky's gentle curiosity.

From then on, each time someone mocked him for his crawling gait, he answered with another tale. Each time they demanded to know why he still carried a blade he could never properly wield, he smiled and told them it was no longer a weapon but a key—a way to unlock worlds without spilling a single drop of blood.

Word spread through the settlements like wildfire: *the boy who traded his weapon for a story.* Some laughed at what they called foolishness, shaking their heads at such waste. Others quietly tied strips of cloth to nearby rails in witness to the transformation they'd seen. Mira firmly refused to transcribe his stories into her endless ledgers, insisting with unusual passion, "They live better in mouths and hearts than trapped in ink." Nessa, lounging against a wall with her signature smirk, drawled, "Let the boy carry his blade if it comforts him—his tongue's grown sharper than that dull metal ever was."

The boy never rose taller than three feet, never escaped the grinding reality of stone against his knees. But his stories traveled farther than any sword thrust could reach, crossing walls and boundaries, lifting hearts that had forgotten how to soar.

And in a city slowly remaking itself through silence, cloth, chalk, glass music, and shared breath, his choice became another kind of law: a covenant written in imagination, promising that words could cut deeper than steel, that creation could triumph over destruction, that even the most broken among them could become keys to unlock wonder.

Chapter 89

Salliwith's Passing

"Where breath leaves, the circle holds."

THEY DID NOT summon bell or banner. They made a circle.

Salliwith lay with her shoulders bare against the shrine's worn boards, the last straps whispering above her like tired wind. Amber light from jars set low along the rail cast a steady glow across her collarbones where cloth once rested. Chalk dust filmed the stone beneath her open palms.

She did not ask for pardon. The Pulse had taken its measure of her long ago—intent weighed, height denied—and she had lived inside that sentence one strip of cloth at a time. Now there was nothing left to tear but breath itself.

Mira knelt first, her ledger sealed against her ribs, thumb blackened on leather. She spoke only to the air: "Witness, keep."

Rael pressed his scar to the stone stair and breathed the old count into the hollow between them—seventeen, four, two —until the words thinned to wind and only rhythm remained.

Karine set her cracked lens on the stone, not to capture a face but the stillness around it. She traced a thin white ring around Salliwith's hands, chalk circling palm and bone. "Held," she whispered, leaving the name unadorned.

Kess moved close without ceremony, a single strip of leather looped through her fingers. She did not tie Salliwith to anything. Instead, she tied the strap to the rail, then to empty air—an open knot, a promise of release. "For slack," she said, voice rough with care. "So nothing binds what must go."

Nessa stood upright at the circle's rim, studs and coin-charm catching jar-light. She did not laugh as was her way. "Look," she said, low and even. "Witness costs until only witness remains." Her chin lifted toward the dark seats where no Tribunal waited to pass judgment.

Children came on quiet knees. They brought no ribbons, no flowers. They touched their foreheads to the chalk ring, then backed away to make room for breath to pass.

At the edge of the rail, two women paused—Untethered, straight-backed, faces set like stone. One wore a dress hemmed too clean for Threshold; the other kept her hands clenched at her sides as if contact itself could stain. Someone whispered, "Her daughters," and the whisper died of its own weight.

They did not kneel.

The older one looked once—at the bare shoulders, the chalked palms, the straps, the amber jars—and flinched as if the sight burned. "She chose stone," she said, but the words found no purchase on the ground. The younger's jaw worked soundlessly. Neither came closer. Neither spoke her name.

Salliwith did not look their way. She turned her head toward the shrine she had fed for years, her breath growing shallow. Her hands, emptied of cloth, pressed flat to the chalk until her skin went grey as dust.

"The body is the last strip," she said. "Take it gently."

Silence answered. Not absence—presence without speech.

Mira set her palm over Salliwith's and matched her breathing to the failing rhythm. Karine's white ring held steady. Kess's open knot waited, patient. Rael's count dwindled to a single word: "Hold." The circle took it up without voices—lungs only, like a quiet tide.

On the inhale, Salliwith's ribs rose like thin wings. On the exhale, they did not rise again.

No one reached to close her eyes. They had never looked away.

Nessa lifted one hand, not to command but to still the small, automatic grief-sounds at the circle's edge. "Witness," she said, and lowered her arm.

The two women at the rail turned and left without speaking. The square did not follow them with its eyes. It followed the last of Salliwith's warmth as it left her skin and entered the night air, where breath keeps what names cannot.

MIRA TOUCHED the ledger's cord but did not untie it. She

pressed her thumb hard until the leather took another crescent of black. "Kept," she said.

Karine leaned forward and marked a second, finer ring around the first, then set her chalk aside. "Kept," she echoed.

Kess loosened the strap she had tied to nothing until it lay across the board like a line drawn for a hand that no longer needed to hold. "Released."

Rael breathed—one, two—and the children answered with the gentlest exhale, a hush that moved across the circle like spreading light.

They did not lift Salliwith then. They did not carry or wash or wail. They stayed until the stone under her palms cooled and the chalk took her complete imprint. Only then did they raise her by many hands, low and careful, clothless as she had lived her final days, the circle walking her body once around the shrine so every rail and ribbon and jar could bear witness.

At the place where the chalk ring had held her hands, the children traced her palm-shapes darker, packing dust into the lines until her absence became a map of what had been.

No decree named the rite. No prayer finished it. Breath did.

And when the circle finally opened, it opened the way a knot opens—without tearing, without sound—leaving the place where she had lain marked by rings of white, a loose strap, and the steadied air of a square that had learned how to honor what consequence takes.

Salliwith had carried intent. The world had carried its cost. The people carried her the rest of the way.

Chapter 90

The Last Tribunal

"Every stage ends when the actors cannot rise."

THE DAIS that once bore the Triad like a throne sagged beneath their diminished weight, marble groaning like tired lungs struggling for one final breath. Robes that once proclaimed dominion no longer draped with grandeur—they clung like burial shrouds to bodies already half-withdrawn from life.

The Chief Arbiter hacked himself raw, each cough shredding the carefully prepared decree clenched in his withered grip. The vellum disintegrated before a single word escaped, ink bleeding into spittle until it ran down his fingers like tears unworthy of witness.

The Defender Magistrate pressed her hands together as if in prayer, but her lips trembled with soundless syllables, a voice that had once tethered thousands reduced now to the faint rasp of fabric fraying in indifferent wind.

The Canonister scraped himself forward on elbows worn to blood, dragging a broken banner pole like driftwood. He raised his head and shrieked: *"This square is mockery! These vows are nothing but ash!"* But the roar cracked into wheeze, collapsing into silence before it reached the first row. His mouth gaped for one more proclamation, yet nothing came. Silence, thick and final, poured out instead.

Below, the people did not jeer. They did not cheer. They watched, patient and grave, as one does at a death already long accepted.

Children pressed chalk circles around the dais, solemn as undertakers sealing a tomb. Knot-binders tied strips of cloth to the marble steps—bright, deliberate, but low, a farewell without allegiance. Jar-bearers set vessels at the foundation, fireflies pulsing steady as vigil-candles, beating with a rhythm no decree had ever commanded.

Mira stood with her ledger closed, thumb black upon the leather spine. "No record," she said, her whisper cutting sharper than a bell. "Their absence is epitaph enough."

Nessa tilted her chin toward the collapsed figures, silver studs and coin-charm catching dawn like sharpened stars. "Look at them," she called, laughter sharp as shattering glass but emptied of cruelty. "They cannot even rise for their own lies." The murmur that passed through the crowd was not outrage, nor triumph, but the final exhale of a story ending.

Karine crouched low with her cracked lens, chalk trembling in her hand. She pressed so hard the stub snapped against stone, but still she carved a single word beside the fallen rulers: **Ash.**

Rael, scarred cheek against the stair, whispered his vow into the silence: *"Hold."* Hundreds of lungs answered as one, breath swelling into chorus, releasing the word together until it grew larger than any tongue could command.

The Tribunal never rose again. No decree left their mouths. No banner lifted above their heads.

The dais sagged into ruin, not toppled by riot nor flame but by the slow inevitability of truth. And with it, the last illusion of rule collapsed.

What remained was not crown nor gavel, not parchment nor staff. Only the honest ground, and the people who had learned to listen when it breathed.

Breathmark (all): *"Even names burn to ash; only witness endures."*

Chapter 91

Hunger Oath

"Hunger itself is a vow none can break."

THE SQUARE HAD long since shed its banners and scrolls, its hollow decrees crumbled to dust. What remained was emptiness—an ache blooming in every chest, a gnawing that carved hollows in every belly. Yet from that stark emptiness came the first true oath of the new age.

They gathered around low tables carved from scavenged beams, surfaces scarred with chalk spirals and bound with fraying cloth. No bread crowned these makeshift altars. No grain lay golden in waiting bowls. Only mason jars pulsed with the dim amber of trapped fireflies, their gentle light catching on ribs sharp as cage-bars, on cheekbones that jutted like knife edges.

One child, thin as a reed, pressed his palm flat against the bare wood. "I will not hoard." His voice cracked with hunger's brittleness, yet it carried farther than any royal feast's laughter ever had. Another followed, fingers trembling like autumn leaves: "I will share until I have nothing left to give." More joined the chorus, their vows spilling into air that tasted of ash and desperate want:

I will feed a neighbor before I fill my own mouth.

I will not eat alone while others starve.

I will carry hunger with you, as you carry it with me.

The five bore witness as they always had:

• **Mira** sealed her ledger with deliberate care, pressing her black thumbprint across the cord—refusing to trap these living vows in dead words lest they calcify into the very decrees they had cast aside.

• **Nessa's** silver studs caught the firefly light as she leaned forward, her whisper cutting through the silence: "Better to hunger bound together than feast on plenty that divides us."

• **Rael** pressed his weathered scar against cold stone, counting each vow as heartbeat, as breath drawn, as the very rhythm of survival itself.

• **Karine** mapped the empty bowls with her cracked magnifying lens, naming each barren circle on the table as if it were an undiscovered continent awaiting her careful cartography.

• **Kess** sat among them this time, straps wound around her forearms like living cord, raw hands resting on the table itself. She cut one strip free with her blade and tied it around an empty bowl, binding absence as if it were weight. "Even hunger can be carried," she said, her voice rough with fatigue but steady. "But only if the load is shared."

And there too—woven invisibly through the hunger and the breath—lingered **Salliwith**. Not in cloth, for it was gone. Not in voice, for it was silenced. But in echo. Her absence pressed upon every vow like a hand upon the shoulder, quiet, magnanimous, magnificently enduring. Her gift was to make the hollow itself sacred.

When the last trembling voice fell silent, something extraordinary happened. The hunger itself transformed—no longer a weakness to be hidden, but a covenant to be shared. It spread across Threshold like a law older than any tribunal's judgment, binding as the breath that sustained them all.

No royal decree had written it into being. No banner proclaimed it from watchtowers. No scribe had recorded it in official ledgers.

Yet it held.

The vow of hunger had become the city's truest covenant—not carved in stone or inked on parchment, but etched in the hollow spaces between their ribs, sworn in the language of empty stomachs and open hearts.

Chapter 92

Ritual of Division

"To divide with witness is to multiply what remains."

AT FIRST, there had been chaos—desperate hands grabbing, shawls torn in frenzy, children clawing for crusts until nothing remained but bruises and the hollow silence of defeat. But from that shameful ruin, the people carved something sacred: a ritual as deliberate and reverent as any temple prayer.

They gathered at dusk in the Ash Market, where vendor mats had once sagged beneath the weight of plenty. Now only bowls of rough stone and fired clay marked the sacred center—empty vessels that became holy the moment they were ringed with white chalk and circled by strips of faded cloth.

When food appeared—a scrap of day-old bread, fruit bearing the purple thumbprints of bruising, a meager handful of boiled roots still steaming—it was placed in the bowls under the watchful amber glow of firefly lanterns. Division began not with grasping hands, but with careful words. Each portion was named aloud before a single finger touched it:

"This bread for the fever-sick."

"These roots for the bent-backed elders."

"This fruit for the hollow-cheeked children."

Each vow was spoken into air thick with shared hunger, each word reshaping how the meager feast would move through the community.

The five witnesses made the ritual law through their presence:

• **Mira** tapped her ledger shut with finality, refusing to trap this living ceremony in dead ink, but nodding gravely as each portion received its sacred assignment.

• **Nessa** stood sentinel with arms crossed, her silver studs catching the lantern light like stars, watching for the first flicker of greed with eyes sharp and unforgiving as blade edges.

• **Rael** whispered his steady count—one, two, three—his rhythm becoming the heartbeat that steadied each passing hand, each trembling reach.

• **Karine** drew rough maps of the bowl arrangement with stub chalk, tracing each vessel's position until the market itself became a living diagram of compassion.

• **Kess** sat cross-legged beside the bowls, straps wound tight around her work-scarred forearms. With deliberate care she tore one strip free and tied it around a cracked vessel, binding it as if to make absence itself endure. "Fiber fails when left alone," she said, voice hoarse but steady. "But bound to others, even emptiness can carry weight."

And though she was gone, **Salliwith's absence** weighed heavier than cloth ever could. Her bare shoulders, remembered, became part of the ritual itself. Every division was marked by the cost she had borne, her witness echoing in silence that no ribbon or ledger could replace.

When every morsel had been named and every portion assigned, a profound hush settled over the gathering. No one lifted food to lips until the witnesses drew breath together in unison. Only then did the meal begin—not a feast, never plenty, but enough to remind them all that division done in full sight of the community held more power than any decree bellowed from palace balconies.

The ritual could not banish hunger from their bellies or fill their children's cheeks with the glow of abundance.

But it ended the chaos. It replaced the shame of desperate scrambling with the dignity of deliberate sharing.

And in a world stripped of so much, that transformation was law enough.

Chapter 93

Children's Portion

"What the smallest hands choose becomes law for all."

It was the children who demanded their own share—not as charity bestowed by pitying adults, not as scraps thrown to the small and helpless, but as a right earned by their very existence in this hollow world.

They gathered in tight circles pressed low to the ground, mason jars casting trembling amber light across faces still round despite the hunger gnawing at them all. Their bowls were pulled close like shields, as if to test whether the adults' sacred ritual could withstand the scrutiny of those too young to remember abundance.

At first the elders hesitated, weathered hands hovering uncertainly—afraid of what small appetites might demand in a world where starvation lurked behind every meal. But the children spoke with crystalline certainty, hunger unsoftened by nostalgia for better days.

"We will divide for ourselves," announced one girl, her knees chalk-white from play turned solemn. Her voice carried the matter-of-fact tone of absolute truth. "So you can see exactly how we hold together."

The witnesses bent low to observe this unprecedented challenge:

• **Mira** kept her ledger firmly shut but pressed her ink-stained thumb against its leather spine—a silent acknowledgment that these young ones had earned the right to record their promises in breath and action rather than dead words on parchment.

• **Nessa's** silver studs and hammered charm caught the jar-light as she leaned forward, a knowing smirk playing at her lips—not mocking, but approving. "Let them prove themselves," she murmured. "Better their clean hands than ours, already stained with compromise."

• **Rael** whispered his steady count into the expectant hush, slowing it so each child could follow the sacred rhythm that governed all their sharing.

• **Karine** crouched close to the circle, her cracked magnifying lens fogging with her breath as she traced chalk arcs around their small bowls—naming each vessel sacred as altar stone. Under her breath she echoed what Salliwith had once given them all: "To witness always costs something." The words were no longer hers alone.

• **Kess** shifted forward, her palms scarred and strong, laying a strap across her knees. She tied its frayed end to one child's bowl and then to another, binding them together. "Even hunger can be held level," she said, her voice steady. "This strap carried burdens once. Tonight it carries fairness."

The children's method was startlingly simple and devastatingly pure: one precious scrap set aside for the fever-sick who could not leave their beds, one portion for those too weak to crawl to the market, one small offering for the shrine itself—a tithe paid without being asked. Only after these obligations were met did they claim what remained.

They did not fight over the remnants. They did not clutch portions to their chests in fear. Instead, they passed bread crusts between them like treasure, shared boiled roots like holy relics deserving reverence. Their small hands moved with a gravity that put adult ceremony to shame.

When at last they lifted food to their lips, their laughter rang out—thin as spider silk but bright as struck flint. That sound cut through the market's perpetual silence more sharply than any decree ever had. Even the Tribunal's hollow-cheeked remnants, bent low in the shadows, turned their faces away, unable to bear the quiet judgment it carried.

From that night forward, no ritual was considered complete without the children's portion. It became law not carved in marble or inked on scrolls, but etched in the steady movements of small hands and the unwavering clarity of young voices who had never known a world where sharing was optional.

And it held—perhaps more firmly than any adult promise ever could.

Chapter 94

Accord of Silence

"Silence becomes covenant when all breathe it together."

THE MARKET SQUARE had known many accords: ash scattered on bitter winds, cloth tied until it frayed, breath counted until it became rhythm. But none carried the profound weight of this night.

When the last scraps were gone and jars guttered low, the people gathered not to divide, not to chant, not to kneel. They gathered simply to be still.

Mira laid her ledger shut before her bent knees, ink-stained thumb pressed to its binding cord. She offered no words. Her refusal was testimony enough.

Nessa touched the silver studs at her ears, her father's charm brushing her jaw. For once her laughter fell away, leaving something sharper, steadier: reverence without noise.

Rael pressed his scar against the cold stair. His lips did not count, did not name. They only shaped breath itself, rhythm carried into the lungs around him.

Karine set down chalk and cracked lens. For once she did not map, did not name. She let the fractures remain untitled, a silence her map could not break.

Kess sat at the shrine with her scarred palms resting on the stiffened straps she had once bound into use. She did not tie, did not mend. She simply held the leather steady, alive in the hush, her body proof that invention could outlast noise.

And Salliwith—bare shoulders now gone to memory—lingered in absence. Her cost pressed upon them all like unseen cloth, the reminder that witness demands surrender until even silence is paid.

No one stepped forward to lead. No voice rose to decree. Even the children hushed their usual games until only the sound of lungs remained—inhale, exhale, a covenant written in breath.

The square itself seemed to lean inward, stones heavy with listening.

At the edges, the husked Tribunal sat in their ruins, condemned to silence not chosen but imposed. Their muteness was judgment; the people's quiet was law.

When dawn paled the marble, no word had been spoken for hours uncounted. Yet all knew what had been sealed: silence as bond, silence as strength, silence as law itself.

It was called the Accord of Silence.

And it held.

Chapter 95

Breathmark of Witness

"A breath shared becomes a record no ink can erase."

THE CIRCLE BEGAN NOT with decree or chant, but with the simple rhythm of lungs. One child drew breath slowly, then exhaled as if in prayer. Another matched it. A third followed. Soon dozens, then hundreds, until the whole square pulsed like the heartbeat of a vast, unseen body.

Mira did not open her ledger. She pressed her ink-black thumb to her cheek, marking herself not as Recorder but as witness among witnesses.

Rael counted softly, voice frayed but steady. *Seventeen. Four. Two.* The numbers steadied the rhythm, but the breath itself—shared, synchronized, sacred—was the deeper covenant.

Nessa stood upright at the circle's rim, her studs catching faint jar-glow. For once she did not laugh. Her chest rose and fell with the others, silent proof that law now lived in breath, not decree.

Karine traced wide spirals of chalk around their gathered bodies. Not maps of fracture this time, but arcs large enough to enclose them all—the geometry of air made visible.

Kess sat near the shrine, her scarred palms resting on its straps. When children pressed their hands to the stiffened leather, it seemed to creak in rhythm, as if even fiber remembered how to breathe.

Salliwith's absence ached, but strips of her vanished shawl fluttered from rails and posts. Each faint tremor of cloth joined their exhale, her witness still stitched into the night.

Above, the Guards lowered their staves and listened. On the dais, the Tribunal's seats sagged empty, shadows deepening like epitaphs.

No one spoke. No one needed to. Each careful inhalation confessed hunger endured; each exhalation promised endurance still to come. Children's lungs carried the rhythm bright and strong, elders' lungs wheezed like bellows, but together they inscribed one covenant:

The Breathmark.

Not written in ink. Not carved in stone. Recorded in the air itself.

When dawn touched the stair, the circle dissolved. But the record remained. Every chest that had risen, every lung that had joined, carried it forward like scripture too vast for any book to hold.

The city itself had become archive.

And the witness held.

Chapter 96

Ledger Refused

"Sometimes the blank page bears more weight than ink."

THE LEDGER LAY open in Mira's lap like a wound, its pale pages luminous in the last jar-light. Around her, silence lingered from the night's great circle—every chest that had risen and fallen together leaving invisible lines already written in the air.

She dipped her pen, lifted it above the page. The nib trembled—not from weakness, but from recognition. To trap the Breathmark in script would reduce it, shrink it into something smaller than it was.

"No," she whispered.

The sound rippled outward like a stone across still water. She closed the book with force, pressing her ink-stained thumb hard against the spine until the black crescent spread like a seal.

From the crowd came unease:

"If you do not write, how will it endure?"

"How will our children know?"

Mira raised the sealed ledger high. "Because it endures in us. In our lungs, not parchment. In silence freely chosen, not testimony compelled."

Rael pressed his cheek to stone and whispered the word that steadied him always: *Hold.* His vow ratified her refusal.

Nessa laughed, sharp but approving. "Even the Recorder knows when words get in the way of truth." Her earrings caught the faint light, glinting like witnesses of their own.

Karine crouched low, chalk snapping in her hand as she scrawled across the stair: **REFUSED.** The cracked lens on her brow caught the jar-light, turning denial into record.

No decree followed. No elder spoke against it. The refusal itself became law. The ledger shut, its blank pages heavier than any filled book could have been.

The people leaned into the silence.

And the silence held.

Chapter 97

Lanterns Beyond Oceans

"Light carries farther when borne by many hands."

THE SEA WAS black that night, heavy with salt and prayers unspoken. No beacon marked safe passage. No royal lantern burned on any tower. Only jars—once alive with fireflies, now filled with oil, tallow, or luminous moss—bobbed against the tide, their glow small but defiant.

It began at Threshold. Children carried vessels from the square to the river's edge, lighting scraps of cloth for wicks. They set them drifting, each flame a vow that silence would not be forgotten. The current bore them outward, scattering stars across the dark water.

From there the light multiplied. Bridges hung with ribbons gained their own lantern lines, trembling like constellations stitched across the city's wounds. Merchants carried jars aboard boats with no cargo but hope. Pilgrims tucked them into baskets, walking until river became delta, until river met sea.

In Havana, fishermen lowered jars into surf, watching them dance among breakers like freed constellations. In Aleppo, children placed them atop ruined walls, light falling into hollows where windows once framed sky. In Murmansk, sailors lashed jars to ice-rimmed docks, their glow stubborn even against the polar wind. In Jeddah, bright ribbons snapped from lantern handles, flames bending sideways yet refusing to die.

Each place renamed the light. Some whispered *seventeen, four, two* to the rhythm of waves. Others spoke only *hold,* letting the sea itself answer back. Everywhere the vow transformed—not chained to ledgers or decrees, but drifting in vessels low enough for any hand to touch.

Mira heard of the lanterns but refused to open her book. She pressed her thumbprint black against its spine and whispered, "Let it live in eyes, not ink."

Rael pressed his cheek to the wall, his vow carried outward on the salt wind.

Nessa stood high on the parapet, earrings flashing like twin sparks above the surf. She laughed, sharp with wonder: "The oceans belong to us now. Not to maps, not to empires. To light carried low enough for all to claim."

Karine traced their routes by glow, her cracked lens fogging in sea air. She drew no borders, only circles where flames gathered like stars come to rest.

Kess stood at the river's edge with her hands blackened from labor, guiding children as they lashed cloth to the jar handles. Her voice was rough but sure: "Keep them low, keep them steady. Even light must be bound before it can travel." The leather strap looped at her belt touched water first, tethering the first lantern before she released it to the current.

By dawn, the horizon itself was changed. No longer black sea against black sky, but a field of drifting lanterns—a second heaven, born of human hands.

Not decree.

Not verdict.

Only light, floating outward.

Law written on water.

Chapter 98

Ribbons on Bridges

"A strip of cloth can hold more weight
than stone."

THE BRIDGES SAGGED under years of flood and neglect,
their stones darkened by salt spray and the endless passage
of dragging knees across worn spans. Yet what truly kept
them from collapse was neither mortar nor imperial decree,
but ribbon—countless strips of cloth that bound them
stronger than any mason's art.

At each dawn's breaking, children scrambled barefoot to the
highest rails, tying strips torn from winter shawls, from
threadbare hems, from whatever precious cloth their families could spare. The river wind snapped the fabric like
battle banners, yet no royal emblem or noble crest adorned
them—only honest fray, proof of hard use, proof of witness
borne.

One bridge bore scarlet strips, each dipped in broth so thin
it was more memory than nourishment, the color of hunger
transformed into hope. Another fluttered with indigo rags
torn from Salliwith's final bolt—cloth still carrying her
ghost-scent of tilled earth and forge ash. Across the third

span, ribbons bleached bone-white by endless rain trembled like spectral hands raised in wordless chorus.

Travelers crossed with reverent slowness, calloused palms pressed to railings where fabric whispered secrets against weathered skin. Each deliberate touch became sacred vow: *Hold fast, endure all, return whole.*

At the central span's heart, Mira placed her leather ledger but left it sealed in silence. Above it, she knotted a single strip of cloth blackened with her own ink—the only mark she would permit the world to read. "This alone," she said to those who gathered close, "records all we need remember."

Rael dragged his broken body to the parapet's crumbling edge, pressing scarred cheek to ancient stone, counting not his labored steps but precious breaths: *seventeen, four, two.* Each exhale misted the morning air, and each ribbon seemed to dance in perfect rhythm with his whispered vow.

Karine crouched near, her ever-cracking lens raised like a prayer, sketching bridges not as mere spans of dressed stone but as living tapestries—woven crossings where cloth had replaced cold architecture with something warmer, more forgiving. She named them softly as her chalk traced their forms: *Bridge of Ash. Bridge of Hunger. Bridge of Witness Born.*

In the midst of it all, Nessa stood defiant and upright, shiny silver studs catching jar-light like captured lightning, her voice blade-sharp as she mocked the shadows of vanished Guards. "Your precious decrees dissolved in river water. Our humble ribbons hold stronger than all your dressed stone." Wild laughter answered her from both muddy banks.

When darkness finally claimed the sky, jar-bearers emerged like fireflies, lining every bridge with vessels of glass nestled between dancing cloth strips. The wind carried their combined radiance far downriver, so that even those too broken or weak to cross could witness light dancing above dark water—a constellation brought low enough to comfort.

It was whispered that the bridges had at last discovered their truest weight—not in quarried stonework or iron rein-forcement, but in offered fabric, in touching hands, in shared breath that bound stranger to stranger across the flowing divide.

Not verdict.

Not decree.

Only ribbons, knotted low and humble, carrying the wounded city safely across its own deepest fractures.

Chapter 99

The Strap Returned

"Even the strongest fiber frays, but bound together it holds."

THE RIBBONS MULTIPLIED across the scar and bridges, bright scraps fluttering like a thousand promises. Yet among them hung one darker thread: the last length of Kess's strap, worn smooth from years of binding, frayed to near breaking.

She held it in both hands, the leather trembling like something alive. For a moment she hesitated—this strap had borne children across floodwater, had hauled broken bodies from the Crawlways. It was the last tool she could still call her own.

Then she pressed it flat against the bridge rail, knotting it among the bright cloth. The leather looked dull beside the ribbons, but the crowd hushed as if seeing it blaze.

"This one held weight," Kess whispered, her voice raw as scraped stone. "Let it hold us still."

Children reached to touch it, small fingers tracing the scarred surface. Mira closed her ledger without a mark, ink refusing to lessen the moment. Karine circled the strap with chalk, writing one word: **Bond.**

Rael whispered hold, and the leather seemed to creak in answer.

Nessa tilted her chin high, earrings flashing. "Even the strongest fiber frays," she said. "But when it binds with the rest, it becomes law."

And so the strap, once sling and shrine, became ribbon too— woven into the city's memory, a final bridge of leather among cloth.

Chapter 100

Constellations Beyond Threshold

"Stars drawn low can guide more truly than those out of reach."

THRESHOLD HAD LONG BEEN MARKED by the familiar signs of their new covenant: mason jars pulsing with fireflies, bright ribbons snapping in the wind, chalk spirals traced on stone, and marble scars that had been transformed from wounds into sacred seams. But when night fell clear and cloudless, the people inevitably looked upward—only to remember with fresh ache that the ancient stars remained distant, indifferent, utterly untouchable by human hands.

So they made their own constellations instead.

Jar-bearers climbed the bridges and rooftops with careful purpose, setting their glass vessels in deliberate patterns that spoke of intention rather than accident: three lanterns along a crumbling parapet, four arranged in a protective circle around a silent shrine, five placed in a crooked line that playfully mimicked the hunter's belt their grandparents had once pointed out in clearer skies. Children laughed with pure delight as they named these new star-patterns—*The Broken Sling, The Shawl's End, The Ledger's Refusal, The Ribbon's Knot*. Each luminous shape held stories too fresh and immediate for ancient sky-myths, yet already strong enough to shine guidance through the encompassing dark.

Karine knelt at the marble stair's worn base, her cracked magnifying lens fogging with the warmth of her breath as she meticulously mapped every single point of light. Her chalk arcs connected rooftop to bridge, shrine to market square, until the entire city revealed itself as a living sky laid flat and accessible. "Constellations," she whispered with wonder, "but drawn at our own height, where we can reach them."

Mira watched this transformation unfold without once opening her leather ledger to record it. "What the ancients wrote in distant fire is too far from us to matter," she said, her ink-stained thumb pressing the familiar cover shut with finality. "But what we set burning here and now—this light we can actually reach when we need it most."

Rael whispered his eternal vow into the expectant silence —"*Hold*"—each familiar number of his sacred rhythm measured out carefully across the glowing points until the earthbound constellations seemed to pulse like the visible breathing of some vast, benevolent creature.

Nessa tipped her chin upward toward their handmade firmament, her earrings catching fragments of jar-light until they glittered like stars come down to earth. "Better our constellations than theirs," she declared with satisfaction. "At least these ones listen when we breathe, respond when we call."

From the most distant markets and settlements, word of the light carried outward like seeds on favorable wind—a luminous map that no empire could erase with decree or conquest. Pilgrims began tracing their way into the city by following these low stars rather than the high ones, reading patterns of glass and flame that told them they had finally reached a place where witness still lived and thrived.

Threshold became something unprecedented: not merely a scar of broken stone marking ancient failure, but a firmament deliberately remade at the height of three feet from the ground. Here were constellations stitched together from humble jars and scraps of cloth, stars placed low enough for any hand—child or elder, strong or frail—to reach up and touch their warmth.

Not tribunal verdict. Not royal decree. Not official proclamation.

Only light drawn into shapes that remembered what mattered, carried faithfully by those who refused to let their chosen silence remain shrouded in darkness.

Chapter 101

Circle Unbroken

"What holds once can hold again, if breath is shared."

THEY GATHERED where the Crawlways knit together like bones that had broken and learned a new shape. Stone there was smooth from years of knees and palms; rails shone with the grease of countless ribbons tied and retied. Chalk ghosts lingered in the seams. Jars breathed a low amber.

The circle was smaller now. Salliwith's strips still fluttered along the iron—prayers without the shoulders that once anchored them. Across the rail, a single dark length of leather—Kess's last strap—ran through the brighter cloth like a vein, quiet and strong.

Mira set her ledger in the dust and kept it closed, inked thumb pressed hard on the binding as if sealing breath inside. She did not speak.

Nessa took the rim, the only figure still upright. Her silver studs held the jar-light; her laugh, when it came, was softer than before, but it still cut clean. She lifted her chin, and the crowd steadied.

Rael leaned his scar to stone. The old rhythm moved in his mouth without need of voice—seventeen, four, two—and the nearest children caught it, passing the count outward on the tide of their lungs until it belonged to all.

Karine crouched and drew sheltering arcs around them, chalk curving like ribs. Through her cracked lens the glow broke into constellations laid low enough to touch.

New witnesses folded in—pilgrims from the delta, stray families from bridge-settlements, children who had learned the ritual from stone itself. Each tied a strip, set a jar, took a place. No herald called them. The city had taught them.

They breathed together.

Inhale: hunger's weight, the ache of names not spoken, the freight of cloth that had gone to other hands.

Exhale: the vow that nothing would be hoarded—not breath, not witness, not pain.

Above, no banners moved. The Tribunal seats, long abandoned, were only shadow. Overhead, their own low stars—lanterns and jars arrayed along parapets and rails—held the geometry of home.

The breath went round once. Twice. A third time, unbroken. Hands found rail. Foreheads touched stone. Ribbons lifted and settled as if the square itself were a chest rising and falling.

Mira kept the ledger sealed.

Nessa stood.

Rael's measure held.

Karine's arcs closed.

Salliwith's cloth whispered without her. Kess's strap did not fail.

When the final tide of air returned to where it began, every lung answered with the same quiet certainty:

The circle held.

No decree named it law. No ink pinned it down. Yet the covenant stood—the kind that lives in bodies and therefore cannot be edited away. What they had once kept through hunger and ash they could keep again, and again, for as long as breath consented to move among them.

They did not cheer. They did not pray. They only breathed, and let the city breathe with them.

Chapter 102

The Empty Dais

"What is forgotten in silence dies more completely than fire."

THE DAIS still stood at Threshold's crumbling edge, its marble surface spider-webbed with cracks like veins in brittle bone. Once it had borne the Triad in their robes of height and command. Now the three seats loomed vacant, not waiting for return, but hollow in the way ruins are hollow—stripped of all weight, all relevance, all breath.

Whispers lingered in the shadows about the rulers who had sat there: the Arbiter coughing his decrees into silence, the Magistrate pleading to ears that had already turned away, the Canonister shrieking pronouncements until his voice cracked like glass. Now children muttered their names only as curses scrawled in chalk, jokes that dissolved into laughter before they even finished the syllables.

The truth was plainer than stone: the Tribunal had not fallen to revolt, nor been toppled by riot. They had been husked—mocked, pitied, ignored—until their voices thinned to nothing. What remained were only shadows cast by empty chairs.

Mira refused to open her ledger. Her blackened thumb pressed against the spine with deliberate force. "Absence is record enough," she said. "Ink would only give them weight they no longer hold."

Nessa stood at the rim, silver studs catching jar-light, her laughter sharp as flint but emptied of cruelty. "Vanished? No. They collapsed under the echo of their own noise." She turned her back on the dais, as though to prove it did not deserve her gaze.

Rael pressed his scar to the stair and whispered hold—but never for them. His vow was for the circle that had endured in hunger and breath, not for rulers who had squandered both.

Karine crouched low, cracked lens fogging with her breath as she marked the dais with chalk. She drew one stark line across the platform and wrote a single word: Silence.

Then Kess stepped forward. Her palms were raw from labor, leather coiled between them like a vein cut from the earth itself. She knelt at the first wide crack that split the marble stairs. With steady hands she looped her strap through the break, knotting it tight until the stone itself seemed bound into witness. The leather groaned as it tightened, old fibers straining against a ruin too long ignored.

"Even stone needs binding," she said, voice low but sure. "Not to keep it whole, but so we remember where it failed."

Children rushed to her side, their own ribbons bright against her dark strap. They tied scraps into every fissure, mocking marble with cloth the Tribunal had always despised. Laughter flickered, but it was different now—not cruel, not triumphant, only certain. The dais was no longer throne or stage. It had been stitched into the same fabric as Crawlway scars and shrine rails, nothing more and nothing less.

No witness lit jars in the Tribunal's honor. No cloth was tied for them alone. The knots belonged to memory, not to rulers.

By dusk the once-mighty dais sagged beneath the weight of its own irrelevance, bound with straps and ribbons like a wound marked for healing rather than height. Above it, the empty chairs gathered dust. Below it, the people breathed in unison, bound not by decree but by the work of their own hands.

The Tribunal had not been conquered. They had been outlived.

And the final word was not judgment shouted from on high.

It was Kess's knot pulled tight, leather rasping against marble, proving that what frays alone can still hold when tied into witness.

Chapter 103

Accord of Silence II

"When silence repeats, it ceases to be pause and becomes covenant."

THE FIRST ACCORD of Silence had been born of exhaustion—lungs too weary to form words, voices too frayed to command. But silence, once discovered, revealed itself as law. And when twilight returned, the people chose it again—this time not as accident, but as covenant.

They gathered without summons, without decree. Cloth strips lay folded in weathered palms. Mason jars rested dim at their sides. Breath rose and fell like a tide, steady, deliberate, patient as prayer.

Mira set her ledger down in the dust and pressed her ink-black thumb hard against its cord. She did not open it. She did not explain. Refusal itself had become record.

Nessa stood tall at the circle's edge, studs faint with the last of the light. She smirked once, sharp as ever, then let her mouth close on silence. The hush rang louder than her laughter ever had.

Rael pressed his scarred cheek against stone. He whispered nothing. The children who had learned his rhythm breathed it forward for him, their lungs carrying the vow into the square until every chest echoed the old count without words.

Karine crouched low, cracked lens clouding with her breath. She drew chalk arcs around the circle—shapes without letters, signs without names. Blank geometry, silence traced into visibility.

Kess stepped forward among them, her raw hands binding a strip of cloth to the rail. She tied no emblem, marked no words. Only knots—stubborn, plain, enduring. When the leather groaned, she pressed her palm flat to steady it. "Even silence needs binding," she murmured, voice rough but whole. The knots answered in stillness, creaking as if they, too, breathed.

The people followed. They tied ribbons but left them blank. They placed jars but did not light them. They bowed low, their inhalations and exhalations weaving the square into one unbroken body. Silence thickened until even hunger hushed itself, until grief itself held its breath.

No word was spoken. No decree announced. Yet when dawn struck the marble stair, every witness knew the truth without doubt:

Silence had ceased to be accident. It had become law.

The Accord of Silence was chosen, confirmed, and kept.

Chapter 104

Breathing City

"When walls exhale, the city itself becomes witness."

AT FIRST IT existed only as whispered rumor spreading through the markets like wildfire: that the flooded Crawl-ways sighed audibly at dusk, that ancient stairwells drew breath like massive lungs carved from marble, that the ribbon-draped bridges trembled with a rhythm that had nothing to do with wind and everything to do with the steady pulse of inhale and exhale.

Then one night, when silence had settled deep as snow across the square, the impossible truth revealed itself to all who had gathered in witness.

Children crouched in perfect stillness, counting Rael's sacred rhythm against the cold stone beneath their knees. When their synchronized breathing reached that familiar cadence—*seventeen, four, two*—something extraordinary happened. The walls themselves answered their call. Air began moving through hairline cracks and ancient drainage channels in perfect unison with their living lungs, as if the city's bones had remembered how to breathe alongside its people.

Mira felt the miracle beneath her weathered palms as she pressed her leather ledger shut against the trembling marble —stone rising and falling as though each word she had deliberately refused to write had somehow been inscribed instead in the moving air itself, recorded in breath rather than ink.

Nessa laughed—not with her usual sharp mockery but with genuine awe, her silver earrings catching fragments of lantern-light as they trembled with wonder. "We don't simply live inside the city's boundaries," she whispered into the breathing darkness. "It lives and breathes inside us now."

Rael pressed his familiar scarred cheek against the wall and whispered his eternal *"Hold,"* and for the first time in memory the echo that came back was not from human mouths but from the masonry itself—stone and mortar carrying his vow deeper than any voice ever could.

Karine bent low over her work, her cracked magnifying lens fogging with excited breath as she traced new chalk arcs across Threshold's worn stairs. "Constellations," she murmured in amazement, "but woven from shared breath instead of distant stars."

Everywhere the witnesses looked, the miracle multiplied before their eyes: bright ribbons fluttering in perfect time with collective exhalation, mason jars flickering as invisible drafts pulled air through their broken glass, strips of shawl and lengths of sling-strap shivering as though touched by lungs vast and unseen but undeniably present.

For the first time since the devastating Pulse had shattered their world, the gathered people did not feel merely grounded to earth by gravity and grief. They felt carried, lifted, sustained by something larger than their individual struggles. Not by royal decree or official proclamation, not by the vanished Tribunal's hollow authority, not even by their own fragile human accords—but by the city itself choosing to draw breath alongside them, to join its ancient rhythm to theirs.

When dawn's first pale light touched the eastern horizon, the miraculous sound gradually ceased. The breathing walls fell silent again. But no one who had witnessed this transformation could doubt what they had experienced together.

The city had joined their covenant of silence and breath. The city itself had become alive with them, through them, because of them.

Not tribunal verdict. Not imperial decree. Not official proclamation written in gold ink on precious parchment.

Only breath shared freely until even the stone remembered how to live.

Chapter 105

Breathnote: Epilogue

"What holds in silence becomes the city's breath."

THE CITY HAD BEEN PULLED low, stretched thin, bound in hunger and cloth, carried by jars and vow.

Every strip, every mark, every shard of glass had asked its price.

Now the six threads lay side by side, no longer scattered, no longer alone.

The ledger closed in silence.

The earrings gleamed in ash-light.

The vow circled lungs like tides.

The cloth lay bare but not forgotten.

The straps hung broken, raised as shrine.

The maps widened until they touched the sea.

From these fragments, the city inhaled.

Not decree.

Not verdict.

Only breath—shared, low, unbroken.

And so Book II closed: not with a fall, not with a rise, but with a held breath waiting to be carried forward.

Toward what the city would become.

Toward the shape yet unseen.

Toward the long descent of memory into law.

Breathmark — The Held Shape

NOT VERDICT. Not decree.

Only silence bound.

The city held its breath, woven in ribbon, carried in jars, etched in chalk.

Walls exhaled, bridges trembled, lungs answered in unison.

Stone had spoken once. Now breath itself spoke.

And it waited—not for collapse, but for release.

Part Three

Book III - The Breath That Remains

Where witness endured beyond measure, and dignity did not bend.

Not ruins. Not remnants. Only the breath that endures.

Breathnote — The First Breath

"Not silence. Not decree. Only breath shared."

THE CITY EXHALED, slow and steady, as if the stones themselves had lungs.

Every fracture traced, every strip tied, every vow whispered had settled into rhythm.

What was once scattered now pressed close, a shape made whole by witness.

No banner flew. No council spoke.

The ground itself carried the weight of law.

And in that stillness, breath gathered—

not to end, but to begin again.

Chapter 106

The River Mouth

"Where covenant drifts to sea."

THE DELTA OPENED WIDE like a scar that had learned to sing. Where floodwater once gorged and receded in violence, the river now moved with a rhythm steady as lungs. Salt and silt braided together, curling through shallow channels where abandoned boats lay tilted on their sides, ribs exposed like relics of another age.

Cloth clung to the ruined docks—faded ribbons that had drifted downriver from Threshold's bridges, binding splintered timbers into strange new shrines. Mason jars bobbed against pilings, many broken, but even in their cracks light had pooled: oil lamps, moss embers, scraps of flame clinging stubbornly to glass that should not have held anything at all.

The air here carried both hunger and promise. Ash taste lingered on the tongue, yet wild reeds grew thick in the marsh, pushing their green shoots upward through blackened mud. Stone stairs, once cut for imperial patrols, sagged low into water where children now launched jars as lanterns, sending them toward the sea as if to chart constellations on the tide.

The city's breath reached this far. Each wave against the banks exhaled, each reed bent in rhythm, each gull's wing-beat fell into cadence. The mouth of the river no longer marked boundary or end. It became threshold—the place where covenant left the square and entered the world.

No banners rose.

No verdicts rang.

Only breath, carried outward by water until even the ocean seemed to wait for it.

Chapter 107

The Cistern's Crack

"Thirst shortens patience faster than hunger."

THE CISTERN HAD SPLIT a finger's width along its belly, thin as a cruel smile. All morning the city gathered to watch water count itself—one bead swelling, a hesitation, then the fall. Stone remembered each drop with a bruise, marking an abacus of need along the wall.

No banner hung to name the crisis. No decree explained distribution. Only the square, the rail, the chalk marks, and jars breathing low under tarps, saving their light for night.

Mira sat already on the Low Bench, ledger sealed against her knees. She pressed her black thumb into its spine as if to seal silence into law. "We divide by breath," she said, not loud but certain. "Not by fear."

Karine leaned her cracked lens against the cistern's lip and marked the stone with blunt honesty—short white dashes at knuckle, palm, and elbow height. She drew a final line at three feet: the city's truest measure. "Law begins where bodies meet walls," she said.

Rael pressed his scarred cheek to plaster beside the leak, whispering his rhythm into the falling bead. "Seventeen... pause... four." The crowd matched his breath. "Two." He tapped twice. A ladle tipped. Water moved.

They called it the Weight-of-Water division before noon was over. Not new law—only old mercy taking new shape.

Children formed the first ring, bowls low. Elders knelt behind them, hands open to prove nothing hidden. The Untethered lingered restless at the edges.

Nessa stood sharp in the sun, mother's silver studs in each ear flaring, father's single charm brushing her right cheek. She did not glance at the Tribunal's hollow dais. She kept her eyes on the crack. When a man from the Upperways tried to shove forward, Mira rose only to one knee. "She drinks when her turn comes," she said. The murmur bent toward assent. Rael said "Hold," and the drip silenced more than any gavel.

Kess moved among the children, a coil of damp ribbons looped through her belt. Her hands, scarred from years of leather, showed them how to thread cloth through each bowl-handle, how to knot it tight enough that no one could double back and steal a second measure. She tied each strip with deliberate patience, then let small hands try, correcting them only with the tilt of her callused fingers. "Water slips," she murmured, "but knots remember." The phrase passed through the square like breath itself.

The work steadied the people: Karine's chalk set the pace, Rael's rhythm kept time, Mira's thumb sealed witness, Nessa kept the line true, and Kess's knots made each share visible. Even the restless Untethered had to admit the ties held firmer than threat.

By dusk, bowls bore their ribbons like fragile standards. The drip slowed, the queue thinned, and the last cloth strip fluttered dark with wet. Mira pressed her thumb to Karine's lowest chalk mark. "Witness taken," she said. "No words."

The jars were covered, the light banked. Children traced spirals around the cistern's base, chalk dust smearing into their hands like flour.

Kess sat back on her heels, breath heavy, her palms raw but steady. She looked at the children's knots—crooked, imperfect, but holding—and allowed herself the faintest smile.

"Tomorrow," Nessa said into the fading air. "We pour again."

And the city exhaled, bound not by decree or parchment, but by ribbons wet with need, knots tied by living hands, and water measured to the rhythm of lungs.

Chapter 108

The Narrow Feast

"Hunger teaches what abundance forgets."

THE MARKET WAS NO MARKET. No grain bins stood, no shouting traders, no bright cloth to tempt an eye. Only stone, smoothed by bodies dragging themselves lower each season, and the hush of bowls scraped clean days ago.

Yet they called it feast.

Not for food—there was none to warrant the word. But for the act, the rhythm, the ritual. Even scraps gain weight when divided by law.

Children chalked the ground into rough circles, each one smaller than the last, spirals tightening until only a hand-span remained at center. A single bowl was set there, empty but waiting, as if to remind them all what fullness once meant.

Mira sat nearby, her ledger bound and sealed, thumb black against the cord. She refused to trap hunger in ink. "Some pages," she whispered, "must stay blank. Absence holds its own truth."

Rael leaned his scarred cheek against the cold pillar at the market's edge. "Seventeen," he breathed. "Four. Two." Each number stretched thin as famine, but still he gave it. The crowd answered with lungs, not voices.

Karine crouched with her cracked lens, sketching the stalls that no longer held anything. She named them nonetheless, her chalk catching dust on stone: Stall of Salt. Empty Grain. Shadow Jar. Names for what was gone, because even absence demanded record.

Nessa stood tall, earrings catching the last of daylight like defiant sparks. A man muttered, "She laughs at our hunger." He was wrong. She did not laugh. She bit it back. Restraint was her witness, and it cost her more than words.

At the rail, children lifted what strips of Salliwith's cloth remained—faded, fraying—and dipped them in broth so thin it carried only scent. They pressed the damp witness to their lips before tying it back. No taste, only ritual, yet eyes closed as if threads alone could sustain.

Kess moved among them in body, alive and scarred, her palms callused from years of binding. She knelt with the youngest, showing them how to knot ribbons steady against bowls and rails, her hands correcting theirs with patient care. "Hunger frays quicker than cloth," she murmured. "That's why we bind." Each knot held not food but promise, and the children touched her wrists as if to steady themselves with her strength. Her last strap hung beside her, salt-stiff and worn, proof that labor could endure even when bellies did not.

They called it feast because each one took nothing, yet none left empty. Breath was portioned where bread was not. Silence carried weight when bowls could not.

By nightfall, a murmur traveled the Crawlways—children passing the word as if it were sweet: *We feasted.* The sound filled more than mouths.

Above, no banners stirred. Below, chalk spirals glowed pale under jar-light. Between them, the city breathed into hunger and called it law.

Not abundance.

Not banquet.

Only the narrow feast that proved they still remained.

Chapter 109

Ritual of Division

"To divide is not to diminish, but to remember."

THEY GATHERED NOT in the market, but in the long shadow of the cistern, where water once dripped steady enough to be measured. Now it left only a damp scar on stone. Hunger, like thirst, had learned to sit among them as a guest who would not leave.

The bowls were set in a circle. Not full, not empty—each held a crust, a boiled root, a shred of cloth dipped in broth so thin it carried only scent. What mattered was not the portion but the act: each offering laid down where all could see, no hand hidden, no bowl concealed.

Mira refused to open the ledger. She bound its cord tighter, thumb blackening the knot until the stain cut into leather. "Ink will not decide this," she murmured. "Breath will."

Rael bent close to the floor, scar pressed to cold tile, whispering the cadence that had become their measure: Seventeen. Four. Two. Each pause was a division; each number, a portion. The rhythm spread through lungs until even the faintest sigh aligned with his count.

Karine marked arcs around each bowl with her cracked lens, the glass fogging in the cool air. Chalk circled crumbs as if they were altars. She named them softly—First, Second, Third—not of rank but of order, a map of survival drawn in dust.

Nessa kept watch at the edge, earrings catching low jar-light, silver sparks flaring like warnings. When a man pressed forward, hand closing over more than his share, she lowered herself to her knees so his greed seemed taller than it was. "Take it," she said evenly, "but every eye here will see the size of your hunger." He let the portion fall.

Children enforced the ritual with cruel precision:

"Ribbon shows—move on."

"Count with the wall or go without."

"One bowl, one breath."

Their voices were merciless, but merciless in the way gravity is: exact, unbending.

Salliwith's rail still bore its fluttering strips; one was dipped in broth and tied back wet, dark against stone. Beside that memory, Kess worked, gloves marked with chalk, a coil of straps slung across her shoulder. She cut them into narrow lengths and knotted each bowl after its share was measured —knots plain, visible, undeniable. Her motions were steady, exacting, each tie a seal against want.

"Fiber holds where flesh frays," she said, voice rough but unshaken. "Let the knots show what words cannot."

When the last portion was divided, no one was satisfied. But no one was forgotten. The ritual had held.

And it was this holding—more than fullness—that gave the city its law.

Not decree.

Not verdict.

Only division made sacred by witness.

UR-IX: The Widow's Step

(Upper Registers — Depositions of the Untethered)

He had only to speak the words. He was a commander once. I heard him give orders that cut deeper than blades. Orders meant to break men, to kill them slow. He thought words were not weapons. The Pulse proved otherwise.

The day it came, he dropped at my feet. My husband, face to the earth, hands clutching empty air. I did not fall beside him.

I am Untethered, they say. I wish I were not. Survival tastes like betrayal. I stood only because I never meant harm. Not once. I spoke harshly, I turned cold—but never with the weight of killing behind it.

Now when I walk, I take small steps, knees bent, as if I too were bound low. My neighbors see pity. It is not. It is penance.

He meant to kill. I did not. That difference keeps me upright, and keeps me from peace.

Interlude X— The Bell Foundry

"Metal remembers the sound it once carried."

THE FOUNDRY HAD GONE cold long before the Pulse. Its furnaces stood as hollow husks, molds choked with ancient soot. Bells lay shattered across the floor, their bronze mouths brimming with rainwater, their silence heavier than any sound they had ever cast.

Children moved among the ruins like scavengers, gathering bronze shards in small, careful hands. Over crackling fires, they melted these pieces of the past, pouring the liquid metal into clay jars and weaving it into cloth strips— remnants of what had once summoned armies to war. No clarion call would ever ring from these scraps again.

But when a jar pulsed with captured firefly-light, steadied by threads of bell-metal, its glow ran deeper than mere illumination. The light seemed anchored to something older, something that remembered.

A boy crouched among the broken bronze, his voice barely a whisper: "Let the bells keep their silence."

And so they did. The city no longer needed their sound—it had learned to carry its own music in the quiet spaces between heartbeats, in the gentle pulse of makeshift lanterns, in the footsteps of children who built light from the ashes of noise.

Chapter 110

The Children's Law

"What is claimed without pity becomes unshakable."

THEY GATHERED NOT in the market, but in the long shadow of the cistern, where water once dripped steady enough to be measured. Now it gave only a damp scar on stone. Hunger, like thirst, had learned to sit among them as a guest who would not leave.

The bowls were set in a circle. Not full, not empty—each held a scrap, a crust, a boiled root, a shred of cloth dipped in broth so thin it barely carried scent. What mattered was not the portion but the act: each offering laid down where all could see, no hand hidden, no bowl concealed.

Mira refused to open the ledger. She bound its cord tighter, thumb blackening the knot until the stain cut into leather. "Ink will not decide this," she murmured. "Breath will."

Rael leaned close to the floor, scar pressed to cold tile, whispering the cadence that had become their measure: Seventeen. Four. Two. Each pause was a division; each number, a portion. The rhythm spread through lungs until even the faintest sigh aligned with his count.

Karine traced arcs around each bowl with her cracked lens, the glass fogging in the cool air, chalk circling crumbs as if they were altars. She named the lines softly—First, Second, Third—not of hierarchy, but of order, a map of survival drawn in dust.

Nessa watched from the edge, her earrings catching low jar-light, silver sparks flaring like warnings. When a man tried to press forward, hand closing over more than his share, she stepped into the circle—not laughing, not mocking, but lowering herself to her knees so his greed looked taller than it was. "Take it," she said evenly, "but every eye here will see the size of your hunger." He let the portion fall.

Children enforced the ritual with cruel precision:

"Ribbon shows—move on."

"Count with the wall or go without."

"One bowl, one breath."

Their voices were merciless, but merciless in the way gravity is: honest, without exception.

Salliwith's rail still bore its fluttering strips; one was dipped in broth and tied back wet, dark against stone. Beside her memory, Kess crouched low, gloves chalk-dusted, a bundle of straps across her lap. She cut them thin and tied one to every bowl after its share was measured—visible knots proving each portion was sealed. Her motions were steady, deliberate, each knot a seal against want.

"Fiber holds where flesh frays," she said, voice rough but certain. "Let the knots show what words cannot."

When the last portion was divided, no one was satisfied. But no one was forgotten. The ritual had held.

And it was this holding—more than fullness—that gave the city its law.

Not decree.

Not verdict.

Only division made sacred by witness.

Chapter 111

Accord of Silence

"When voices rest, breath itself becomes agreement."

THE SQUARE FILLED but did not roar. No chants, no shouts, no demands. Only the soft shuffle of knees lowering to stone, as if gravity itself had called assembly.

The Accord began not with words but with quiet.

Mira did not open her ledger; she laid it flat on the bench, cord tied, as if to declare that no ink would own what was about to pass. Her thumb rested black against the spine, a seal that said: this silence is its own record.

Rael leaned his scar against the wall, counting inward instead of outward. Seventeen. Four. Two. The numbers stayed in his chest. His lips barely moved, but those nearest breathed with him, lungs finding rhythm until the whole square inhaled as one, exhaled as one.

Karine pressed her cracked lens to the floor and drew no map. Instead she traced a single unbroken line of chalk circling the assembly, a boundary to mark the silence sacred. Beside it she wrote one word: Hold.

Kess sat among the bowls, her gloves dusted white. She threaded narrow strips of leather through the handles and tied each knot slow and deliberate, as if fastening silence itself to the circle. "Fiber steadies even when voices fray," she whispered, not to command but to remind. Hands nearest her followed the example, binding scraps of cloth to bowls and rails until the hush itself was cinched tight.

Nessa stood at the rim, Untethered still, earrings gleaming like fragments of fallen stars. Her laughter, sharp as ever, did not rise. She crossed her arms, bowed her head, and let silence claim even her defiance. For once, her refusal to mock was itself a vow.

From Salliwith's shrine, cloth strips barely clung, thinned to threads. A boy untied one and pressed it flat against his mouth—not to silence himself, but to show that witness, too, had chosen quiet.

The Guards—those who remained, stripped of staves and hollow of command—stood at the stair's edge, waiting for noise to break. It did not. They lowered themselves, awkward, crawling into the circle, unwilling to remain outside its law.

No leader named the terms. No council called for hands. The Accord bound itself in breath. In its hush, hunger was acknowledged, loss carried, witness shared. What could not be said was still spoken—etched in lungs rising and falling together.

When at last the jar-bearers lifted their vessels, the fireflies inside pulsed once, twice, three times with Rael's count. The silence deepened, then broke like dawn.

Not decree. Not command. Only silence, chosen together—
an accord that held without a single word.

Chapter 112

Breathmark of Witness

"To witness is to breathe twice: once for
the self, once for the other."

THE SILENCE of the Accord did not dissolve when dawn
returned. It settled deeper—into lungs, into ribs, into the
cadence of ordinary movement. Each step, each pause, each
hand laid upon stone carried the weight of having been
truly seen.

In the Crawlways, children traced spirals no longer as
games but as signatures—marks that declared, I was here. I
breathed this air. I remain. Their chalk smudged quickly in
the damp, but dust clung to knees and palms like benediction, proof enough of presence.

At the shrine, jar-bearers lit their vessels one by one in
wordless procession. The rhythm of firefly light pulsed
steady against encroaching dark, echoing Rael's vow
without sound. Witness required no voice—only the trembling constancy of being.

Mira refused ink again, yet this time she placed her ledger
openly on the Low Bench, spine exposed, thumb-mark stark

against worn leather. One by one, the people pressed their hands beside it—not to turn pages, but to leave smudges, fingerprints, the silent signatures of those who refused to vanish into forgetfulness.

Karine bent low over her cracked lens, chalk trembling between weathered fingers. She mapped no fractures this time, but faces instead—crooked lines for mouths that had spoken truth, gentle arcs for brows furrowed in thought, spirals where eyes had met hers in recognition. Not portraits, not careful likeness, but breath-marks: evidence of souls encountered.

Even Nessa stood apart, Untethered still, her silver earrings catching dawn's first light. Yet when a child approached with indigo cloth, she bowed her proud head, allowing small fingers to tie the strip around her wrist—bright color against pale skin. She neither protested nor laughed. The mark bore witness enough.

Rael pressed his palm to cold stone and whispered Hold into the wall's ancient ear. The word carried no echo, but those nearest breathed with him, their exhale stretching his vow into something larger, more enduring. No command rang forth, no decree was proclaimed—only breath, shared and multiplied like loaves among the faithful.

From that morning forward, the law was not written in marble, nor sealed in scroll, nor carved into any ledger's unforgiving pages. It lived instead in breath—quiet, constant, passed from lung to lung like sacred flame.

Witness had become the city's final scripture.

Not verdict. Not decree.

Only the breath that remained, carrying truth for all who still endured.

Chapter 113

Ledger Refused

"A blank page can weigh more than one filled with words."

THE LEDGER LAY UNOPENED on the Low Bench, its leather cord wound so tightly that even Mira's ink-blackened thumb could not undo the knots without drawing blood. All through the morning, people stole glances at it—waiting for her to loosen the binding, to give shape to their silence in the terrible permanence of ink.

She did not.

A boy, emboldened by the crowd's restless murmuring, stepped forward. "Recorder, why won't you write what we've seen?"

Mira's gaze fell on him—not stern, but steady as stone. "Because once I write it, it ceases to belong to you. Ink devours breath. What we have now, this living thing, must remain ours alone."

The crowd shifted uneasily, boots scraping against worn stone. For years, they had trusted her to hold memory, to preserve what might otherwise crumble into forgetting. But the ledger had grown too heavy, too dangerous. If authority could seize words from pages, then silence became their only sanctuary.

Karine crouched nearby, chalk trembling in her weathered fingers. "Then I will draw what you refuse," she offered. Her hand moved in urgent strokes across the stone—faces that had witnessed, spirals that remembered, vessels that held light against the dark. But even as she worked, her marks smudged under the press of passing bodies.

She paused, studied the blurred shapes, and something like relief crossed her features. "Perhaps this is right. Maps should fade, so we might redraw them truer each time."

Near the wall, Rael pressed his scarred cheek to ancient plaster—bone against stone—whispering his litany not as record but as living vow: *Seventeen. Four. Two.* His breath fogged faintly against the surface, vanishing before eyes could capture it.

"Memory isn't ink," he murmured to those who leaned close. "It's the air we share, the rhythm we breathe together."

From the crowd's edge, Nessa watched with calculating eyes, her silver earrings catching jar-light like trapped stars. "So we abandon all books?" Her voice cut through the reverent hush—more challenge than question. "We burn every page because truth might slip from hand to hand?"

Mira did not flinch. She touched the ledger's worn spine once, fingers lingering on cracked leather, then pushed it across the bench for all to witness.

"Keep it," she told them, her voice carrying to the farthest listeners. "But do not open it. Let its weight remind you what silence has saved."

A deeper hush followed—deeper than any written law. One woman pressed her palm against the book's cover, leaving a ghost-print of dust and sweat on leather. Another laid a strip of indigo cloth across its binding, as if to shroud silence in ceremony. One by one, others approached: pressing hands, laying ribbons, even scattering breadcrumbs across its surface.

Before their eyes, the ledger transformed—no longer archive, but altar.

When jar-bearers raised their flickering lights that evening, casting dancing shadows on the gathered faces, Mira spoke only once more: "Not everything belongs to the page. Some truths breathe freer without the cage of ink."

And for the first time in generations, the people understood that memory could survive unwritten—alive in shared breath, in protective silence, in witness carried body to body like sacred flame.

Not decree. Not verdict.

Only refusal, held fast against the world—heavier than any words could ever be.

Codex XIII – The Law of Refusal

"Silence itself became protection."

WHEN TRIBUNALS DEMANDED TESTIMONY, many chose not to answer.

When markets demanded oaths, many remained silent.

Refusal became its own law:

• What is refused cannot be corrupted.

• What is unsaid cannot be twisted.

This was not weakness.

It was strength through silence.

Interlude XI – The Orchard of Breath

"Trees count longer than ledgers."

BEYOND THE CRAWLWAYS, where salt once spoiled the soil, an orchard still stood. Its trees bore no fruit, only twisted limbs and bark cracked from thirst. Yet children pressed their palms to trunks and spoke Rael's rhythm into the wood.

Seventeen. Four. Two.

Each tree inherited a count, a name. Their game became ritual: racing between branches in cadence, chanting until lungs burned. Hunger turned into chant, and chant into law.

Adults followed in silence, watching. No fruit was gathered, but dignity grew in the counting. The orchard endured, not by abundance, but by breath.

UR-X: The Parent at the Rail

(Upper Registers — Depositions of the Untethered)

MY DAUGHTER WAS ten when the Pulse arrived. She had carried a kitchen knife once, whispering vengeance after being struck at school. I saw her then, small and furious, blade trembling in her hand. Intent shone through her like flame. I took the knife away—but the Pulse remembered.

When the ground changed, she dropped. Forever.

I stood, the knife still in the drawer, untouched. I had never meant harm.

Now I live at her height. Chairs cut low, tables sawn short, bedding pulled down to the floor. I kneel each night at the rail of her cot, whispering stories so she does not feel alone.

I could stand, but she could not. So I chose her height.

Chapter 114

Lanterns Beyond Oceans

"Light carries farther when borne by many hands."

THE SEA LAY black that night, vast and breathing, its waves rolling like the ribs of some ancient, slumbering giant. No stars pierced the clouded horizon. No ship's lantern marked safe harbor. Only the jars—transformed now into vessels of light—floated steady against the restless tide.

They had begun as whispers in Threshold, small offerings left trembling at the stair, then carried outward like dandelion seeds on wind: across stone bridges, through crowded markets, up to moonlit rooftops. From there, pilgrims and merchants bore them downriver, past broken docks and fractured ports, until at last they reached the patient, waiting sea.

Each lantern carried its own beating heart:

• Some held fireflies captured at dusk, their ancient rhythm pulsing through clouded glass like trapped starlight

• Others flickered with salvaged oil and braided wicks torn from old cloth

• A precious few glowed with luminous moss gathered from forgotten caves—faint as whispers, yet unyielding as hope

• All bound with ribbon or marked with chalk, each one a promise humble enough for any hand to keep

In distant Havana, weathered fishermen lowered them into churning surf, watching points of light bob and weave like constellations torn loose from heaven's vault. In war-scarred Aleppo, children balanced them atop shattered walls, their glow catching the broken teeth of ancient stone. In frozen Murmansk, sailors lined ice-crusted docks with trembling flames that guttered but refused to die against the polar wind's fury. In golden Jeddah, desert gusts bent their flames like prayer, yet still the light endured, stubborn as faith against encroaching dark.

The vow traveled with them across trackless waters. Some whispered Rael's sacred cadence—*seventeen, four, two*—counting waves instead of heartbeats. Others spoke only one word, breathed like benediction: *Hold.* The sea carried that single syllable farther than any sail, deeper than royal decrees, beyond the edges of every map ever drawn.

Mira, hearing tales of lanterns crossing impossible oceans, closed her ledger with finality and pressed her blackened thumb hard against its spine. "This cannot be written," she told those who still asked for records. "It must be lived, must be seen with your own salt-stung eyes."

High atop a harbor parapet, Nessa stood silhouetted against the star-drunk sky, her silver earrings catching moonlight like fragments of hammered starfire. "The oceans belong to us now," she called out, her laughter sharp and wild as a storm-petrel's cry. "Not to their maps. Not to their decrees. Light drifts farther than any law they can forge."

Through her ever-cracking lens, Karine traced these impossible paths across her expanding map, the glass fogged with salt spray and wonder. She marked no borders now, no boundaries of empire—only gentle circles where light had gathered like schools of luminous fish, drawing coastlines not of conquest but of witness shared.

And always, Rael pressed his scarred cheek to cold stone, whispering his rhythmic vow to the eternal tide. The sea answered in kind—breath matching breath, endless and unbroken as the turning of worlds.

By dawn's first blush, the horizon blazed with ten thousand lanterns drifting in long, graceful arcs across dark water—an ocean of earthbound stars, low enough to touch, bright enough to guide any lost soul home.

Not verdict. Not decree.

Only light, carried farther than oceans, deeper than any darkness dared to reach.

Chapter 115

Bridges of Witness

"What cloth remembers, stone forgets."

By the time lanterns had vanished seaward, the bridges themselves had become altars. No longer crossings alone, they were places where silence gathered, where breath was measured against the weight of stone and found stronger.

The ribbons still clung, frayed and faded, yet each strip spoke of hands that had tied them long before. Hunger-colored red, ash-scented indigo, rain-bleached white—all trembled together in the night wind, a language of cloth no decree could erase.

Pilgrims came without haste. Some pressed their cheeks to weathered rails, leaving warmth where cold had endured too long. Others added nothing, only touched what was already tied, whispering vows into knots they would never know who first made.

Mira brought no words. Her ledger remained closed, her thumb dark against its spine. Instead she pressed a single strip of blackened cloth low against the stone, refusing to raise it higher, declaring in silence: witness belongs where every hand can reach.

Rael leaned into the arch and let his rhythm fall into breath alone. *Seventeen, four, two*—not counted now, but breathed until others around him echoed unconsciously, lungs joined in unison, the bridge itself seeming to hum with their vow.

Karine's cracked lens caught only fragments, yet she lowered her chalk to mark the parapet with new names: not fractures this time, but spans redeemed—*Bridge of Ash. Bridge of Hunger. Bridge of Witness.* Circles instead of lines, bonds instead of borders.

And Nessa, Untethered still, stood tall against the jar-light's glow, her silver studs catching fire like twin sparks. She did not laugh sharply this night. Her voice carried steady, low, and sure: "These knots hold where their decrees drowned. Cloth remembers. Stone forgets."

When darkness pressed deepest, children loosed fireflies into the air above the spans. Their glow threaded between ribbons, constellations born low enough to be touched, high enough to guide. For a moment, it seemed the bridges themselves breathed—stone, cloth, and lungs aligned in one patient rhythm.

No gavel echoed here. No Tribunal thundered. The bridges bore their own testimony.

Not verdict.

Not decree.

Only witness—bound in ribbons, carried in breath, stronger than stone.

Chapter 116

Constellations Beyond Threshold

**"When the ground is too heavy, we draw
our maps in stars."**

NIGHT OVER THRESHOLD was never truly dark. The Crawlways flickered with jar-light like scattered prayers, the bridges rippled with ribbons that snapped in wind like muted temple bells, and the shrines glowed softly with cloth dipped in consecrated ash or blessed broth. Yet above it all, the sky remained vast, indifferent, and achingly whole.

It was the children who dared claim it first.

On moonlit rooftops they gathered in breathless conspiracy, tipping glass jars upside down with ceremonial care, releasing clouds of captured fireflies into the boundless night. The insects rose in wild, uneven patterns—some darting swift as startled thoughts, others drifting slow as lazy prayers—but together they stitched glowing arcs across the darkness, weaving low constellations from nothing more than fragile wings and stubborn light.

"That cluster's ours!" one boy shouted with fierce joy, pointing toward insects hovering like fallen stars above the Tribunal's long-abandoned hall. A girl with chalk-dusted fingers began tracing star-shapes across roof tiles, her marks echoing the drifting lights above. They named their creations with fearless invention, voices ringing clear: *The Scar, The Ribbon, The Witnessed Hand.*

Far below, Mira stood in shadow with her ledger pressed tight against her heart like armor. "This is the record I cannot keep," she whispered to the patient stones, "the one that belongs only to the sky itself." Her ink-stained thumb left its familiar mark on worn leather, but the book remained sealed, its secrets safe within.

At the stair's weathered base, Rael leaned his scarred cheek against ancient stone, whispering his sacred cadence into the wall's listening ear: *seventeen, four, two.* With each repetition, the fireflies above seemed to pause in their wandering, their scattered light flickering in perfect synchrony with his breathed vow, as if the sky itself had learned to count his rhythm.

Karine knelt on a crumbling parapet, her ever-cracking lens tilted toward heaven's vast archive. She raised trembling chalk to stone, then stopped—her map was already blurred with too many desperate lines, too many failed attempts to capture the un-capturable. Instead, she exhaled slowly and marked only one word beside her tangled sketches: *Endure.*

Higher than any earthbound soul dared climb, Nessa perched on a wind-carved ledge, silver earrings blazing like twin beacons in the jar-light's glow. She lifted her proud chin toward the star-drunk sky and spoke to the listening night: "Your decrees crumbled into ash and memory, but our stars refuse to fall." The laughter that followed her words rang sharp yet joyous—not cruelty, but relief finally given voice after too long silence.

By midnight's deepest hour, Threshold had found its reflection in the heavens: bridges woven from ribbons of light, jars transformed into living constellations, hunger and silence and witness stretched across infinite sky like new law written in patient starfire.

The city below had birthed its own heaven—close enough to touch, eternal enough to last.

Not decree. Not verdict.

Only constellations, low enough to belong to broken hands, high enough to endure beyond any earthly power's reach.

Chapter 117

Circle Unbroken

"What closes is not ending, but return."

THEY GATHERED ONCE MORE where the Crawlways crossed, in that same worn hollow where the first desperate circle had formed in the early days of collapse. The ancient stone still bore faint spirals drawn by children's hopeful hands—half-worn by countless seasons but never truly erased. Ash stains lingered like prayers on the weathered rail, cloth scraps clung by stubborn knots that refused all dissolution, and jar-light pulsed softly where glass vessels had been placed so often the stone itself remembered their sacred shapes.

This time, the circle did not begin with trembling fear or desperate need.

This time, it began with homecoming.

Mira placed her leather ledger at the hollow's heart but left it sealed in reverent silence, its spine darkened by her faithful thumb. She made no claim of authority, spoke no words of power. She simply let it rest as witness—nothing more, nothing less than proof they had endured.

Rael pressed his scarred cheek to that same listening wall, whispering his rhythm softer now—seventeen, four, two— no longer struggling to hold himself upright, but weaving the scattered breaths around him into one sacred cadence. Without command or coercion, the gathered crowd began to echo his count, lungs moving in perfect unison as though the vow itself had seeped into bone and marrow.

Karine crouched low with her eternally cracking lens, chalk trembling like a prayer between weathered fingers. But instead of mapping fractures or tracing breaks, she drew one single, encompassing circle around them all—no names inscribed within its boundary, no divisions marked, no hierarchies drawn. Just one unbroken line that declared in silent eloquence: here we stand together, here we choose to remain.

Kess moved among the children, gloves faintly dusted with chalk, a bundle of straps across her lap. She showed them how to tie short lengths into the chalked boundary, her gestures patient, her knots deliberate. "Fiber holds where flesh frays," she said quietly. "Let the knots show what words cannot." Each child repeated her motion, binding hunger and witness into the circle until it became more than chalk—woven, visible law.

In the gentle jar-light's glow, Nessa stood tall and proud, her silver earrings and the single charm, catching radiance like earthbound constellations. She offered no sharp mockery, no cutting laughter, but let the profound silence rest on her shoulders like a crown finally claimed. "Once we were scattered and divided," she said, her voice soft as falling ash, "but see how we are all still here, still breathing, still choosing to gather."

From Salliwith's distant shrine, a final strip of precious cloth was carried forward by small, reverent hands—tied not to the cold rail but to Karine's chalk circle itself, pinned low enough that every reaching hand could touch its worn softness.

The people pressed inward like water finding its level: hands seeking hands, shoulders touching shoulders, breath mingling with breath. Grounded and Untethered alike lowered themselves to the patient stone, filling the hollow with the sound of steady, synchronized breathing. No Guards remained to scatter them with violence, no Tribunal survived to mock their quiet devotion. Only the circle itself remained—drawn once in desperation, drawn again in hope, drawn now at last unbroken and complete.

And for the first time since the Pulse had shattered their world, the wounded city felt genuinely, miraculously whole.

Not verdict. Not decree.

Only a circle, closed at last in sacred silence, yet somehow—impossibly, eternally—never ending.

Interlude XII – The Ledger of Ashes

"Not every record deserves to remain."

HE HAD BEEN A KEEPER ONCE, proud of the straight lines he'd inked across endless ledgers. When the shelves collapsed in thunder and dust, he saved only one volume—its pages smoke-stained but whole, a final testament to what had been.

At Threshold, he built a small pyre with deliberate hands. One by one, he fed his life's work to the hungry flames. Ink curled like dying serpents, parchment blackened and crumbled, leather spines split with sharp cracks that echoed across the square. He watched the ashes rise and scatter where children now tied strips of cloth to broken posts and drew chalk spirals on cracked stone.

When Mira found him there and asked why, he spoke without turning from the dying embers: "Because law does not belong to paper. It belongs to breath."

She said nothing, but pressed her soot-blackened thumb against her own ledger's spine—a small desecration, a quiet rebellion. His ashes drifted between them, settling into her silence. Two keepers sharing witness without need for words, watching the old world burn so the new one might breathe.

Chapter 118

Tribunal Vanished

"What is absent can still weigh upon the stone."

THE DAIS at Threshold stood abandoned to wind and weather. No imperial banners sagged from its tarnished rails. No royal scrolls unfurled their golden lies into the patient silence. The three seats that once held the Triad sat weathered now by endless rain and drifting ash, their velvet cushions gnawed to threads by hungry rodents, their carved wood splintering like old bones at every edge.

Children climbed them without reverence or fear, playing innocent games where thunderous decrees had once shaken the very stones. They tied bright cloth strips to the chair-backs like festival ribbons, scrawled chalk spirals across marble steps worn smooth by countless supplications, filled the hollowed ceremonial bowls with smooth pebbles and wild laughter. What had been stage for power's grand theater was now simply playground for the free.

Yet the absence itself carried its own terrible gravity—heavier than any presence ever could.

Mira traced the ledger's leather cord with one fingertip and whispered to the listening air, "Here law once dared pretend to speak with heaven's voice." She made no move to open the book, no gesture toward recording. She let the profound silence stand as the only record worth keeping.

Rael pressed his scarred cheek to the worn stone stair, aligning his old wound with its weathered edge like a key finding its lock. He spoke no rhythm this time—simply breathed deeply, letting clean air move through spaces where voices of cruel judgment had once tried to rise like smoke.

Through her eternally cracking lens, Karine peered at the vacant platform and saw no ghostly faces lingering in its shadows—only fractures spreading like spider webs through the marble itself, growing wider with each passing season. She traced their paths in soft chalk, naming them with quiet satisfaction: Husk, Hollow, Vanished Without Trace.

Kess lingered near the lowest step, straps looped carefully across her knees. She did not touch the dais, did not knot anything to its splintering frame. Instead she showed a knot-binder child how to pull leather tight against cloth, her hands steady where the platform above had failed. "This is what holds," she murmured, voice low but clear. "Not their height, not their seats. Only what we bind together." The child nodded, pulling the strap until it bit fast around the rail, a binding stronger than any decree.

Before the empty platform, Nessa stood proud and unafraid, her silver earrings flashing bright as her fierce grin. "They are gone," she announced, her voice carrying to every corner of the gathered space. "And nothing we do—nothing we could do—will ever bring them back." Her words rang with hard-won triumph, but carried warning too: power does not always vanish so cleanly from the world—it lingers like poison in old habits, in inherited fears, in memories that refuse to fade.

The crowd that heard her did not kneel in gratitude. They did not bow in relief. They simply turned their backs to the dais as one body and faced each other instead—choosing the living over the dead, the present over the buried past.

The Tribunal had not fallen gloriously in righteous battle. They had not been executed by revolutionaries or erased by counter-decree. They had been abandoned—first by their faithless Guards, then by their indifferent city, and finally by the very breath of those who had simply stopped fearing their empty threats.

Their silence had become the city's most precious inheritance. Their absence, the new law's only foundation.

What remained was not the echo of their power, but the space they had left behind—space that belonged now to ribbon and chalk, to children's laughter, to Kess's knots, to the patient breathing of those who had outlasted their oppressors simply by continuing to exist.

Not verdict. Not decree.

Only the quiet certainty that they were gone forever, and that what remained—fragile and precious and alive—must somehow learn to hold.

UR-XI:The Last Voice

(Upper Registers — Depositions of the Untethered)

THE MUSIC STOPPED YEARS AGO, but I still see that room. Bass cut mid-beat, and half the floor collapsed onto knees. Some didn't. I wasn't alone—scattered lights caught us upright, trembling, while others clawed through glass and spilled drink.

I said then: *They fell. I didn't.*

I was wrong. Some stood. Some crawled. None of us understood why.

It has taken years to name what that night carved into me. To stand among the fallen is no victory. It is dissonance. A note too sharp to resolve.

Now, when I press my cheek to stone, I hear a steadier chord. Seventeen. Four. Two. A rhythm from below, carried upward until even we who still stand borrow it. Numbers steadier than music, stronger than lights.

I am still on my feet. Only now, I know what standing

means. It means bending when others cannot. It means lowering by choice, not by law.

Seventeen. Four. Two.

Still standing. Still witness.

Kneeling, at last, in the breath between numbers.

Chapter 119

Accord of Silence II

"Absence is not void, but space made sacred."

THEY GATHERED at dusk in Threshold Square without summons, without call—drawn by something deeper than command. The dais loomed above them like a hollowed skull, empty and accusatory, its silence heavier than any thundered decree had ever been. No soul dared climb its weathered steps. No hand reached to light torches on its tarnished rails. The people understood: it was not theirs to resurrect, not theirs to reclaim.

Instead, they formed a circle low upon the ancient stones— the second accord born from the first's ashes.

Jar-bearers placed their vessels at the rim, fireflies pulsing in rhythm with the tide of communal breath. Knot-binders followed, laying strips of cloth across stone, weaving spirals of witness. Chalk-stained hands drew arcs that joined each lantern, each ribbon, each inhalation into a single unbroken shape.

The Six Witnesses held the circle together:

• **Mira** laid her leather ledger at the circle's heart, sealed shut, thumb dark against its cord. Her refusal was altar enough: silence preserved where ink would have been stolen.

• **Rael** leaned his scarred cheek against the stair's foundation, whispering no numbers this time—only breathing steady, offering lungs as scripture, rhythm as covenant.

• **Karine** crouched with her cracked lens and marked a single encompassing circle in chalk: no names, no divisions, only one line that bound them whole.

• **Kess** knelt with straps folded across her lap, showing children how to braid cloth into leather, weaving strength into fairness. "Stone breaks, banners rot," she murmured, gloves chalk-dusted. "But what we tie holds."

• **Nessa** stood at the outer edge, Untethered still, earrings catching the last ember-light, coin-charm brushing her cheek. She gave no laughter, no scorn, only bowed her head —silence resting on her shoulders like a crown she finally consented to bear.

• **Salliwith**, absent in body, spoke through what remained: her last strips fluttering from the shrine, carried forward by children's hands to the chalk line where they tied them low enough for every palm to touch.

When the jars dimmed and darkness pressed close, the circle did not break. They breathed as one—lungs steady, silence unbroken. What had begun in hunger and fear now stood as law: chosen quiet, deliberate witness, the binding of presence and absence into a single covenant.

The Tribunal was confirmed gone not by decree, but by the patience of those who had simply outlived them.

Not verdict. Not command.

Only the second accord—six threads drawn tight in silence, unbroken as breath, eternal as the pause between heartbeats where all true law is born.

Chapter 120

Breathing City

"A city endures when lungs outlast law."

DAWN POURED like honey across Threshold, golden light clinging to Crawlways, bridges, and weathered rooftops as if the ancient stone itself were exhaling after a long, held breath. No banners stirred. No decrees rang from marble heights. Yet the city lived with fierce vitality—its rhythm no longer dictated from above, but flowing from the steady covenant of shared breath.

From the Belowline rose the familiar symphony of survival: hands scraping along worn stone, knees dragging through narrow passages, lungs straining together in the damp corridors of night. In stripped markets, bargains spoke the cadence of hunger. In makeshift clinics, healers leaned close, measuring life not by law but by the intimacy of breath exchanged.

Children carried this rhythm upward like water finding light. They chalked spirals on every reachable surface, tied bright cloth to bridge rails like low-slung banners, lifted jars that caught morning mist like fragile dreams. Brief gestures, each small as butterfly wings—yet woven together they made the wounded city pulse like a single living lung.

Through it all, Mira walked with her ledger sealed, thumb black with witness pressed against its spine. She no longer ached to write. Stone remembered. People carried memory in bone. Silence had become the city's most faithful scribe.

Against walls grooved by bodies in desperation, Rael pressed his scarred cheek. His vow softened into hum: *Seventeen. Four. Two.* No longer plea, but tide, heartbeat, season.

At the square's broken edge, Karine crouched with her lens fogged by dew, chalk circling stone. Her maps traced not only fracture but also spirals of ascent, ribbons binding stranger to stranger, lanterns that marked the path of hope. "The city itself is body," she whispered. "And we—its breathing lungs."

High above, Nessa stood untethered, earrings catching sun like shards of star. She laughed once—sharp as glass—yet the sound gentled as it fell, turning from defiance to release. For the first time, her height did not divide her. The same air filled every chest. The same rhythm moved every heart.

By full light the city moved as one. No Tribunal judged. No Guards threatened. No decree fractured the communion. Only lungs rising and falling in synchrony—living proof that life endured and even flourished beyond the wreck of every power once feared.

Threshold was no longer ruled by law. It was law: breathing, living, inscribed in the shared air of those who had learned that some truths can only be spoken in the language of breath itself.

Not verdict. Not decree.

Only breath—rising and falling like the sea, remaking the world with each exhale, writing the future in the patient air between heartbeats.

Codex XIV – The Law of Dignity

"Dignity endured when everything else was lost."

WEAPONS WERE GONE. Height was gone. Ledgers, straps, maps, and shawls were gone.

What remained was breath, and the way people carried each other.

The law was clear:

• Dignity is not in possessions.

• Dignity is not granted by rulers.

• Dignity is carried in the act of surviving with worth.

This was the last law: dignity remained when all else was stripped away.

Breathnote — Epilogue

"Not ruin. Not decree. Only the breath that remains."

THE CITY no longer bowed to marble halls or bent beneath banners strung too high for mortal hands to touch. It moved by breath alone—slow as tide, steady as season, unbroken as the turning of worlds.

Children's chalk spirals glowed faint against ancient stone, soft as candlelight in morning mist. Cloth strips fluttered in dawn air, frayed but unyielding, holding fast to their chosen places. Jars pulsed with patient light, their small flames echoing distant constellations overhead—earthbound stars brought low enough to comfort. No longer fragments of rebellion scattered in fear, these had become the city's heartbeat, visible, steady, true.

Mira's ledger lay sealed, her thumb dark as old blood with ink she would never spill again. Refusal itself was her witness; silence her testimony. Rael's vow had spread into every willing lung, his once-broken rhythm now strong as braided steel, woven deep into the people's breath. Karine's maps, once filled with fractures, now bloomed with circles and constellations—orientation born from brokenness, beauty revealed in the spaces between cracks. Nessa's laughter, once a blade of defiance, had softened into release, her commanding height no longer a wall but a crown shared in common air. Salliwith's cloth endured in grateful hands, threads worn yet unforgotten, proving the ground itself remembered those who had loved it well. And Kess's straps —once burden, then shrine—were tied among the ribbons, fiber holding still, proof that invention could endure long after strength was spent.

The Tribunal vanished like frost at first light. Guards dissolved into memory's dust. Decrees washed away like salt in rain, leaving only the freedom of those who no longer feared their hollow thunder.

What remained was not silence as absence, but silence as presence—dignity carried low to the ground, breathed through lungs that knew endurance from surrender, steadied in hearts that refused to break though the world had broken around them.

The city's center was not in monuments to power but in the humble rhythm of souls breathing together through darkness into whatever light awaited.

Not verdict carved in stone.

Not decree thundered from heights.

Only breath—rising and falling like prayer, like tide, like hope itself.

And in that shared breath—patient, persistent, un-defeatable—the wounded city discovered itself miraculously, impossibly, eternally whole.

Author's Statement — The Grounded (Rider Edition)

I did not write this book to imagine another apocalypse. We have enough of those.

I wrote it because the world we already inhabit is one where children are murdered in their classrooms, where wars consume cities and fields until maps themselves go blank with grief, where "thoughts and prayers" have become currency cheaper than silence.

Every time a life is taken, an entire constellation of futures collapses. Families vanish in an instant. Communities shatter. Humanity loses not just a heartbeat, but generations of breath that will never be drawn, words that will never be spoken, love that will never be given.

Governments, kings, and dictators thrive in chaos—they declare it purpose, wielding height and power as if standing taller could render their cruelty invisible. But even the worst among us love something, and they gamble that their love will survive their violence.

What I saw, what I could not stop seeing, was the absence of consequence. No tribunal of nations. No council of laws. No divine intervention. Only repetition—crisis to crisis, war to war, shooting to shooting—while the architects of violence remain untouched by the weight of what they have wrought.

So I imagined a world where consequence arrives. Not with fire from heaven, not through human judgment, but through the simplest physics of breath and earth. A world where those who choose intent to harm and destroy are lowered, permanently, to a place where height can never again be their advantage.

The Grounded is not fantasy—it is moral physics made manifest. Not judgment but refusal. Not decree but consequence. It asks: what if the universe itself said no?

If there is hope in these pages, it lies not in the powerful but in small hands that tie cloth to broken posts, in makeshift jars that carry light across darkened waters, in breath shared between those who choose to remain human when cruelty demands they become less.

This book offers no solutions. It bears witness. And in that witness, I hope you find not comfort, but the fierce dignity of those who refuse to let darkness have the final word.

Taloa Douglas Ross

—◎—